ALL DEMONS' DAY

ALL DEMONS' DAY

The Havana Pirate Manuscript

A Novel

Herman Portocarero

iUniverse, Inc.

New York Lincoln Shanghai

ALL DEMONS' DAY
The Havana Pirate Manuscript

iUniverse books may be ordered through booksellers or by contacting:

iUniverse
2021 Pine Lake Road, Suite 100
Lincoln, NE 68512
www.iuniverse.com
1-800-Authors (1-800-288-4677)

Because of the dynamic nature of the Internet, any Web addresses
or links contained in this book may have changed
since publication and may no longer be valid.

This is a work of fiction. All of the characters, names, incidents, places,
organizations, and dialogue in this novel are either the products of the
author's imagination or are used fictitiously.

ISBN: 978-0-595-46571-2 (pbk)
ISBN: 978-0-595-70340-1 (cloth)
ISBN: 978-0-595-90867-7 (ebk)

Printed in the United States of America

EDITOR'S NOTE

The MS on which the present book is based was located in a vast collection of late 18th century legal documents, including the transcripts of various piracy trials, kept in the Cuban National Archives, in the collection *Documentos de la Administración Colonial Española en Las Floridas y Louisiana, 1746-1821.*

It remains a mystery how it found its way there. After reading the book, the reader may speculate on the implications of this location. However, as the MS was the only document in English in the whole collection, it may have been classified by error.

The author of the MS, my remote namesake Rey Portocarrero, was obviously not a native speaker of English, having picked up the language on the road and on shipboard. His often erratic spelling and punctuation have been corrected. Some obscure passages have been clarified. Where I felt it to be necessary, some background on historical events alluded to in the text has been added. Otherwise, the peculiar flavour and rhythm of the writing have been left intact, preserving Rey's own voice.

I hope the reader may conclude, as I did, that the contents of the tale justify its numerous literary flaws.

La Habana, Cuba, summer 2003.

HP

ALL DEMONS' DAY
CARIBBEAN LOCATIONS

1. The 'Vision Quest' at Port Royal, Jamaica, December 1765
2. Rey 's landing at Bahia Honda, Cuba, and adventures in Havana, January 1766–January 1767
3. Rey and Epifania in Savannah, Ga., January–February 1767
4. Captain Trench at Charleston, S.C., November 1766
5. Rey and Epifania in New Orleans, La., February 1767–?

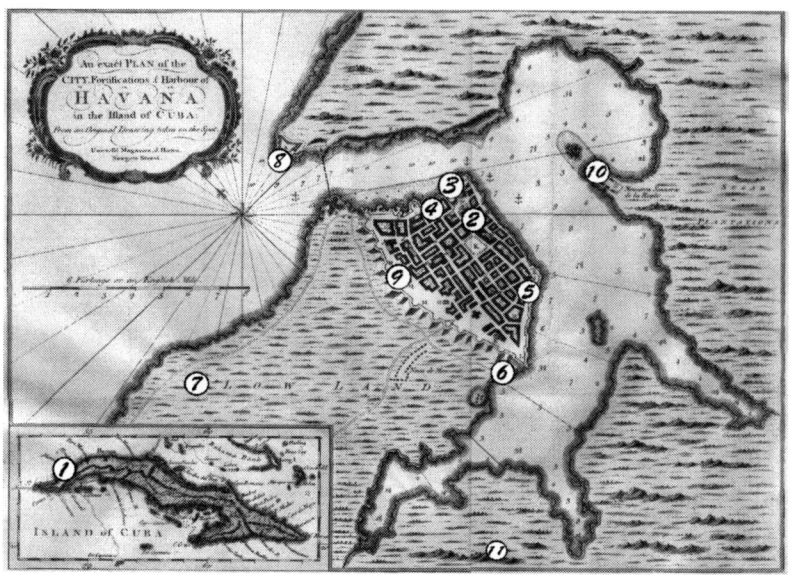

HAVANA LOCATIONS

1. Rey's landing
2. Rey's lodgings
3. La Fuerza
4. Pedroso Palace
5. Alameda de Paula
6. El Fanguito & El Hueco
7. El Vedado
8. El Morro
9. Epifania's hideout?
10. Regla & Solar Sarabanda
11. Runaway settlement

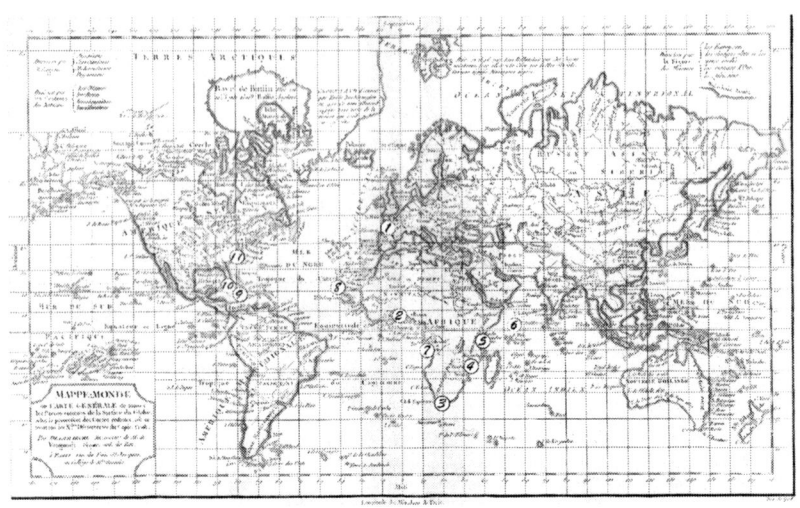

**WORLD MAP
TRAVELS OF THE 'DRAGON'**

1. Leaving Bordeaux, October 1, 1763
2. Trading on the Slave Coast, late 1763
3. Victualling at the Cape, January/February 1764
4. Capt. Dandélion disappears, March 1764
5. Reshaping the ship and retraining the crew, 1764–1765
6. Taking of the "Sultana", July 1765
7. Careening the ship, September 1765
8. Taking of the 'Barbersteyn', November 1765
9. Marauding in and around Jamaica, late 1765
10. Reaching Cuba, January 1766
11. Savannah-Charleston, spring-summer 1766

BOOK I

San Cristóbal De La Habana

CHAPTER 1

▼

It was a delicate mission. A vote was taken, as our Articles required. Unanimously, the crew voted for me. They had sound reasons to want me off the ship with only the slightest prospect of a safe return. I was the darkest of them all and the only one fluent in Spanish. I could also read and write, which is rarely forgiven. They acknowledged my skills, but I clearly felt now that I had never been regarded as truly one of them. On the night of January 5th, we approached the coast to within half a mile, and two deckhands rowed me ashore.

It was a cool, moon-lit night. The coastline west of Havana has numerous deep coves, sheltered by wooded cays. Anxiety almost overcame me while the ship fell away. At any moment I expected Captain Trench to discover as yet my secret, appear on deck and shout the order to kill me. But nothing happened.

The bottom was sandy where I jumped overboard. There were no wishes or goodbyes. I waded through the reeds and climbed up the grassy embankment below the road. When I reached the crest of the slope, I stood for a while, dripping on my own shadow, and saw the boat emerge in a vast expanse of moonlight on the quiet waters, moving swiftly halfway between shore & ship.

The shadows were deep all around me under the moon, absorbing even the small noises of cicadas and owls. After months at sea, my feet were unsure. My nose itched at the deep and unfamiliar smells of mud & straw & pollen. While assuring that the contents of my pockets had stayed dry (the two packages I was carrying had been sealed and wrapped in oiled leather pouches), I took my bearings.

There was a narrow valley separating the bay from the hills. I faced east, towards the city. To my right, I made out half-harvested fields of sugarcane, reaching halfway up the foothills. Small slave shacks were dotted against the hillsides—dark silhouettes humbly married to the vast landscape. Rows of stately palm trees, wet with moonlight, lined the oxcart tracks through the sugarcane fields, granting royalty to even the poorest estate. In front of the shacks there was the intermittent glow of cigars being smoked in the doorways.

A sudden chill interrupted my observations, and I started to walk. At that precise moment, a drumbeat echoed from a cluster of shacks in the hills, and a man's nasal voice started an African chant:

> *"Asokere, asokere Eleggua.*
> *Asokere, asokere Eleggua*
> *Alaroye ... "*

The beat was taken up by two more drums: *one, two—one, two three; one, two—one, two, three* ... A high-pitched girl's voice yelled pleasure or pain, followed by a rooster's chant halfway muffled or strangled. The rhythm persisted.

Unconsciously, I fell in step with it as I walked on, my wet shoes sloshing against the beat.

CHAPTER 2

▼

Walking swiftly and begging rides as I went, I made it to within view of Havana by mid-afternoon on the next day, being my birthday, January 6th, and the feast of Epiphany. People on the road had warned me: in Havana, it was the day of the *cabildos,* the yearly carnival of the slaves and the free Africans.

The warnings came from the white overseers, who stood on muleback, whips in hand, at the edge of the sugar cane fields. The harvest was in full swing: cane leaves were being burned, the cutters progressed among the high stalks in irregular rows, wielding deadly machetes, apparently docile yet ever so often glancing over their bent shoulders with eyes of hatred and defiance. Oxen were struggling on the muddy tracks, pulling carts loaded with the cut canes. Even the main road—though hardened by incessant traffic—was strewn with crushed cane and cluttered with lumps of sticky red clay falling off the wheels as the carts moved towards the mill.

Above the hills, above the forests of cane still standing, the horizon was dotted with plumes of smoke locating the various *ingenios* where the boiling of the cane juice was in progress.

The overseers' voices shouted orders and warnings at the working slaves, using their given names and their tribal affiliations: "*Ven acá, Antonio Macuá! Cuidao, Julian Arará!*"

The road ran between the seas of cane on my right, and the great silvery indifference of the smooth ocean on my left. Not a sail in sight: the *Vision Quest* had retreated while still under cover of the night. The air was crisp and clear, the shadows deep and sculptured. After the monotony of sea and sky on shipboard, the colors of the land—the green of mango trees, the red of hibiscus flowers—seemed supernaturally saturated. And in the midst of all this beauty, here was I, walking the open road as a messenger between worlds, a temporarily free soul; and the merciless business of the harvest grinding countless other souls—sweat to sugar, sugar to gold.

Approaching Havana from the west, I stopped and sat on the outer bank of the river *Almendares* and cleaned my person and my clothes of the dust and mud of the road. A young boy came along singing, carrying yucca and plantains on his head. On the higher ground behind me, mango and papaya trees were growing profusely. Women dressed in calicoes and madrases sat chatting and laughing under a lone palm tree.

Across the river, the fort of *La Chorrera* stood on coral cliffs guarding the estuary. Battles had been waged here when the British attacked Havana a few years earlier. Some burned buildings about a hundred yards inland from the fort still stood witness to a bombardment from the sea. But like the other and grander fortifications of Havana, the *Chorrera* fort had proved useless. The British had surrounded the city from the north and the east both by sea and by land, and the inept Spanish commanders—given to the sleepy formalities of their colonial routine—had been unable to make a stand.

All of this was familiar, because the news of Havana's fall had travelled the oceans as the major event of an epoch, and had been widely commented on by men of all nationalities involved, as having a deep impact on their own lives. For the end of such a war meant that thousands of soldiers, mercenaries and sailors became redundant and were pushed into adventure. As I will have occasion to relate, Captain Trench's own career as a pirate had been a direct consequence of an earlier such peace treaty, abolishing lucrative hostilities and never delivering the announced benefits.

Having cleaned my boots as the last detail of my outfit, I stood and surveyed the wider horizon. From *La Chorrera*, the coast followed an elegant sweep with the *Morro* castle, the entrance to the port and the *Casablanca* hills to the far left, and the city proper, looking deceptively well protected at the deep end of the harbour, to the right. Tall masts of ships stood out against the sky behind the towers and buildings even from this considerable distance. I counted eight churches from north to south. The countryside beyond looked wild and mostly neglected, except for a few small farms and quarries on the immediate outskirts of the city gates.

As I stood wondering how to face the guards at the gates with my hidden goods, one of the women who'd been chatting under the royal palm tree came toward me carrying a large basket filled with oblong packages wrapped in banana leaves. She asked: *"Compañero, quieres pasta de guayaba?"* She put down the basket, half unwrapped one of the packages and showed me the goava jelly inside. It was a brownish-yellow, semi-translucent and sticky substance.

Conversing with the woman—an elderly *mulata* dressed in white muslin robes and wearing many colourful necklaces—I found out that she made the jelly at home and sold it on the road to earn some money of her own, as it was about the only product not controlled by the government monopolies. Looking me over curiously, she enquired about *my* business. I said I was a Traveling merchant, looking in her eyes as I said it to test her reaction. She laughed and said: *"Compañero*, work your story before you face the guards!" I bought three packs of the jelly and thanked her for her advice. She joined her friends under the tree and the laughter started again, all the women now looking over their shoulder at the Traveler without a story who'd bought a six-months' supply of goava.

Turning my back to the women I sat down and carried out a plan suddenly inspired by the sight of the jelly. I took the packages I had brought from the *Vision Quest* out of my belt and unwrapped the oil cloth. Yes, the substance was remarkably similar to the jelly. I recalled the description of the high-quality product as it had been given to Captain Trench by a China Sea trader who had been our hostage: '*moderately firm texture, capable of receiving an impression from the finger; of a dark yellow colour when held in the light, but nearly black in the mass, and free from grittiness.*'

The only stroke against the plan was the strong smell of my contraband, as opposed to the blandness of the jelly. But that risk I had to take. I joined the contents with the jelly and wrapped the whole mass in one bundle of banana leaves. I thought the result had an innocent enough aspect and I felt quite satisfied with myself. When I looked up, there were four elderly women, including my goava seller, surrounding me and shaking their wise heads: "*Compañero,* without a better story and with such clumsy contraband, you won't go anywhere." They sat me down and offered me a cigar, which I smoked in considerable confusion while they unwrapped my bundle and remade it so as to give it a far more convincing innocence. "Any soldier at the gates would have seen immediately that you had rewrapped the package yourself. See, you have to fold the leaves like that, like weaving them. Now it's home-made again. And now let's work that story of yours."

C H A P T E R   3

▼

The women were right, of course. I made it through the gates and
entered the fabled city of *San Cristóbal De La Habana* as the sun was
setting. Underneath my clothes and behind my mask of a freewheeling trader, I was feeling solemn and anxious. The crowds on the
streets absorbed me reasonably well, although I saw some quick
glances identifying me as a foreigner, from girls and women as well as
men. This was a very fast-thinking city to be sure.

The streets were muddy and chaotic, the people a rich mixture of
skin colours, of glitter and misery. Enquiring my way around, I was
offered a variety of services and goods in deep whispers, private rooms
being second on the list after sundry forms of sex, and preceding contraband tobacco, snuff and rum. I promised a coin to one streetboy to
get rid of the others, and he walked me all the way to the port and led
me to the house of Sra. Marisél in *Calle de los Oficios.*

I filled out my name in a musty register. Señora Marisél had a *patente* or license to rent rooms to travelers, she explained, and her house
was of a good reputation, being conveniently near the *muelle* yet away
from the inner streets worked by countless *jineteras* at night. She was a
white woman of about fifty, with tired eyes and bitter about the
mouth. She deciphered my name with difficulty, then looked up in
surprise but said nothing. As I had always been known as 'Rey' only
on board the *Vision Quest*, going by my family name seemed a safe

enough course in Havana. But I soon found out that this name was all but discreet here. I paid for a week of lodging in advance, hoping that would be sufficient time to sell my wares and leave the city. Sra. Marisél left with her register and now I had the room to myself and I surveyed my new surroundings.

Calle de los Oficios or *Oficios* as it was commonly referred to, ran parallel to the waterfront with the customs office and the warehouses. Various shipping agencies occupied the neighbouring buildings. My room was on the third floor, a bare space with a bed, a table and a straight leather-backed chair, the leather eaten by the mildew of many a tropical summer.

Next I counted my money. I carried a considerable sum, part of my shares of last voyage's prizes, but I had had to abandon a larger part of it in the captain's hands. Obviously, Trench had taken my money hostage for my return from this mission. The sum was important, yet would not have been enough to compensate the ship if I had decided to go it alone with the value of the merchandise I carried on the crew's behalf. Hence, Trench must also have thought he had my loyalty—or at the very least he thought me enough of a man of honour for such dignified blackmail to trouble my conscience. I will go into these complex questions at length later on, for this issue of the captain's trust, the binding value of my oath to the Articles and my betrayal of the crew were not easy matters for me to come to terms with. Confined to my room after the movement and the excitement of the open road, I became painfully aware of my multiple treasons and the enormous risks I was now taking.

Darkness came early. At the stroke of seven from the bells of the Franciscan convent, honest citizens had deserted the streets around the *Palacio Pedroso*, and the din from the gathering crowds grew steadily louder. I leaned far out of my window to see throngs of dressed-up people disembark from a ferry landing, apparently coming in from the other side of the inner harbour. As I was about to leave my lodgings, I stood hesitating for a long while about whether or not to leave the packages in my room.

There was no safe hiding place there. The landlady had done nothing to inspire my confidence. In fact, I supposed she was in league with the Guards and would have my room searched as soon as I turned my heels, since her own credit with the authorities no doubt depended on denouncing suspicious newcomers to the city. If my wares were found and examined, I was in for deep trouble. After much debate with myself, I resolved to carry the merchandise on my person as the least dangerous option. I fit the two packages, now again wrapped in their oiled leather pouches, inside my belt. As it was rather chilly outside and I was wearing my long overcoat, the swelling around my middle was not too conspicuous.

The evening chill had no visible effect on the scantily clad black and *mulata* girls who were converging onto the Plaza. They came in tight groups escorted by their own drummers and musicians, yelling and laughing as they went. As I was to learn later, the procession formed at the *Castillo de la Fuerza*, where the various African nations paid their respects to the Captain-general before marching off into the city. I looked up and down the respectable houses: the white women had deserted the balconies from which they otherwise surveyed the world. The doors were closed. Their menfolk stood in the downstairs doorways of the buildings, arms crossed, smoking cigars, watching the rowdy and colourful crowds with eyes full of distrust and disdain. They seemed to live in a different city, or on another planet altogether. But in the courtyard of one of the palaces, long tables had been set up for gambling, and one could glimpse liveried servants dressing sideboards with pitchers of sweet wine and lemonade, entire hams decorated with strips of white paper, huge red snappers in thick sauce, preserves of mango and goava, colourful cakes smothered in whipped cream. At the far end of the patio, an orchestra consisting of black musicians was setting up: a clarinet, three violins, a bass, a flute and two *timbales*. They were rehearsing the minuet which would always be played to open these dances or *romper la danza*, as Habaneros called it. Strangely enough, the nightlife seemed to belong to the uppermost and lowest levels of the society, the serious-minded people caught in the middle class closing and barricading their doors.

Once in a while, a carriage bearing a coat of arms drew up at the entrance of the Pedroso Palace, and someone in the crowd would recognize a fashionable lady or a powerful aristocrat and yell a name in a mock-ceremonial tone: *"El Conde de Casa Bayona! La Marquesa de Montehermosa!"* Havana's quick streetwit would inevitably add quips and puns. The *marquesa's* beautiful name provoked sarcastic comments about her remarkable ugliness: *"Móntate, fea!"* As I penetrated the crowd, I absorbed its rough and ragged beauty, its urgent sense of pleasure.

The official part of the carnival was over after the respects paid to the Captain-general, and now the real dancing had begun. All the dancing women were beautiful, in truth not always because of physical attraction but because their movements saved them from the laws of gravity and their radiant faces, already wet with perspiration in spite of the evening chill, interpreted the radiance of the crowd as a whole. Flasks of rum were passed hand to hand. The crowd moved slowly towards *Empedrado*, with spontaneous stops when a really beautiful girl would dance a sensuous solo with her beau or with various pretenders circling her. Small subsidiary crowds would then form within the crowd, whirling within the whirl. I was drawn into various such groups, handed flasks of rum, taking burning sips and passing on the flasks. I was encouraged: *"Toma! Toma, asere! Te gusta el chispetrén? Tómate un trago más!"*

The warmth of the *chispetrén*—the cheapest white rum—soon made me forget my self-consciousness about wearing my long overcoat in the middle of this gathering of semi-nude girls and smoothly muscular men. I remained concerned, however—even in my growing drunkenness—about the contents of my belt, regularly checking its tightness around my waist even as I was drawn into the dances myself, giving in to the hypnotic syncopated rhythms of the African drums with the sweet illusion that I had become part of this crowd and its collective soul.

Now shouts went up from various sections of the crowd, answered each time with a flourish of drums in a different, recognizable pattern: "*El Cabildo de Angola Real! El Cabildo Gangá Arriero!*"

These shouts seemed to be rallying cries, the drums coded messages to various tribal groups now dispersed in the crowd.

Next to me, a very dark-skinned girl shouted back in response to the Angola cry: "*Kuna Mbanza! Kuna Mbanza!*" And one of her neighbours, a middle-aged man wearing a red handkerchief around his neck, trying to take advantage of a shared secret language accosted her: "*Oye, carabela!*"—and tried to circle her waist. But she, playing hard to get, pushed him back and looked him up and down with disdain: "*Déjame, negro fula! No soy tu paisana! Mírame: yo soy mulata!*"

Full of such solidarities and tensions—an immense moving snake of souls with their fun and abandon and mistrust, their sensual provocation and their loneliness—the crowd moved along *Empedrado* and then turned left into *Compostela*, leaving behind the aristocratic palaces and now penetrating the deeper layers of the Old Havana, shacks and hovels sticky with sweat and mud and sex, mired in the hypocrisies of power and slavery, yet on this night stubbornly resisting despair. Torches and candles were lit everywhere, the humblest window and doorway decorated with palm fronds. The open doors revealed the interiors, the small rooms proudly organized about a single piece of good furniture, wide-eyed children laughing, old women looking on warily yet still shuffling their feet and moving their shoulders to the rhythms of the passing drums.

CHAPTER 4

▼

"Your expensive merchandise is dancing down the street, Don Francisco", said Mateo Pedroso teasingly. "Those niggers and their horny bitches are beyond control, Don Mateo", answered the other *gentleman*.

They had retreated to the back of the patio together with the other members of their class, while their women were dancing the minuet with their lovers present and aspiring, conveniently freeing husbands to discuss trade and politics.

Mateo Pedroso, one of the owners of the palace, was Havana's most powerful man. He was a merchant, but one of those who had bought himself into the colonial administration, run itself as a commercial monopoly by the Spanish Crown. He had consolidated his position during the recent British occupation of Havana in 1762, when skilful collaborators had turned the short-lived foreign domination into a distinct advantage for the *criollo* aristocrats and the newly enriched traders. At present Pedroso carried the title of *Regidor Perpetuo*, or Permanent Alderman. This was a royal commission, bought and sold (as opposed to the elected city councilmen). He had made his brother José the *Sindaco Procurador* or attorney general. Controlling both the city administration and the judges, the Pedrosos ruled discreetly, but firmly, leaving only the visible duties of power to the Captain-general Antonio Bucarely. The latter had taken up his position after the British occupation, and had thus found the whole web of interests and intrigues so embedded in the city that he had to accommodate himself to it. At first he did so reluctantly, reminding the Pedrosos of his royal commission and even showing them the parchment carrying his title. Mateo, who knew Bucarely was a civil servant without personal fortune, asked:

"Is the document ... edible, Excellency?"

"*Edible?*"

"Well, Don Antonio, it better be if it's your Excellency's purpose to live on it in this city."

Bucarely lost his composure. Here he was, the King's governor of this city and this island, being threatened with starvation by a civil servant who was in theory under his command, but his resistance lacked conviction. He knew better than Pedroso that His Majesty conferred grand titles and failed to pay the corresponding wages.

Next, Pedroso introduced to the Captain-general the other major conspirator: Francisco de Arrango y Parreño. He was a sugar baron and a major slave importer, the most prominent defender of the trade.

The British had given up Havana after only one year of occupation because the Jamaican plantation owners—who had the King's ear in London—feared that the development of the much larger island of Cuba as a producer of sugar would ruin their interests. The easiest way the British could stop Cuba's development after the occupation, was to create a shortage of slave labour. Thus, the British navy intercepted more and more slaving vessels bound for Havana.

Soon, humanitarian pretexts would be invoked for these acts—whereas, paradoxically, the shortage of slaves in Cuba was also in part caused by the frequent manumissions, a legal possibility inexistent under British law. Arrango owned most of the eighty or so sugar mills on the lands around the island's capital. Consequently the situation threatened his fortunes.

"What does this year's *zafra* look like, Don Francisco?" Pedroso now asked, while the two men watched the minuet and smoked.

"Too early to tell, Don Mateo. The cutting started late because the weather stayed hot beyond November. Then there is the eternal problem of milling the cane before fermentation sets in. We had rains: the land and the roads are muddy and the oxen move too slowly. I will make my rounds of the *ingenios* next week. But I can tell you already that every *mayoral* at every mill will complain about being short of hands."

"So the situation has you ... preoccupied?"

"To say the least."

"And what do you suggest we do about it?"

"Let's go upstairs, Don Mateo, so we can talk at ease."

CHAPTER 5

▼

The dancing crowds carrying me along were now converging on a plot on *Calle Compostela*. Louder and louder shouts went up: *"Pa'l solar Arará! Pa'l solar Arará!"*

Inside the *solar*, not even the pretence of still being in Cuba was upheld. I was in an African island within the island now. I was also too drunk, too deep into my own abandon and my private ecstasies to take detailed notice of the surroundings. I was absorbed in a continuous whirl of hot and sweating bodies, mesmerized by the rhythms and the shouts.

Yet I vaguely started to recognize faces and bodies, as if the crowd repeatedly came full circle around me. I was no longer aware of the fact that I was still an object of curiosity in my long coat. Three times I felt particularly piercing eyes resting on me, and every time when I turned around I saw a pretty head wearing an elaborate blond wig blending again into the crowd, leaving the image of a naked back, a supple waist and a sensuous shaking of young breasts moving like mangoes in a storm.

The rhythms, commanding the madness, gave purpose to the crowd. Sets of three drums of various size were used to issue ever more complicated patterns. The drummers sat against the far walls of the *solar*, holding the drums horizontally, and sweating even more profusely than all of us. Men danced up to them, challenged them, sprayed spurts of rum from their mouths right onto the wooden flanks of the drums as girls were shouting: "*Iyá! Itótele! Okónkolo!*" In my own growing madness, I *felt the drums speaking their secrets and saw their spirits rising* above the colourful cylinders decorated with caurie shells and small copper bells.

As I passed before the drummers, rotating with my section of the crowd, in spite of my dissipated attention I was struck by the sight of a child of about ten years old leaning against the wall next to the drummers. He was a street boy in rags of a dirty red colour, short and muscular, with weary red eyes and an expression much older than his years. He was leaning on a slightly crooked wooden staff and smoking a cigar in between shots of rum. His bloodshot eyes rested on the crowd with mischief and provocation and none of the playfulness of his age. In a curious way, he seemed to take in the crowd like a king reviewing troops, as if collective honours were due to him and came to him naturally, so strong and slightly menacing a radiance emanated from his presence. When his eyes rested on me, I felt unpleasantly exposed and revealed, and for all my drunkenness I understood that he immediately recognized me as a stranger with a secret. But his perception was not benevolent as had been that of the women on the banks of the *Almendares*. More still, I felt he had located the invisible packages in my belt and possibly even identified their content. But I whirled on, out of sight, with immense relief.

Now I felt a more structured madness coming over the crowd as a chant grew from their midst and gradually concentrated the whirling and dissipated energies. Also, with another sudden and unpleasant flash of sobriety I noticed I was the only soul in the crowd unable to join in the chant, as I knew neither the words nor the language. The sounds, however, soon reminded me of the chant I had heard coming from the hills just after landing the night before, and now I gathered my spirits and began to join in the chorus, imitating sounds the meaning of which remained mysterious to me but whose magical effects seemed obvious under the circumstances:

"Eleggua, Eleggua, asokere Eleggua
Eleggua, Eleggua, askore Eleggua
Alaroye, Alaroye ... "

Now a commotion was created in front of the drummers, as an old man became possessed and started a wild and shaking solo dance. People stood back in awe and respect, others encouraged the spirit riding the man who was now behaving like a malicious young boy, the stiffness of his considerable age miraculously evicted from his limbs. As his behaviour became more markedly diabolical—attacking young girls and ripe women alike—a subtle shift in the drums prodded the crowd to change the incantation:

"Echú baragó
Echú baragó
Moforibale ... "

The women ran and shouted: *"Achelú! Achelú!"*
All the concentrated energies of the crowd changed to a less cheerful mood, and currents of fear and repressed violence ran under my own skin, same as I saw them reflected in eyes all around me. In the midst of this growing collective anxiety, two men all dressed in white stepped forward. One carried a machete, the other a ripe coconut. The *machetero* struck the coconut in the hands of his ritual companion twice, the second stroke at right angles with the first. The strokes were powerful yet subtle, the *machetero's* muscles retracting at the very moment of the impact, so as not to harm his colleague's hand.

The coconut was held aloft for a short while, then thrown on the floor with great energy. It split in four sections. The crowd edged forward to see how the pieces had fallen, and the machete-man shouted: *"Alafia! Alafia!"*—pointing triumphantly at the four coconut fragments *lying all four with the inner white lining upward.* Unbelievable as this may seem, the anxieties were at once dispelled, and the crowd became jubilant again at what I immediately understood to be a favourable oracle.

The men in white retreated. Their place was taken by two costumed devils all in red and black and wearing pointed hoods extending down over their faces like penitents' masks with narrow, beaded eye slits. The shouts now became: "*Iremé! Iremé! Los Diablitos!*"

The little devils started to attack women with children, pretending to take away the children and eat them. Women screamed and lifted up their little sons and daughters protectively, real panic in their eyes.

Next, I was drawn by the crowd into a closed chamber at the far end of the compound. Inside, the sweat of hundreds of compacted bodies cemented us into one collective beast. A slender and beautiful *mulata* girl, dressed all in transparent yellow and gold, was dancing with a strong, muscular man in red and white. The shouts became: "*Ochún! Ochún! Shangó! Shangó!*" At first the girl just acted the obvious teasing coquette, but as her spirit penetrated deeper, she started to take off her clothes.

The man, for his part, both domineering and imploring, also turned an initial caricature into a vivid, almost painful portrayal of masculinity. I witnessed, with increasing clarity, a ballet signifying the holy principle of desire, acted out between strong and very physical characters representing the opposing and complimentary sides of the female and the male forces.

I also stood admiring the yellow girl's reckless abandon, her utter wish to expose herself against all the laws of church and society whose repression is so often labelled as decency. In her ecstasy, the girl wanted to beam on us the creative and liberating force of her nudity; and, acting out the repression her innocent force was subject to in the outside world, her handlers rushed around her with dark veils. What remained was a tantalizing ballet, not so much intended or scripted, as *resulting from real opposing forces at work in the collective frenzy*. I was more and more certain that this night was full of deep revelation—and danger. When the mystic union was finally performed, the girl fell to the floor exhausted and was carried outside, where already new shouts went up:

"Letra del año!"

A group of priests stood in the middle of the yard, their leader a solemn man in his sixties, dignified and grave. He read out a proclamation from a scroll of parchment:

"Los sacerdotes de Ifá reunidos en esta casa templo sacaron la Letra del año ..."

The crowd yelled, the man motioned for silence with an imperial gesture. Then he spoke the following enigmatic words, which, even in my drunkenness or precisely because of it, I registered for later decipherment:

"A los hermanos Oriates, Babaloshas, Iyaloshas e Iworos!
Al pueblo religioso!
Divinidad regente: Elegguá!
Signo regente: Ogunda Ogbé!
Profecia: Osobo Ikú Intorí Arojé!
Flag of the year: black, yellow and red!
Increased contraband and corruption!
Do not believe in sweet and poisonous dreams!
Fear the dragons coming from afar!"

CHAPTER 6

▼

"Has your Excellency been properly honoured by his most loyal subjects?"

The Captain-general, after taking the salute from the *cabildos* at the *Castillo de la Fuerza*, had joined the Pedroso brothers at their palace on the plaza next to the Jesuit chapel. It was about eleven. Downstairs in the patio, the dancing and gambling were in full swing. Gentlemen, ladies, officers and even priests were playing *monte*, shouting and smoking as they lost their civilized restraints. The music also had grown wilder now, the musicians sweating as they played more and more syncopated rhythms such as the popular *guarachas*, the dancing now dominated by scandal-courting young *mulatas* turning the heads of heirs—and their fathers. The Pedroso brothers, Arango and now Bucarely looked down with weary eyes on the night-time behaviour of their own class.

"Spare me your sarcasms, Don Francisco: you know this is a burden of my office."

"And an expensive one, at that," said Arango, "Given all the coins your Excellency has to throw to those dancing Africans ..."

Bucarely choose to ignore the allusion to his tight personal finances, coming from this arrogant sugar millionaire.

"Francisco, Francisco," said Pedroso, "Let's not irritate his excellency on a night like this."

"That is the very least of my intentions, Don Mateo. I said it by way of introduction to a ... proposal of mine."

"A proposal?"

"Yes, your Excellency. As a matter of fact, a proposal to ... reverse your Excellency's situation in regard to the dancing niggers out there."

"Explain yourself, Don Francisco."

"Instead of throwing good money at them, there is a way to ... *extract gold* from every *ebony piece* sailing into your Excellency's harbour."

Being a good businessman, Arrango knew how to time teasers and offers. Bucarely was already at his mercy. But he wanted to enjoy the moment, and he widened the conversation to a more general subject, also because—in spite of his usually strong self-control—the night, the wine and looking out over the city from the high balcony gave him a sense of power and connectedness.

He said: "*Do you smell the ocean out there, gentlemen? Imagine for one second all the invisible lines crisscrossing the waters of the globe. We have faster and faster ships sailing the seas. Every day we explore new routes for universal trade. We find new opportunities, create new engines, discover new goods and better ways of producing old ones. Our kings rule, may God bless them, but we men of business fill their treasuries. Our bankers invent new documents and formulas. I can now sign a paper here on my desk, and thus insure a ship in Malabar or abandon a cargo in Malacca ... Trade will become more and more universal. Borders will blend, armies will still defend boundaries but the real power, my friends, will gradually shift elsewhere. And who knows that better than we Cubans, who live here in Havana on the very crossroads of the Empire? Frankly, it took the British to show us our own assets.*"

"You cannot do away entirely with politics, Don Francisco," protested Bucarely, who vaguely understood the direction of the millionaire's visionary musings, and concluded there would be little future for self-respecting civil servants if Arrango's ideal world came into being.

"Oh, of course not, your Excellency. There will still be good and bad wars, and peace treaties containing the causes for the next war and so on. We will still proclaim principles, maybe even believe in them on Sunday mornings ..."

He stood silent for a moment, and both Pedroso and Bucarely were impressed. Then he turned slowly around and faced them squarely. Pedroso, who knew Arrango well, was nevertheless amazed at the sudden expression of infinite scorn with which the millionaire looked down on the Captain-general.

"Bucarely," he said—and his tone was not more courteous now than if he were addressing an overseer in one of his sugar mills— "Bucarely, *you will work for us from now on.* This is the deal: whatever Madrid or London say, you allow every Dutch, French and Portuguese ship carrying Africans to enter port. We need every slave we can get into this island. I for my part guarantee you one fifth of the price of every live head sold off the ships."

CHAPTER 7

▼

Now with its rites and prophecies behind it, the crowd fell back to its primary purpose: wild and shameless fun. Streaming out towards *Empedrado* and the *Alameda*, strengthened in its defiant attitudes by the revived African connections, the carnival took over the entire city. Again I was carried along by the crowd's snakelike progress—past barricaded doors and shut windows and balconies, past shady hideouts where unspeakable deals were being made between a whispered lie and a bloody knife. The young girls' abandon was total now, their breasts and bellies and buttocks come to independent life, their eyes ecstatic. Entire flocks of very young semi-prostitutes—'*mulatas de rumba*'—flaunted totally unchristian sex for their own pleasure, men being pushed into secondary rôles in the collective pantomime.

Moving towards the city wall and the notorious lowlife zone beyond the Arsenal, the crowd began to shed small groups to taverns and brothels along its trajectory. I remained firmly embedded in the middle, where the hard-core *rumberos* and their drummers and musicians maintained the discipline of their madness. The rhythms were ever more insistent and mesmerizing. My mind dictated furiously: "*Dance, world, dance! All you planets and gods, obey the commands of the drums, the universal law of Motion or Death!*"

By now, I had drunk and danced myself into a state of semi-unconsciousness. I thought myself safely cushioned by layers of friendly bodies around me, till I noticed that a circle of dancing young men, all dressed in wide, striped pantaloons and short, sleeveless vests worn without shirts, pressed closer and closer, more so than the density of the crowd seemed to warrant. At the same time, while I was still whirling around and around, I thought I saw, beyond the circle, the young street child with the dangerous aura around him whose aspect had struck me during the ceremonies inside the *solar*. Next, I remember a fleeting glimpse of the pretty near-naked girl wearing an elaborate blond wig who had also been around inside. Then the circle was closed even tighter, and I was separated by it from the sheltering crowd and drawn to a dark corner just off the *Alameda*. There was an overwhelming stench of urine as I fell into the mud when they started to beat me up.

The last thing I remember was my coat being pulled off.

CHAPTER 8

▼

You may well imagine the state I was in when I woke up early the next afternoon. I had vomited on the floor, my head hurt worse than a leather punching-ball, I had a black eye and bruises all over, my clothes were in disarray—and my merchandise was gone. The extent of this latter disaster became only apparent to me now. In my drunkenness, even the attack and the blows I had suffered had been absorbed in a loud, brightly coloured and unstable universe where all the daytime laws of cause and effect were deeply distorted. But hangovers are the revenge of gravity.

Instead of a free spirit roaming possible worlds—as I had felt only the previous day, approaching Havana from the countryside—I was a lost soul in a hostile city. So much for the freewheeling traveller cherishing the illusion that he can penetrate the souls of foreign places: let him be himself and carry lightly the burden of his otherness. My life wasn't worth a penny without my contraband: Trench and the crew would never believe that I—the man of letters!—would be so stupid as to lose their fortune on my first night in Havana. Or, if they did, their judgement of my inadequacy would be as severe as the one they would have pronounced on my treachery. Not that I had ever intended to return to the *Vision Quest*: but the value of my merchandise would have allowed me to disappear and start an honourable life elsewhere. As I was stuck in Havana, the crew would hunt me down sooner or later. I was a dead man for sure.

When I called Sra. Marisél to ask for a pitcher of water, she stood in the doorway and looked at me as if her worst suspicions were confirmed, what with the black eye and my torn clothes: I was the kind of foolish stranger lost already in Havana's underworld after the temptations of only one night. If not for the week's rent I had paid up front, I would have faced an immediate eviction. She could not know all my money was gone; probably she was rarely paid for a whole week in advance. On her sour face, the predictable battle between her love for the hard cash and her shallow pretence at respectability was almost comical.

Muttering curses under her garlic breath, she brought the water. I undressed and washed. Discarding the outer layers of clothing superfluous in the warm weather, I regained a sufficient appearance of cleanliness to face the street. But I was utterly lost as to my next move. Standing by the open window, I took in the hustle of the port and viewed the landscape beyond the bay. Right in front of me was the *Muelle de San Francisco*, the most busy anchorage where various ships were being unloaded under loud whistles and in apparent good humour, half the men working, the others knowing better and giving free advice.

East of the port channel, beyond the vast expanse of the inner harbour, low hills rose to prolong the fortifications of *El Morro* castle and the extension works in progress. After the occupation by the English, Madrid had decided to make the city absolutely impregnable, and now a massive military complex was being laid out. At the foot of the hills, facing the *Alameda* and the Arsenal on the city side, was a small church surrounded by vague buildings and a small sugar mill: this, as I was to learn later, was the village of *Regla*, fated to play such an important part in my further adventures.

As I stood by the window, the activity on the street and the bright sunshine absorbed my attention to such a point as to make me forget my worries. Chatter from gossiping women; men whistling after girls;

disputes from balcony to balcony; three guards chasing a pickpocket, then catching him behind a corner, out of view of the victim, and going off with the loot. These streets were theatre for sure. In the middle of all this brightly coloured hustle, my eye fell on a young girl coming from the side of the *Plaza de Armas*, walking swiftly on loud, high-heeled wooden *chancletas*, greeting men, children and dogs as she went, smiling brightly and shouting comments to other women. She seemed to be a character of the neighbourhood, louder and brighter than the average, exuding confidence and seduction, feisty and enjoying her powers to the full. To my astonishment, she entered Sra. Marisel's house and a few moments later I heard a loud knock on my door, and her voice chanting: "*Permiso?*"

I opened the door.

"Wishing you good afternoon, brother," she said. "I have something you lost on the street last night ..."

Her dark face, framed by countless braids of long, light brown hair, was merry and open; she seemed honestly pleased with herself and convinced she was doing something worthy and agreeable at the same time.

"And who be you, little sister?"

"Oh, beg pardon. I thought we had been introduced. My name is Epifania."

She curtsied and shook the braids away from her eyes. She was constant motion, quick as a lizard.

"And pray, what's your business?"

"I am a thief, and I also sell pussy. At your service." She curtsied again and cracked up. "And what's your name, *mi chino?*"

"I am Rey."

"*Coño, hermano—un nombre de muchas campanillas!* A real king! And right after Kings' Day. I'm in luck."

I stood hesitating what to say to this amazing bird. Her shameless honesty seemed total; so was her self-assurance as she produced one of the leather pouches from behind her back and proudly put it in front of me.

"That was stolen from me, sister. I think you owe me an explanation."

"Oh, of course." Her smile grew even wider now. "Fact is, I stole it from the thief stole it from you, see? You got lucky. You owe me a reward, I think. Few people in this city would have retrieved this for you. Other girls, not to mention. Brother stole this from you named *Pompi el Palero,* dangerous character from the *Palenque.* Deals in everything, and works for the police as well. *Cimarrón, negro curro—y tremendo chivatón además!* A runaway, a sorcerer and a police informer all in one ... But I know how to handle him. He wants to be with me, of course, *pero yo no estoy en na'*—all men want me, but I am strictly my own person. Do I get my reward now?"

I tossed her a *Real,* which she caught in mid-air, bounced off the windowsill to check the sound, then bit it, nodded and put it in her dress. As I nervously opened the pouch and unwrapped the oilcloth—desperately hoping to find the hidden content—Epifania stood watching me.

"Won't you go now, sister," said I, annoyed at her presence and the darting, inquisitive glances shooting from her restless and pretty eyes. "I have given you your reward, right? I might complain about the whole situation, as you were obviously in league with my attackers. But let that rest ..."

"Complain? To the guards? You don't look like they'd pay you any mind." She rested those streetwise eyes, fast as insects, on my face and my clothes for one heartbeat.

"What's the stuff?" she now asked with a half-smile, standing provocatively bent over the table, pushed-up breasts generously pouring over the off-white calico of her low-cut dress. "It looks like ... *pasta de guayaba* ... what did the English call it again ...—goava jelly, right?" She added, maliciously: "But, if it's worth that *whole Real* you gave me for it, it must surely be something more interesting ..."

"Maybe."

I smelled the stuff: it *was* goava jelly. My first illusion gone, and against my own better judgment, I took my pocket knife and delicately cut through the middle of the pack. But of course the blade of the knife encountered no resistance. I had lost everything except for having recuperated one of the now useless pouches.

"You look like you could cry," said Epifania, and leaned even deeper over the table. *"Partes el alma—it's soul-splitting".* In spite of my anger, I made out the fine, colourless down growing between her smooth, very dark breasts, bared practically down to the nipple. But I revolted against the ease of this seduction. I had been enough of a fool during the carnival and would not be taken for granted again.

"Why don't you tell me the whole story?" She insisted.

"Get out of here, you whore!" I shouted, exasperated at myself.

"Yes, that's what I am," she said proudly, "and a thief as well, as I told you when I came in. So I steal and I fuck, is what I do. But you know what? I'm also honest and fun to be with, and the loss is yours, brother. *I did you a real favour—you don't even understand.* This is a difficult city. A place way too tough for you by yourself. I can see what you think you are—oh yes, I have more eyes than you know. But forget it: you are not."

She collected herself—lively face, dancing braids and tempting breasts and all—and left the room with a slow and provocative gait, rolling her hips and her buttocks to underscore my loss.

I sat down and slowly rewrapped the pack of jelly. I suddenly felt very alone and dejected. Soon I realized I had been a fool again, chasing the only person who might know where all my goods had gone. But also the girl's cheerful presence and her openness, her bright eyes and pretty breasts had impressed me more than I cared to admit. Too late, I moved to the window and scrutinized the street, but obviously there was no trace of the girl now. I lay down on the hard bed with the lumpy mattress, and lit a cigar, trying to fight the mounting access of despair and self-pity.

I slept badly for most of the day and the following night, drifting in and out of confused dreams.

The next day, the entire city seemed to participate in my dejected mood. The sky was clouded, the air heavy and unbearably humid. I didn't recognize the buildings which, at my arrival, had stood bathed in honey-coloured sunshine. Now the walls looked a dirty grey, the woodwork eaten by humidity and termites, every construction attacked by saltpetre from the sea. The very stone of the city, full of marine fossils, seemingly wished to re-melt into the formless ocean. An all-pervading stench of mud rose from the streets, stronger towards the *Alameda*, the Arsenal and the shipyards and taverns beyond. Likewise, the people had lost their easy glitter and appeal: in the bad light, all eyes appeared full of either defiance or distrust.

Not a breeze was stirring. In the leaden heat, a moral torpor invaded one. Symbols of this mood, mangy street dogs of the breed particular to despair, were fighting over small heaps of refuse on street corners. I would learn that such deep swings of mood were peculiar to Havana—perhaps because the city's foundations were so shallow and its government so corrupt that the very buildings accepted the humours of the ever restless and scheming inhabitants.

But I gradually collected my spirits, and resolved I *had* to find Epifania. I convinced myself that I was not nearly as defenceless as my foolish behaviour during the carnival night seemed to indicate. Hadn't I passed through many adventures already, always protected by my good fortune in the end? My confidence slowly re-establishing itself, I sat by the open window, smoking and waiting for Epifania to appear: she had seemed so much at ease in the neighbourhood, she certainly belonged around here.

The strong and aromatic tobacco gradually induced a dream-like state. I needed to convince myself that my luck had not run out. Reviewing my trajectories, I travelled to the past, richly, with complex memories and connections.

Outside, time kept moving forward, the rhythm kept by the church bells, and at night by the singing voices of the *serenos* or watchmen, assuring the good people of Havana that all was well, and their sky clear and unclouded—*el cielo claro y despejado.*

CHAPTER 9

▼

The city of Antwerp had once been the key to the Spanish Low Countries. But after the Peace of Utrecht in the year 1713, the blockade of the city and the port by the Dutch under the Barrier Treaty had ruined trade, and the Catholic church had stunted its spirit.

I came into the world in this provincial backwater, a city the ghost of its former self. Once the river Scheldt had been a lifeline to the world, proud masts of countless ships crowding the anchorages around the Markgrave's castle. Once the wind on the river banks had carried smells of the oceans; now the stagnating waters smelled of mud and accumulated shit.

Having succeeded the Spanish, the Austrians ruled the city in league with small-minded local shopkeepers, the more enterprising souls having fled north beyond the blockade. There is no greater treason to a city than to close its port. Antwerp's soul had been briefly revived with the establishment of the Flemish East India Company in the year 1723. But the river remained barricaded, the Company moved to Ostend and went bankrupt in 1727. In 1743, the Austrians sealed the betrayal of Flemish interests when they cancelled the Company's charter to please Britain and Holland.

Younger sons of Spanish nobility—the former masters of Flanders—were stuck in the city after the Austrian takeover. The more ambitious Spaniards moved on to the Americas where there was a future. The ones staying behind were the hopeless *hijitos de papá*, content to vegetate on mediocre allowances, grand names of past glory, a horse on credit and two sets of elegant clothes.

There were enough local girls to be impressed: since the middle class was ruined, poverty was rife. I came into this world in 1741. A new war with France was being fought, the so-called *War of the Austrian Succession.*

My mother was such an impressionable girl, born in the fortified village of *Lillo* north of the city, near the line of the blockade. *Lillo* was one of the forts built to defend the approaches to Antwerp during the religious wars.

The new war brought a short-lived new influx of Spanish nobles and mercenaries to Antwerp, dreamers of glory in a new confrontation with the Dutch protestants, would-be liberators of Antwerp and its river, or simple opportunists. My father, they say, was one of them, a Portocarrero from Extremadura. But Antwerp saw no battle and its river remained closed. Having missed his claim to glory, my father left shortly after my birth—for the Spanish West Indies, they say.

My mother was confined in a public orphanage near Venus Street in the city. The austere front of the building carried an image of the Virgin Mary with the Spanish legend: *Nuestra Señora de la Soledad.* 'Our Lady of Solitude'! What a patron saint to be born under! But admittedly, there were better omens, too. For one, my father had accepted to give me his name before he disappeared. Plus I was born, as you already know, on the sixth of January, the feast of Epiphany or King's Day, and my mother later told me that my father's first name had been Gaspar, the name of one of the three kings or wise men. To view such trivial facts as cosmic coincidences was not just a game to me, but a desperate search for certainties.

I have to sing the praises of my mother. She was as free and open a spirit as her surroundings and circumstances allowed for. It would have been difficult enough to raise a fatherless child in a narrow-minded and gossipy place like Antwerp; but the grandiose name, when confronted with her reduced circumstances, made it even worse.

Thus I grew up in society's margins, given to private worlds and their self-made pleasures and disappointments. Yet, as was to happen over and again, circumstances and events of my life would also be determined by political events in foreign and even hostile worlds far beyond my reach. With a secret arrogance, I sometimes claimed these events as somehow directed at me, imitating the behaviour of spoiled house cats who are convinced that every move of their masters is related to their exalted persons. My father's presence in Antwerp had been a small result of world politics. His disappearance was caused by colonial expansion in the West Indies. Thus both my coming into this world, and my poverty as well as the grand and meaningless name I was burdened with, were ripples remotely caused by Empire.

All along my life's path I would be tossed about by currents and tempests stirred up by kings, yet I would stubbornly stay my own course. Wasn't I one of the *real* kings of the *Día de Reyes?*

CHAPTER 10

▼

My mother's fortunes were unsteady to say the least. She made some money as a seamstress and embroiderer, but since she wasn't and couldn't become a member of the Guild, she had to work as a subcontractor for master tailors who paid her a pittance for the beautiful work she delivered. She did laundry for a while, till her pride revolted against sorting the dirty underwear of the rich.

One day as she crossed Kipdorp Street, leading to one of the city's medieval gates, a bent old woman whispered to her: do you work during the day? Work for me at night, you'll make more money!

But she didn't accept that offer and for a while our fortunes went all the way down. Bailiffs came and took the scant furnishings of our rooms. My mother had to beg my grandmother for some money to buy back the bed and the table as our possessions were auctioned off on Friday Market Square.

To spare my mother the humiliation, I went by myself to the auction, a sweaty hand grasping the pieces of silver borrowed from my grandmother in my trouser pocket.

Friday Market Square was moderately crowded when I got there and started looking for the bailiffs who'd carried off our stuff. It was a random crowd, consisting of the curious idlers always attracted by human misery, well-to-do burghers hunting for bargains, victims of the bailiffs like myself, desperately trying to retrieve some driftwood from the shipwreck of their lives; and the bailiffs and auctioneers, empty-eyed, given to their routines. The rainy sky over the square and the city was just as grey and indifferent, offering salvation nor escape. The very tower of the cathedral, on the right off the square as I entered it, pointed toward a heaven without depth or promise. Making my way among the idlers, I had a deep and desolate feeling *of not belonging here*, neither on this square nor in this city nor in this narrow life. In spite of the solidarity and indeed the love I felt for my mother, I decided then and there, under that empty and hopeless grey sky, to escape someday and chase brighter colours and live loudly. I would always distinctly remember this moment; later I thought it had been the first call of my father's blood luring me to risks and adventures.

In the drizzle, most of the confiscated goods offered for sale looked pathetic: for the scant profits they would make, creditors might have saved themselves the expenses of the bailiffs. But profit, I vaguely understood, was not the main motive of this here ritual. It was about the almost indecent exposure of the daily trappings of failed lives, issued as a warning how deep one could fall once outside the snug codes of respectability.

I discovered our furniture and stood biding my time shamefully, feeling even more sorry for the table and the bed, looking so shabby and naked here, than for myself. When the time came, I was the only bidder and I got everything back. There was a man with a dogcart to make deliveries, for which my wise grandmother had given me copper coins I had kept in the other pocket. But now the man argued I'd have to wait till the end of the market before he could carry the things over. So I joined the idlers and looked around a bit more. Burghers in furs were going through a pile of brilliant junk—mirrors and chandeliers obviously come from some disgraced mistress' quarters.

A boy about my own age, dressed poorly but with a kind of elegance about him, stood admiring himself in a full-length mirror. As I looked over his shoulder, I saw his face was smeared with black ink. So were his hands. He smiled at himself and took attitudes. He seemed totally absorbed in himself and his own private fun, oblivious of the crowd and all the circumstances of rain and misery. His eyes caught my gaze in the elaborate whore's mirror. He spoke without taking his eyes off the glass.

"Hi there, comrade. I was being myself. My real self, that is. Since we are what others see, right? My name is Inky. I work at the printers' shop over there." And he pointed at the façade of a substantial building in the far left corner of the square.

"The printer's shop?"

"You from the country, brother? Yes, *the* print shop. The venerable house of Plantin and Moretus. House of the Polyglot Bible and Mercator's atlas. And a few more such books from long ago, and a lot of crap with His Majesty's patent and the *imprimatur* of the Holy Inquisition. Yes, man, the *mother of all print shops.*

What's *your* story?"

"I'm here to buy furniture."

"Word? Running off with a broad? Setting up house?"

"I'm a little too young for that, no?"

"It's been done at our age, brother," he said with a certain offended dignity. "There's even books printed about it."

I felt I had touched a sensitive subject (maybe he *was* dreaming of eloping), so I made a humble statement:

"Truth is, I had to buy back my mother's stuff taken by the bailiffs."

"Oh yes, the story of this square," Inky sighed. "Not so original, not so deep. Heartbreaking, but wouldn't sell twenty copies in print, not on the cheapest paper it wouldn't."

Now *I* was slightly offended and it must have shown.

"Story of this city too," he said quietly, making his eyes look older and wiser—and checking the effect in the mirror. "Your father gone north, too?"

"Mine went south, or so they say."

"Whatever. Welcome to the club."

A man's voice called from the entrance of the printer's shop: "Inky! Inky!"

"Have to go now, brother. Keep the bosses happy."

He started off towards the building, then turned around abruptly and said: "You wanna know of the printing business? Be here tonight at eleven. Beware of the guards: after ten they pass every fifteen minutes."

And he ran off.

CHAPTER 11

▼

The nearby church of St. Andrew struck eleven as I reached the door of the Plantin building. The narrow streets around Friday Market were deserted, small lamps burning under ornate statues of the Virgin at street corners, rhythmic marching and ritual shouts of the night watch resounding from various points in the labyrinth.

I scratched the window nearest to the entrance. After a short wait, Inky opened the door fitted into the gate. He had an excited, conspiratorial air about him and was carrying a darkened lantern. The shouts and the steps of the guards now sounded dangerously close. He dragged me inside and closed the door.

In the semi-darkness, I noticed many unfamiliar smells. I had never been inside or even close to a printer's shop, and absorbing the fragrances of ink and paper was like discovering new worlds. Inky's grand airs of superiority only added to my excitement. He was as eager to initiate me, I felt, as I myself was to discover the secrets of his trade.

We passed an open door in the gangway. Inky shone the thieves' lantern inside, over dark panelled walls solid with leather bound volumes in neat rows. "Bookshop", he whispered, and ran his lantern over various busts of what must be great writers of the past, I thought. He rested the beam on a bearded face: "Mercator", he whispered "Great man. Quietly made the first atlas while the Holy Inquisition was still insisting the world was flat and Rome or Jerusalem or what-ever lay in the middle. Respect!"

Next he showed the binders' workshop, the proofreaders' room, and the print shop itself, the presses solid wooden machines, incom-prehensible to me as the shadows cast by the dark lantern transformed them into spidery monsters. All the time, I was registering more pun-gent smells, which I tried to identify: leather, glue, rope ...

I would have thought the room with the presses was the holiest of holies of Inky's world, but in that I was mistaken. He whispered: "Printers think they're the masters of the trade. Bullshit. Is just the final stage. Real thing goes on in here, in the back: is where the pages are *set*. That now is real magic, look!'" And he shone the lantern upon endless rows of font in neat cases along the walls, above pages half-set on wooden trays resting on slanted desks. "Is the most difficult part, he whispered, 'cause you have to think and see everything *in reverse.*'"
I was speechless with excitement.

Inky stood admiring the effects of his initiation. Now he took off his cap and scratched his head. He seemed to be considering a next step. "Comrade," he finally said. "I don't know you or your whole story. I trusted you on sight. I've learned from dogs. You're not *com-pletely* trustworthy, of course—your eyes are way too intense for that, is the first thing I saw when you saw *me* in that mirror.

But then again—I have to take chances sometimes. That's also part of my trade ..."

I didn't exactly get the point of all this, except that more revela-tions might follow. Having been raised by women, I easily fell for the allure of secrets and intrigues.

"I came here on trust as well," I said to stand my ground. "You might have robbed or raped me."

"Robbed? You have holes in your shoes just like me, brother. No, it's actually more straightforward and simple than that."

He sighed, and then deliberately took my arm and sat me down in the darkest corner of the room. "Now listen carefully", he said.

CHAPTER 12

▼

Inky went on: "This here business of the bosses, it's all legitimate they say, and incredibly *dull* at that. In the old days of the first Plantin, we printed *excitement*. Now it's all about licking ass: there are censors among the proofreaders, and every word is checked to please Pope and King. The Austrians even took away our monopoly: it's now a Brussels printer, Frickx, who can call himself *Imprimeur de Sa majesté Catholique et Impériale*. You know how sensitive we in Antwerp are to such insults by lesser cities! We're reduced to print breviaries for fat priests, and prayer books for pale virgins."

"Now about six months ago, travelling trader come from Holland, disguised as a beggar monk, showed me a little book he carried in his pocket. Cheap, paper-bound volume, no name of publisher on it, only 'Tot Amsterdam'. Name of the writer clearly fake: *Turco Magnifico*. And the title: **A Night in the Sultan's Seraglio.**"

"Now I am not a bad reader: I've not been to school much, but imagine—with all these words stored around here, I would be a moron if I hadn't taught myself, right? But when I opened the little book, all of a sudden, I felt illiterate again, for I'd never seen words such as these in print. In short, it was a sex story, and a very good one at that, and very precise about acts and organs—hence all the new words. Now the fake monk—I only know him as Hans—asked me a series of questions. Was I paid well? What were my working hours?

Did the bosses trust me? Of course, anyone but a fool would have understood what he was aiming at. I didn't want to be taken for granted, but his only *real* question soon followed: did I have a key to the printery? I didn't answer that right away, for I know how to negotiate, or don't I? His offer was as follows: I would print copies of the text on my own time and smuggle them out; he would cut, sew and bind them and sell them around the city; we would share the profits."

"My mind was working fast. The risk was enormous, of course. If we were caught, it was the Holy Inquisition and the galleys. The guards were forever on the outlook for subversives from the north infiltrating here—they always blamed the strikes and the riots on them, whenever the misery of the weavers exploded. I had no doubt many of the good citizens of Antwerp would love Hans' pornography, but most of them were cowards, and even assuming they would buy, how much would they pay for such dangerous stuff? So I said I had to think it over."

"Of course, I did not have my own key—but getting into any building at night around here is no big deal—all these houses are very old, grown together by outhouses and such, and you don't have to be much of an acrobat to get in. The prospect of the money, such as it would be, was attractive—for you know how an apprentice is treated by the bosses, especially one who can never dream of entering the trade on his own account. Still, in truth, what convinced me was something entirely different. Here I was working as a printer, among millions of words—and so few of them saying anything *real*, understand? It was all prayer books and lives of the saints. Some of the sex was gross, but it was real: it's what people do, or can do. Every other book I'd seen was about what we were supposed *not* to do. So I said yes to the offer and we started our business."

CHAPTER 13

▼

"Hans was living in a room nearby, behind St. Andrew's church. He had worked out an elaborate system to maintain his street character as a begging friar, and spend nights drinking and whoring. The nights in the taverns and the brothels helped him to meet his buyers, he said—for many an orderly citizen was courting the devil at night. At the same time, the whores kept him poor, so he in turn kept me under pressure to print more copies of his book."

"The business was risky enough for me, because the inventories of the supplies—paper and ink—were checked monthly. Paper was costly, but I developed my own system to avoid suspicion. Hans' customers were not very demanding as to the quality of the paper or the printing. So I laid aside my own supplies of papers cut from the margins of the full-sized sheets (Turco Magnifico's book was *in-octavo*, meaning the smallest size), and I recuperated pages from proofs and misprints, which were normally used in book-binding and to reinforce covers, but were not inventoried. With ink I had my own ways, since inking was my first task as an apprentice. I made sure the quantities I needed for any given job were always slightly higher, and this added up to cover my own supply."

"All in all this system—together with the manipulation of the press at night—imposed great discipline. The bosses think they rule any given trade with their laws—but when you start operating in the shade you have to double their skills, setting your brain and your fingers to technique as well as dissimulation, without the glories of recognized success or esteem. The true masterpieces are made under the table, mate."

CHAPTER 14

▼

"We did well enough for about five months, till Hans told me one night he found fewer and fewer buyers for his sex book. I suggested he go to Amsterdam and bring back a new one, for I thought it normal that people got tired of the same descriptions over and over, however juicy they were. Going to Amsterdam was too risky at that time, he said, but he had another idea."

"He showed me a far more imposing book, easily four hundred or so pages, and of greater size than Turco Magnifico's harem tales. This was a illegal version of Captain Johnson's *General History of the Pyrates*, translated and printed in Amsterdam after, so he said, it had become a semi-clandestine bestseller in London."

"The fact that he brought this up, and the very character of the book, made me think very different about the fake friar. Up to that moment I had considered him simply a lowlife with his own system of survival. But when he prodded me to read Captain Johnson's book, and as I progressed with my reading night after night, I gradually came to see him as a deep and dangerous soul, biding his time under the frock for some violent scheme way beyond exploiting the secret vices of the middle class."

"For it was only on the surface that Johnson's book dealt with pirates and prizes. It did so under the flimsy pretext of warning the reader not to stray from the narrow paths of Faith and the Law. Most of the piratical careers described in the book duly ended with hang-ings. But the real purpose of the book as I saw it (and as no doubt Hans had intended me to read it) was to explore the *politics* of the pirates, their claims to absolute freedom and their forays into practical anarchy. Hans still denied all that. He pretended he was only inter-ested in promoting a bestseller, before Amsterdam would start print-ing thousands of copies as the original copyright was running out. He was a black market professional all right: he knew the price and the profits of danger."

Inky paused and studied my reactions. Outside, the guards passed through the square. Inky held his hand over the beam of the dark lan-tern. When the marching of the soldiers' boots had passed, he put down the lantern, got up and disappeared in the shadows behind the desks. When he came back, he was carrying some sheets of print.

"This is from chapter twenty-eight of captain Johnson," He said. "Read!" He set the beam of light on the page, and I deciphered the text:

> 'You are a sneaking puppy, and so are all those who will submit to laws which rich men have made for their own security. Damn them for a pack of crazy rascals. They vilify us, the scoundrels do, when there is only this difference, they rob the poor under cover of the law and we plunder the rich under the protection of our own courage ... I am a free prince, and I have as much authority to make war on the whole world as he who has a hundred sail of ships at sea, and an army of 100.000 men in the field, and this my conscience tells me ...'

"It's from the story of Captain Bellamy", Inky said. "Strong stuff, ain't it? And do you imagine what I had hanging over my poor head if the bosses discovered *this*? Turco Magnifico was one thing, sex was sin but this was straight rope for the gallows."

"So right from the start I had my doubts about Hans' new idea: first, this would not sell nearly as well as the sex book. Next, it was a larger book, far more difficult to print on the sly. The good burghers with secret vices and money would buy sex at a moderate prize—but would anarchists and revolutionaries hiding in cellars and garrets spend their scant pennies on an expensive book preaching their own ideas? Some people with money, like the Masons, they probably were against kings and emperors, especially of the Austrian kind, even stiffer and more remote than the Spanish had been—the Spanish, say what you may—were *adventurers* too. Look at you—you're Spanish yourself, ain't you? But the fucking *Austrians?* Hand kisses and tralala operas. But even if many people in Antwerp were against them, their cowardice would always outweigh their convictions. See, comrade: I knew my public. Guy like Hans, he could afford to go into politics, for he could hope to disappear to the next city when things got too hot under his fake friar's sandals. But me, being too young to run, I had to make a living right here in Antwerp."

"While I was considering all this, what had to happen, happened. Hans was caught with ten copies of his sex book and was put in irons in the *Steen*, where they probably tortured him a bit out of respect for good tradition. My ass was saved by the fact that every copy I had printed still mentioned Amsterdam, and also by Hans' courage: apparently he never mentioned his Antwerp connection, not even when they deported him to the salt mines in Silesia, as I later heard from one of the guards of the *Steen*."

"All of this happened only like two months ago. I lay low for a while. I have copies of Turco Magnifico stashed here, and a set of proofs of Captain Johnson, which I had started to print on Hans' insistence, but am not sure what to do with now. And that's my story."

CHAPTER 15

▼

I began to understand why Inky had lured me to the printery and had made all these confessions to me. He was obviously looking for a new street partner to continue Hans' business.

"How can I do what you expect of me?" I said. "I'm too young to hang out in taverns and brothels".

"Wrong places, mate," Inky answered. "The guards will be on the lookout for pornography in every night spot now. So we have to move to different markets."

"Like where?"

"Think."

I felt I was dragged into Inky's trade against my will. But something in his eyes told me he would not let me go without a struggle after revealing his secrets to me. I thought I could stand my ground in a fight with him, but I also felt attracted to him and his trade and his cocky pride.

"Wherever many people come together? I risked."

Inky nodded: "Yes, but we need to be more precise."

"We want men, not women."

"Excellent, comrade! "What else? Something obvious. Remember, we're selling books."

"They have to be able to read."

"See? We have all the requirements. Now where do we find such men in large numbers?"

"Church?"

"Nice touch, to be sure. But churches are also full of women. The ones guarding husbands in the pews, and real whores in the back. That's a no go."

"High schools?"

"Very good. Students are vicious. Teachers even more so. Not all of them have spending money, though. But we keep schools on the list."

Where we go next?"

"Jails?"

"Brilliant, brother! Sex starved males in confined spaces, and with nothing to lose! Cash may be a problem there, but on a more subtle point, we'll sell to the jailers themselves: implicate the law, corrupt the Holy Inquisition! From his salt mine in Silesia, Hans shouts approval in the name of Holy Anarchy! Next?"

"Libraries?"

"The spirit is upon you, brother!"

Thus I became Inky's partner in the dirty book business. We perfected the product. Turco Magnifico's wet prose was bound in small volumes with the pages uncut and with false titles of a book on mathematics. I peddled them with irregular success near schools and libraries, and Inky helped me gain access to the *Steen*. We made money. I started helping out my mother with household expenses, and she could pay back my grandmother the money she had borrowed to recuperate our furniture.

Inky had kept his fears and his doubts about printing and selling Captain Johnson's pirate book. But I knew he was tempted. Some strange kind of honour bound him to Hans now toiling in the Silesian salt mines—if he were still alive. To bring Captain Johnson's book of absolute adventure and anarchy into circulation in the good city of Antwerp would be fulfilling Hans' parting or dying wish. Also—Inky himself was becoming more and more impressed with the contents of the book. His original fears, turned into challenges, only strengthened his temptation. As for myself, I was proud of my illegal achievements so far, and the money made off Turco Magnifico's harem tales was worth far more to me than the spreading of anarchy in the Austrian Netherlands. Soon Inky accused me of falling into routines, and teased me about my crushing sense of *responsibility*.

True to the nature of the drifting young males we were, we unavoidably took the path to spoil our own advantages. I felt irritated at Inky's comments, and felt I had to rise to a further challenge too. Once this feeling was registered by Inky, he felt he had to up the ante even more. Defying each other's courage, we were perfect fools—and also played to perfection the part of reckless energy driven by the male juices in our loins: the noble and blind, ever renewed urge for action, without which this planet would die of wisdom and boredom within a few generations.

We were unable, however, to print and sell the whole of Captain Johnson's book. It was too important a volume to abscond the necessary quantities of paper and ink. We put together a shortened version focused on the philosophical pirate Captain Bellamy—the one giving the fiery speeches against kings and kingdoms—and spiced up with the tales about the pirate republics in Madagascar, and the cynical comments about multiracial sex in the Brazils. As we left out all the pirate trials and hangings, in fact we produced a far more dangerous book than the original, since we did away with all the edifying pretexts hiding the hard core.

CHAPTER 16

▼

Piracy and anarchy would have been delicate subjects anywhere. But there was a specific reason for the Censors and the Police to be more vigilant in the Austrian Netherlands. As many recent wars had illustrated, seafaring adventures, when officially sanctioned, allowed governments to enlist idlers & downright criminals by the thousands, and send them off on shipboard.

The Ostend East India Company had been such a venture of the Austrians. The Company had flourished, sailing an impressive fleet, even establishing trading posts in India. But in the year 1743, it had been closed down as part of the Peace Treaties. The loss of this safety valve had made the Austrians more sensitive about the lure of naval adventures *not* sanctioned by Authority.

Ostend had been a corsair base for a while in the past. Now the port was greatly diminished, and calls to re-issue Flanders-based *letters of marque* to state-sponsored privateers were politically very dangerous. Our music-loving, hand-kissing Austrian rulers did not want to irritate the French, the Dutch or the British. The Austrians, slow and bureaucratic as they were by nature, were artful defenders of a naval status quo—controlling the waters and maintaining immobility down to the backwaters and the ditches surrounding Antwerp. At the lowest end of these policies, riffraff in port cities were regularly rounded up and sent to the salt mines. Like our friend Hans, potential pirates were buried alive in sediments of prehistoric oceans—a cruel irony indeed for those who had craved the freedom of wind and waves. In Antwerp any boat—even a skiff—became a dangerous symbol of abolished liberties. Deeply continental people themselves, our masters had an instinctive mistrust of the uncontrollable waters. Blockade-running, even smuggling eggs and butter from farms along the river just north of the border, was a major offence. What then with the glorification of piracy on the vast oceans! Once again world politics—although seen through an Austrian microscope—was going to determine my fate.

Our version of Captain Johnson's book—a fifty-page leaflet entitled *Algemeene Historie der Pyraaten*—found its way to the censors' desks after a notorious smugglers' tavern near *Lillo* was raided. Few if any of the smugglers were literate. But the landlord was a one-legged war veteran, a former petty officer of the Navy, who had bought the book from me out of sheer nostalgia. As for me, ignorant at that time of the vast schemes above my head, I had thought the tavern to be a good selling point, and I returned there one drowsy afternoon in June, with three more copies of the book hidden in my clothes.

Taking a shortcut around the *Lillo* windmill through muddy fields of sugar beet, I found myself at the backdoor of the inn—and facing two uniformed guards loitering in utter boredom in front of the sealed door. As they were convinced I was one of the smugglers, and as their boredom needed a sense of purpose, they immediately tried to grab me. But I was way faster than them, and ran off.

Fear, deadly fear gave wings to my poor shoes. If they had searched me, looking for eggs and butter no doubt, they would have found enough piracy and anarchy on me to send me and Inky to Silesia or worse.

CHAPTER 17

▼

In total panic, I fled away from the city, carrying only the clothes on my back, and some money from my last sales. I had only one thought in mind: to escape from this eternal hypocrisy and repression, and to reach Holland, where thinking and the printed word were free. I started to run along the river, going north through the abandoned wharves and shipyards, past decaying warehouses, ghosts of de-masted vessels aslant in the river's mud, and the rotting skeletons of a million barrels—startling entire colonies of scavenging seagulls when I threw my books in the river.

I stopped to catch my breath after walking and running like a madman for hours, or so it felt. I sat down, leaning against a poplar tree on a dyke and surveyed the grand and empty landscape around me.

The city had disappeared behind me. Only the tower of the cathedral was still visible above the lowlands, a vain sign under immense skies. For a split second, as I sat sweating and panting, I felt a pang of regret at not being a believer, having to face all the fruitless beauty and challenge of the world without the support of a higher purpose. Next a deep wave of sadness about leaving my mother and my grandmother moved me to tears. How small and abandoned I felt all of a sudden! The open spaces turned my head, I became so dizzy I had to cling to the tree for support and I thought I would faint.

When I came to my senses again, the afternoon had advanced, the sun was halfway down to the horizon—and as man's moods follow their own cycles under the planets, I found a sort of acceptance of my immediate fate, and the renewed energy to move on.

There were scattered farmhouses and summer stables on the land protected from flooding by the dykes and the canals. Spying from behind the poplars, I could make out the flags of the Dutch garrisons along the river, and their barges blocking the traffic downstream from the city, just below the wide bend westward.

Now, as the sun streamed down at a lower angle, its rays caught the course of the river, and the golden reflection designed an undulating banner of yellow silk snaking through the lowlands. The waters scintillated from afar: the tide was moving. As I stood watching, the ditches and the canals below the dykes came alive. As cosmic force moved the oceans, the North Sea filled up and pushed the flow past the islands and creeks of the delta out there beyond the Dutch troops, into the estuary. The flood was now soaking reed-lands and tidal marches, moving countless blind creatures in the muddy depths, carrying a myriad fishes and eels feeding off the mud, and—expanding the cycle to the heavens—sending off gulls and storks in fancy flight on their daily hunt.

And all of this discreet but all-powerful force on the move resulted in the small, gurgling noises of the water rising above the mud in the ditches and around the sluices. It was the blood of a sleepy giant reaching his fingertips drop by drop; and I couldn't help, standing there alone and forlorn and spying on these vast processes unnoticed in the city, that the Dutch and their barriers were but a futile and unnatural attempt to stop the regular flow of life of the river and the plain, which should so obviously benefit the city at its receiving end.

As the long summer evening dragged on and on, my loneliness felt as vast as the floodplains and the tidal flats around me. I cruelly missed Inky, our conspiracies and our wary friendship. But I also cried over all the things I had hated in Antwerp, resulting from the narrow limits of our existence. Now I valued the small routines and understandings with my mother, the occasional complicities and meagre joys shared, the very poverty of our lives creating a sense of solidarity against the world. Till darkness came, I didn't dare to leave the cover of the rows of poplar trees, lest I fell upon a Dutch patrol. The air was balmy, but I was drawn to the stables in the meadows to find a sheltered place to sleep. On the other hand, if I wanted to reach Holland I could only hope to do so under cover of darkness. But I was paralysed by indecision. I passed hours in fruitless contemplation, acute despair now rising, then receding again.

When night had finally come, I climbed down the dyke, jumped over several ditches and lay down in the leftover hay in the corner of a stable. Lying on my back, I counted stars through a hole in the roof. The straw was itchy at first, and with my raw nerves made my eyes and my nose run. Gradually I calmed down somewhat and must have fallen asleep.

Somewhere in the deepest regions between midnight and dawn, a large and slow presence entered my confused and desolate dreams. It radiated warmth and benevolence, and an immense comfort against loneliness. It softly laid itself down against my exposed back. All my muscles gradually relaxed, as if I were bathed in warm oil. I developed a marvellous erection and felt like I was having sex with night itself.

Not till daybreak did I realize that a calf had entered the stable, and had instinctively sought my company, being lonely itself. Strange as it may seem, this unexpected sympathy from such a massive creature and one so utterly peaceful and free from evil, completely changed my mood. In the morning the calf looked at me with deep soft eyes, its wet nostrils smoky in the cold sunrise, its flanks quivering as the first buzzing flies entered the stable. Then it slowly licked my muddy shoes. Maybe the soles tasted of city salts unknown to farm animals. But this sign of benevolence saved me from sinking in myself. I lay motionless as the rite of bonding was in progress. I felt like a pagan hero spontaneously befriended and protected by wild beasts. I turned thankful and proud. My imagination rose, I wanted to live.

Outside, a low fog hung over the canals, under diffuse rays of sunlight. The air smelled of smoke. There was total silence around the buzzing of the flies. I stood and stretched and embraced the world.

CHAPTER 18

▼

Three days later, sitting by a roadside, I took stock of my situation. I had been unable to cross into Holland—there were patrols everywhere. But as unwelcoming as the supposed Land of the Free was to drifters from the south, the situation on the roads of Flanders was not much better. The countryside was full of suspicion. My dialect almost gave me away. In the countryside, I discovered, people spoke different from village to village, and local guardsmen and provosts could locate any passing person's origin to within a mile, based on accent and vocabulary. Three times I narrowly avoided arrest for vagrancy thanks to the money in my pocket: anyone not carrying at least some silver in good coin, was sent to the nearest poorhouse and put to work. Obviously, I needed a story.

I had no means of proving a legitimate trade or skill, such as being a travelling apprentice. Discarded veterans and mercenaries of the recent wars were everywhere, many of them crippled, camping out in makeshift tents in the countryside, or begging their desolate way from nowhere to nowhere. The guards rounded them up regularly and sent them to the farms of the abbeys, they told me, where they had to provide free labour for the monks, who for only payment fed them remnants from their well-stocked kitchens. And here was I, a mere boy still, lost among the sorry driftwoods of history.

I remembered Inky's description of Hans, and it set me thinking about a similar disguise. While I was too young to turn myself into a begging friar, there were other religious cloaks available. In particular I now thought of the groups of pilgrims of all ages I had often seen setting out for Santiago in Galicia from the steps of St. James' Church in our city. This now seemed an excellent pretext to be on the road. Problem was, though—so far I had been drifting *to the north*, away from Galicia—and suspiciously close to the Protestant lines.

Hoping to avoid the Dutch patrols, I had ventured away from the river and had been erring through rich farmlands for a whole day. I joined another vagrant sitting in the generous, sunlight-dappled shade of an oak tree off the main road. He was a one-armed man in semi-military rags, prematurely aged but with eyes still vivid. He had lost his left arm, he said, fighting on the Spanish side. He regretted ever having taken up arms except for his own causes and profits. He had been a sailor too, he pretended, out of Amsterdam, forced on board a vessel of the East India Company after a wild night with the whores in a tavern on the *Voorburgsche Wal*. He told me about Holland: have no illusions about freedom there, they just practice the opposite side of the Austrian hypocrisy, promoting the export of their own ideas while fighting just as much the import of others not convenient to their own interests ... He interrupted himself, stared at my face and asked: "Are you Jewish?"

Young as I was, instinctive defences were at work around such vital issues of identity, and I answered without answering: "I am only my own person."

"You *look* Jewish. Is that why you want to go to Amsterdam?"

"I have my reasons."

Dropping the subject, he went on about the Dutch: "They preach free trade and they block Antwerp. They mean, of course—free trade *for themselves.*" Yet he said he hadn't minded being on their ship. Yes, it was awful in many ways—but several notches up from being at war on land, and he had been lucky: *the sea hadn't taken another limb.* What could a poor man expect?

His cynicism was refreshing, but the look in his eyes made me doubt the veracity of his sailor's tale. He sensed my thoughts and showed me his tattoos: five points in the triangle between thumb and forefinger of his remaining hand; an anchor on his chest; a heart and the name YOANDRA on his upper arm. On his other shoulder, a very provocative drawing of a totally naked black-haired girl bound hand and feet to a tree with heavy rope. "This one's a charm'," he explained, "To keep one's woman steady while one is at sea. Doesn't work—not with *my* kind of girl it don't."

While he showed me the latter inscription, the ragged sleeve revealed yet another sign higher up toward the shoulder. I saw only the shortest glimpse of it, but could have sworn it was a grinning skull. I could never decide if he had shown me the last tattoo willingly, as a mute warning or a temptation or both. All the while the man was talking and giving advice. He concluded: "Forget Holland, there's no such thing as freedom on land anywhere. Try to make it to Ostend, join a ship."

Following this advice, I made it to Ostend and with great difficulty lived through the autumn and winter of the year 1758, resorting to petty thievery more than once when no one hired me on the docks to unload barges or move crates of fish.

The coming of spring revived my energies. I felt like the seagulls, sheltering inland from the cold but drawn by instinct to the open waters as soon as the air got a little balmy again. Coastal traders and their captains—retired officers running away from sour marriages, or smugglers with doubtful mariners' certificates—were recruiting sailors and deckhands in various taverns on the portside: *In De Stad Doover, Het Gouden Haantje.*

Fishermen had their own inns away from these recruiting grounds. The fishermen rightly considered themselves serious mariners, working the faraway Iceland Banks at great risk, and they looked down upon the coastal trading boats and their crews of outcasts and smugglers. Thus my own lack of seagoing credentials was no objection. I found a berth on board a coaster called *Pigeon Voyageur.* I approached the sea gradually, my first ship never leaving sight of land, going mostly back and forth between Ostend and Calais, the cliffs of Dover clearly outlined on bright days, and carrying whatever traffic was on offer: butter, flour, chickens, cloth, sugar beets, potatoes; and underneath, the occasional fugitive, guns smuggled all the way from Liège, contraband tobacco. It was all performed with a quiet and homespun brand of illegality which I increasingly recognized as a part of my own heritage—indeed, as the very nature of my countrymen, the result of repression and foreign occupation.

I had resolved to become a sailor for good—what other options were open to me? The question of contacting my mother haunted me. But how could I get in touch with her without compromising my safety? To be truthful, I have to add that my sense of freedom chased the sadness. I postponed and postponed again the decision to write her, and to find a safe way to get the letter to Antwerp.

CHAPTER 19

▼

A radical change of Havana's mood interrupted my musings about the past. As I woke up on the morning of my fourth day in Sra. Marisél's house, the city was sunny and breezy again. Gone were the excessive humidity and the motionless heat and the sense of despair they had carried. I went out and walked towards the *Plaza de Armas*, light in the head with hunger—I hadn't eaten a thing in two days, and smoked the more. I remained mindful of the fact that Epifania had appeared to come from that direction when she had entered *Calle Oficios*.

Just beside the enclosure of the *Parroquial Mayor*, as I approached the south-western corner of the Plaza, I was tempted by the smell of fresh bread from a bakery. I spent my very last coin on a warm and crusty loaf which I ate with delight, as being the last pleasure before actual starvation. I sat down in the early sunshine, facing the stark and menacing contours of the *Castillo de la Fuerza*, the seat of government. Slanted sunrays cut deep shadows from the pointed angles of the ramparts, across the dirty moat.

In spite of the early hour, the first whores and dealers were plying their trades already. Sensing me rightly to be penniless now, they left me in peace. These criminal activities were going on right under the government's own walls, the girls and their *chulos* and the whispering sellers of contraband rum and narcotics joking openly with the

Guards with whom they were obviously in league—while lesser offenders, but those without wit and grace, languished by the hundreds in the dreadful dungeons of the *Fuerza*.

Having finished my last meal, I walked across the Plaza towards the seafront. As I passed the ceiba tree at the far end of the Plaza, I saw that an old woman, dressed in rags and apparently out of her senses, was walking around and around the tree, chanting in what must have been her ancestral tongue. Her wide feet were badly calloused, as if she'd grown natural shoes. There were running sores on her legs. Yet when I approached, I saw her eyes and her whole face beaming an ecstatic contentment. She was obviously an aged drifter.

Her belongings, forming the mysterious amalgam such people tend to cherish, lay a few paces away in the shade of the tree. I knew the story of this *ceiba* tree, which the Carib Indians had held holy before the Spanish came and destroyed them. The Africans had taken over the veneration of the tree, and the Church—following its usual opportunistic policies—now said commemorative mass under it on the founding day of the city. As the old woman perceived my presence, she stood and called me: "*Ven acá, hijito!*" And as I was about to reply truthfully, that I had no money whatsoever to give her, she asked sweetly: "*Da me un besito, dale!*" She stood smiling at me, and now I was struck by the remarkable *serenity* radiating from her person.

I approached and gave her a quick kiss on the left check, which she turned quickly trying to catch me on her mouth. She smelled of earth and dry flowers. Her eyes were deep and without illusions.

"*Ay, ahorita me muero contenta!*" she sighed. "I have done what I had to do. I have thanked San Lázaro, and I have been kissed by a handsome boy. Only weeks ago, I was a slave, *mihijo*. I was never any good at work. So I had to wait till I was old and useless to buy myself cheap. I came all the way from Matanzas as soon as I was free. Look what these feet have walked! But they are *mine* now, ugly as they are. And so is this hand and this other one, and this mouth and its remaining teeth, and this head to think its own thoughts. O free, free at last!" She sat down against the tree.

"But you know, *joven*: I won't last much longer in this world. I'm happy to be *en la capital,* I was a city person and never took to the country. But now I'm so weak, so weak. It was such a long walk, and living on sugarcane only … Look, there's some stalks with my stuff there, you want one? No? Well, be so good as to hand me one here, I'm to feeble to stand right now …"

I walked the two paces to her belongings. There were indeed some fresh stalks of cane protruding from one of the straw bags she had been carrying around. But as I grabbed one of the stalks, I got a sudden shock. There, among colourless rags, pieces of metal forming spontaneous amulets and ends of rope woven into patterns was, undeniably—*my missing pouch!*

I hurried back, imploring the lady: "*Por favor, señora*, please tell me, where did you get that leather pouch?" By now the woman had her eyes closed, and she was hardly breathing. Her face was still peaceful, her mouth smiling, but all she could do was whisper. I brought my ear close to her lips, and her smile widened. She sensed my nearness and tried, very feebly, to steal another kiss. "*Ay mihijo, soy tan feliz, tan feliz … pero se me va la vida ya …*" I begged, desperate now: "Please, please, tell me."

She made a great effort and whispered in my ear a repeated succession of syllables, unintelligible at first. Gradually I could reconstruct three words, or so I thought: "*La garza real … La garza real …* " What was the meaning? I thought the poor soul was raving now, and entering a merciful state of hallucination before death, in which she remembered happy moments or beautiful images of her life—because her smile stayed the same, and she pressed my hand three times and shook it weakly, before starting to gather invisible objects around her with all of her dry, bony fingers.

As a child, observing the last moments of a great-aunt, I had seen how the dying collect imaginary things around them, like desperately clinging to something familiar before the great void, or building a little nest for their own bodies. Just as I saw the woman entering that stage, two guards came walking our way from across the Plaza. Failing my instinct to assist the woman in her last moments, I grabbed the pouch and fled into the labyrinth of narrow streets towards the port.

CHAPTER 20

▼

Supposing I had understood her correctly—what had the poor woman's last words meant? Had she been responding to my pressing queries, or had she merely been hallucinating? I knew the *'garza real'* to be a kind of heron or wading bird. Sailors know their sea-fowl, if only because they are often the first messengers of land after long voyages. But I was not familiar enough with the heron to know if its appearance or its habits in Cuba constituted a kind of saying, a symbol or allegory.

Having reached the relative safety of the inner city, I sat down against the wall of the convent of *Santa Catalina*, and tried to allow my intuitions to flow freely, and to think logically from them at the same time. The leather pouch I held in my hands, upon close inspection, still smelled vaguely of the missing substance. But other and more recent smells had penetrated the leather: brine and fish, smoke, strong rum and tobacco. I turned it inside out, and found in my hand a few grains of sand, a tiny fragment of a white sea-shell, scattered parts of a crayfish or lobster's carapace. Had any of these items been transported in the pouch by the thieves, or was it just refuse the pouch had collected at random after being thrown away?

Now my thoughts started to follow a different track. The heron being a wading bird, surely it lived in the mangroves around the city;

and if the poor old woman had come walking from Matanzas as she'd said, she must have passed through those parts.

Now the mangroves were the notable hangouts of Havana's worst cutthroats and highwaymen and their glittery, high-heeled girls, their class referred to by decent citizens—in frightened whispers—as '*negros curros y negras curras del Manglar*'. Not later than that very morning, while buying my bread at the bakery, I had overheard a conversation between two longshoremen, strong & muscular fellows: "*Compadre, yo no voy al Manglar, es un barrio de los demonios, y podemos dejar la piel!*"

Possibly the heron, being a beautiful creature with a fierce eye, and living in the same mangrove forests, stood symbol for the *curros* themselves, who took pride both in their loud elegance and their cruelty. All of this was speculation. Nevertheless, keeping also in mind the place where I had been attacked, it was likely that the thieves were from one of the gangs hiding by day outside the city walls towards the west. Epifania had mentioned thieves from quite another zone. The *Palenques* or runaway settlements were located much farther outside the city. But, fast and clever as the girl had seemed, that may have been a deliberate misguidance.

I was now desperate and resolute enough to start walking in the direction of the *Manglar*.

CHAPTER 21

▼

Behind the Arsenal, where the city had started to burst through its own walls, grids of new streets were being laid out. The zone was dusty and full of garbage, scavenging rats and purposeless dogs. A street ironically to be called *Esperanza* (as indicated by the name written in tar on a piece of board) ran a straight line bearing southwest of the Arsenal. In the shimmering midday light, shadow-less and cruel, it was a highway to nowhere. The workmen, stretched out in their wheelbarrows, were resting under the scaffolding of a nearby building going up. A few hundred yards into the no man's land, *Esperanza* crossed, at right angles, another stretch of a future street, this one to be called *San Nicolás*.

Near this abstract intersection of streets-to-be, there was a cluster of shacks and hovels, one of them carrying a sign: *La Bodega del Cangrejo*. The likeness of a crab was painted under the name, in vivid red. Music, singing and shouts came from the backside of it, where a kind of courtyard was enclosed by small individual huts. In the middle, under a lone cocoanut palm tree, a long narrow table was full of pitchers and bottles, a bare-breasted *mulata* dancing on it to the sound of a creaky fiddle and percussion played in unison on the bottles and pitchers by a group of drunken white sailors—obviously just off their ship—accompanied by their quick-eyed Cuban escorts picked up on the first street corner, testing the resistance of their future victims. The Cubans were singing a *guaracha* which' chorus, endlessly repeated, ran thus:

*'Cuándo, mi vida,
Cuándo?'*

The sailors were quite overwhelmed by the girl's totally natural display of beautiful breasts. But chances were they would never get at those, as these ornaments were strictly bait: in the shade of the individual huts, older prostitutes were biding their time. The sailors, once drunk enough, would end up with them, the beautiful *mulata* gone off with her share of the loot.

There was a heap of refuse next to the entrance of the *bodega*. Under the stinking crab and crayfish shells, under shards of broken pitchers and goblets, I discovered remnants of various cotton bags and torn leather purses. These I understood to be traces of earlier robberies like the one now in progress inside the courtyard. It was a measure of the lawlessness in these parts that the robbers didn't even care to hide the evidence of their deeds. But while I stood thinking this over, I suddenly realized that the old woman must have found my pouch in just such a heap of refuse outside a similar establishment—and hence, that the *Garza Real* was not a symbolic or mythical reference, but in all probability just the name of another lowlife hangout.

As I stood in the full sunshine just outside the courtyard, at first I thought myself lucky that the ruffians and their women were already engaged in their pursuit. But my own poverty now formed a kind of protection, as I was no longer worth a bullet or a knife-thrust. As I had perceived from that morning, the ruffians had a third eye for one's circumstances, and would not attack or even bother one as penniless as themselves. Strangely, the loss of my money and merchandise now gave me the kind of invisibility on the streets I had always craved, together with the serenity brought about by the certainty that one has nothing, absolutely nothing to lose anymore. With these convictions, I ventured deeper into the no man's land.

The sour smell from the nearby mangroves mingled with the salt and minute grains of sand carried by the breeze, stinging face and hands. At the very edge of the mangroves, there was another enclosure of flimsy buildings. And yes: a sign of an even cruder workmanship than the one of the *Bodega del Cangrejo* showed the fierce-eyed, long-necked profile of a wading bird.

There was no action in progress inside the yard. But in front of the entrance, turned towards the city limits, a muscular man with his head shaved and vaguely dressed as a cook was busy behind a shaky table, eviscerating a large red snapper. He seemed a genial fellow, giving me a smile and enquiring my business in these parts. Playing for time, I asked if he was going to cook that fish and he said most certainly he was. I said my name was Rey and could I eat with him, since I had no money and he replied he was called *Sr. Serafín, cocinero*, and yes, I was most welcome to share his meal.

I helped him dress the snapper and kindle a charcoal fire inside the yard, over which he fried the fish in a blackened pan of oil. Soon we sat down to eat. Again and even more than during the morning, I began to see the advantages of my penniless state, and the ease with which this city absorbed me once my pretensions at a higher status had been forgotten.

Sr. Serafín brought out a pitcher of white rum to wash down the fish, and offered me a strong cigar. We chatted and smoked. Only then did he slowly begin to circle around my real intents and purposes, but with subtle and natural diplomacy. Using the most reasonable pretext, I told him I was looking for a certain girl I'd met during the carnival, but had lost sight of. He smiled ambiguously.

"Our girls are forever lost and found, that's how they are."

"Any chance of you giving me some help? I think she's been hanging out around here, from what she told me."

"Are you sure of what you want, *compadre?*"

"Most definitely."

"And the girl's name?"

"Epifania."

Sr. Serafín rolled his eyes and muttered something under his breath. Then he repeated his last question: "Are you sure of what you want?" And again I replied in the affirmative.

He said: "Come to *El Fanguito* around midnight. Bring no weapon, not even a knife. Wear old clothes. Don't speak too much to anyone till you see me. I'll be outside the *Café Cantante*, in the middle of the street on your right. *Oíste?* Understand?"

CHAPTER 22

▼

Remote memories of my first secret meeting with Inky were on my mind for the rest of the day. But this rendez-vous was infinitely more dangerous. At the *sereno's* call of midnight, I left my lodgings and walked swiftly towards the *Alameda*. *El Fanguito,* as I had found out, was a short street of bars and dance-halls just behind the wharfs. It was often flooded, hence its name referring to the mud. As to my appearance, I had followed Sr. *Serafín's* instructions to the letter. I also understood his pressing advice to not even carry a knife. Any weapon drawn in a dangerous neighbourhood is but a provocation if one is not prepared to be the first to stab or shoot.

The *Alameda* was deserted, its shops shuttered, deep shadows under its arcades. The tranquil waters of the inner harbour slowly moved the ships riding at anchor. Their masts and rigging stood densely erect, flickering lanterns at the tops like fireflies in a swaying forest. Potent smells of fish and oil were carried on the breeze, mixing the sour exhalations of excrement and poverty with the breath of the ocean. I reached the shipyard, where the beams of two vessels under construction, standing out against the low horizon, looked like enormous fossils of beached whales.

Darkness was even denser here than on the deserted *Alameda*, yet more men were passing, alone and furtive or in confident groups, many of them mariners given away by their outfits and their swaying walk. Others were lone slumming citizens of middle age, or well-off youths attracted by the promises of the gutter. Along the track we were following, beggars in rags prayed, lamented or shouted, crazed eyes sometimes catching a brief and intense gleam deep inside the shelter of their private darkness.

I was now well past the shipyard. Ahead of me, a shaky wooden bridge crossed the mangroves towards the construction site of the *Atarés* fortifications. Vague reflections of coloured lights slowly drew and shortened our shadows on the muddy street as we approached an alley on the right. Sharp sounds of clarinets and laughter coming from the same direction grew into a consistent din, dominated by the already familiar rhythm of the ever-present hand-clapped *guaracha*. But here the rhythm was more insistent, marked by harder percussion, at the same time more obsessive, more seductive and more desperate. Havana's soul was in the harbour, and here was the soul of the harbour itself: the heartbeat of fast pleasure and ruthless greed. "*But so what!*"—said I to myself; "*Am I a moralist, to stand aside and judge?*" No: I was meant myself to grab life by the breasts; and having come to this conclusion, having turned an adventurous outing into a matter of soul and destiny—I entered *El Fanguito* with more arrogance and confidence than many of my shady companions.

The scene in front of us, as we turned the corner, was tumultuous and provocative in the extreme.

The street was a succession of roughly built dance-halls, lit by colourful lanterns and torches planted in the mud just outside the doors. Muscular men with shaven heads kept a semblance of peace at the entrances, and pretended to control the flow of customers. In fact, the chaos inside each dance-hall created a constant overflow into the street, be it as fights, flirtations or downright sex. The bouncers, nursing their authority with lazy grace, only interfered when there was a good opportunity to show off their strength, or when they were part of some deal with a girl or *chulo* to evict a customer stripped bare of money.

The noise of shrieking voices, clapping hands, drums, flutes and violins was overwhelming. Fast glimpses inside revealed a tangle of bodies: male hands eagerly seeking the contact with half-bared breasts and buttocks of all descriptions, their firm roundness accentuated by fashionably narrow waists. The girls played their bottoms as instruments, ever so often freeing themselves from an embrace or an attempted kiss to turn around and play the animal female in heat with rhythmic tremors of their lower bodies—only to crack up and run away when the clueless male, bursting with desire, was ready to mount.

I read the signs naming the various dance-halls as I walked on: *Salon Rojo, Monserate, Dos Hermanas, El Comodoro, Aché* ... Then I saw the *Café Cantante*—and, sure enough, there was *Sr. Serafín, cocinero,* transformed into one of the gatekeepers or bouncers, his muscular presence, fast eyes and shaven head showing off his personality to great advantage. This particular dance-hall looked by far the darkest, rowdiest and sexiest of them all. Sr. Serafín fronted it with a kind of reassuring attitude, but also with the critical eye of one who understands that men will enter their chosen hell if only to prove themselves. He smiled when he recognized me, looked me up and down and quickly searched me for weapons, finding none, and nodded approvingly for my following his instructions. He motioned me inside while I asked, above the deafening noise coming from the open door: "Is Epifania there?"

"She is where she chooses to be, *compadre*," he answered cryptically.

Upon this, I entered the dance-hall and was at once immersed in its liquid heat, its mass of writhing bodies and the compact smells of sweat and rum. The music was at its highest pitch, the syncopated rhythm danced to ecstasy by one man, in the middle of the dance floor facing the orchestra, gyrating three slender girls at once in complicated patterns, the crowd pressing and yelling around them. As I sought my own way forward, an expert hand grabbed my private parts and started to fondle me. The hand could belong to any one of a group of girls tightly wrapped around me, all taut-breasted, wide-eyed and wet-mouthed in the safe darkness. I freed myself from their attempts, all too conscious of my vulnerability and unwilling to be once again the victim of a stratagem like the one occurred to me during the *Noche de Reyes*. As I pushed my way towards the counter at the far end of the room, my passage still occasionally blocked by the enterprising *jineteras,* two strong impressions stopped me. First, a man turning away from the bar holding a bottle of white rum struck me as resembling—*Mr. Wingate, the mate of the Vision Quest crew!* I saw the man in three-quarter profile, and a moment later he had been absorbed again by the crowd; yet, the impression was a vivid and extremely disconcerting one. The moment was too confused and intense to allow for much reasoning, but I clearly felt the deadly threat Mr. Wingate's presence in Havana would pose to me after the loss of my merchandise. If Captain Trench and the crew were already looking for me, I was most surely lost—for this probably meant that *all of my secrets* had been discovered, and sooner than I had hoped or calculated.

But the second impression, being more urgently related to my present search, was even *stronger.* At the opposite end of the bar, a girl's profile *seemed to be Epifania's!*—only, it may have been her, but strangely transformed from her cheerful, street-happy personality into a much harsher character, unnaturally wild-eyed and brooding, mercilessly surveying potential prey. The girl also disappeared in the whirl of dancing bodies after a split second and I found myself desperately wading through the waves of the crowd, like a drowning man pretending to rescue someone sinking even faster than himself.

I finally reached the bar-counter, where both the ghost of the girl and the one of my former shipmate had appeared. There was no trace of either. However in an even darker backroom, visible from where I stood, much was going on. *Mulatas de rumba* and fifteen-year old black girls were showing their tits for drinks. One of the latter, pressed stark naked against the graffiti-covered wall, let herself be gang-raped by drunken sailors. As she turned her haughty profile sideward, I saw she was biting the thick leather string of an amulet she wore around her neck. Her eyes were wide with drink or drug, her whole body taut, open but somehow unyielding. It was difficult to see her as a victim, as she seemed totally absorbed in her own trance, taking even some deep and secret pleasure in her public degradation—as if her very availability were proof of a higher power over the male race.

While such extreme forms of pleasure were being taken, the deafening music and the provocative dancing went on in the centre of the room. The raped girl might have screamed all she wanted, it would hardly have attracted any notice. Her leather-biting silence was a mere question of self-respect. As I was swept back to the dance floor, I kept on looking over my shoulder, still searching for the two missing ghosts.

But my more immediate imagination was now set afire by the rape scene, and I gave up resisting the crude advances of the other girls. Two of them squeezed me between their hot bodies, searching my pockets while fondling my willingly responding member. I screamed that I had no money left. They cracked up, handed me a bottle of rum and said they would fuck me on credit. I took a long swig and agreed. The rum instantly burned its bright and bitter way deep into my body. After two more swigs, I was ready to sign my soul away, if such had been the condition for a free ride.

Just as I was losing myself once again in this cleverly exploited madness, I saw Sr. Serafín nearby, checking on my situation with the merest hint of a grin on his face. The two girls yelled, and kissed him. He yelled back: "He's my friend, treat him well!"—and went back to his station near the entrance. Now the girls, under approval of the management as it were, redoubled their efforts, and I lost my head even more willingly (having indeed nothing else to lose anymore).

But just as my abandon reached its climax, once again my eyes were instinctively drawn to the darkest corner of the room—and once again I would have sworn that Epifania was watching me from amidst the deepest dregs of the place, herself very much part of them yet full of disdain, as if her own real purposes went deeper and further still ... It was the impression of one fast heartbeat, nothing more. Then my senses took over again and I let the two girls escort me to an alley running along the backside of the dance-halls, which they called *El Hueco*, where they pushed me into a hovel holding nothing but a burning candle and a straw mattress on the dirt floor. There we took our pleasure unrestrained and to the full.

I woke up in the same place towards noon the next day. The two girls had disappeared. I was strangely lucid and refreshed, the sex having burned up the rum in my blood.

Thinking over the events of the night, I was certain now that Epifania had been watching me. But why? If she had wanted to exploit me further, or to form an association with me for whatever reason, she could have sought me out in *Calle de los Oficios*. So she was biding her time, spying on my moves. Did she think that I had more contraband hidden somewhere? Or was she in league with Mr. Wingate and the rest of the crew?—if it was true that the mate of the *Vision Quest* had indeed also been at the *Café Cantante*. These questions were beginning to poison my mood, so I avoided them for a while, and tried to enjoy the total freedom of my present condition between floating and falling.

The entertainments in which I had participated during the night were louder and more crowded and sexier than what I had witnessed in other ports, but not so different as to their ingredients. The difference had come from two characters. Sr. Serafín had no doubt been observing my behaviour, either to confirm what an easy victim I made, or as an agent for Epifania and her plans; and Epifania herself was the strangest part of it all. There was an abysmal difference between the sweet and reckless happiness of her first appearance in my room, and the brooding devil she had seemed to be last night. There was one element however which I recognized from both occasions. The girl had a quick and scheming intelligence, oozing from her eyes either in wit or evil. I was warned.

Wasn't that also the subtle message Sr. Serafín had been conveying to me from the first time I had mentioned her name to him? Sr. Serafín himself I could place with relative ease in the scheme of things. As the daytime cook at the *Garza Real*, he was in a position to lure sailors and slumming gentlefolk to *El Fanguito* where his stature and muscles allowed him to moonlight as a bouncer. Since my stolen leather pouch had been discarded at the *Garza Real*, this was obviously where the thieves, including Epifania, had met after robbing me. Maybe Sr. Serafín was Epifania's *chulo* or pimp—yet I somehow believed what she had told me during her visit, that as a prostitute she worked by herself and was unattached: such had been the total impression of freedom conveyed by either her talent as an actress or her true nature.

Considering all this, the warnings to my safety and my heart were accumulating fast. But consider also that I had no choice but to go forward now. Without my contraband I was a corpse anyway, and Epifania was still the only link towards recovering my goods. The presence of Mr. Wingate, if confirmed, made the matter even more urgent. I did not consider, at that moment, the other potential explanations of his appearance—for as the reader will find out later, I had not penetrated even the uppermost layers of all the intrigues formed on board the *Vision Quest*.

CHAPTER 23

▼

From the *salón* behind one of the balconies of the Pedroso Palace, the three gentlemen were surveying the extension works of the city west of the old ramparts. Both the Pedroso brothers and Bucarely, the Captain-general, wore their best finery: coats and waistcoats, knee-breeches, silk stockings, ruffed cravats, powdered wigs. The weather was turning to hot and humid after the relative cool of the sugar-cane season, and their official dress was a burden. They smelled of wet wool, sweat and lavender water. But inside the balconied room in the Pedroso Palace, they were at least sheltered from the intense sunlight flooding the streets and the construction works they were surveying: the new grid of streets being laid out just east of the ramparts, and the *Castillo de Atarés*, a new addition to the maritime defences, going up to protect the deeper reaches of the inner harbour.

In the merciless sunlight, Bucarely saw men being whipped by an overseer. "Do you employ slaves for the street works now, Don Mateo?" He asked. "The contractors make their own decisions, your Excellency; we merely set the price levels."

"Good Lord, the world out there is ever more competitive and unforgiving," said Bucarely, shaking his head.

Mateo Pedroso raised one eyebrow.

"That's all to our advantage, Your Excellency," he answered. "In the conditions we are now creating, Cuba will be as good as any competitor."

"I was not merely referring to trade, Don Mateo. There is the condition of society in general to consider ..."

His brother José, the *Sindaco Procurador*, not nearly as diplomatic, snorted disdainfully and said squarely:

"What is your argument, Excellency? Do we as authorities exist to maintain order, or to dispense charity? You will forgive me, but let the Church and its Orders dispense charity; it's not our task. Orderly society prospers through the ambitions of its most active members, and the labour of the others."

"On the matter of labour precisely ..."

"Do you want to maintain seriously that freedom—any kind of freedom—can coexist with work on this island, Bucarely? In this indolent climate? Give a little free rein, and all you'll see is every evil passion and disorder raising its many heads. There will be a poisonous snake behind every stalk of cane in every field on the island, so to speak ... They may become fashionable for a season in Madrid, but your so-called *Philanthropists* are laughable. We have to deal with island life. Every man will fight for his own sons, and willingly cut throats of another man's sons in the process. Hasn't it ever struck you, Bucarely, that those Utopians preaching brotherhood of mankind as a whole are invariably people without friends or family? Hence, their universal love imposes them but little responsibility. But I am a patriot, your Excellency: I have the interests of this island at heart, since we have tied our fate to it and since there is no way back now ..." His tone became more confidential.

"Away from the Court in Madrid, Spain herself is poor and agonizing. The American colonies of the British are condemned as we all know. They will either be taxed into destruction, or they will revolt. And what then will become of our Cuba in these new and chaotic Americas, sir? The answer is this: *Cuba will feed sugar to the world, or she will perish with the Empires.*

And here on this rich and ardent soil, in this indolent climate, free trade requires forced labour ..."

Bucarely had heard the speech before. The Pedrosos repeated all the arguments developed by Arango and the other sugar barons. They treated him with scant respect. True, he had accepted their payoffs for admitting the increasing number of slave ships in the harbour—but at heart he remained a loyal civil servant. Their politics were simplistic, he sometimes argued with himself late at night when he was alone and free of their overwhelming controls and insinuations. As gain dictated all their plans, they were blind to the dangers of their scheme. Would not the massive slave imports distort the balance between masters and Africans? The French in St. Domingue, having made the same mistake, were increasingly wary of revolution. And in Cuba the situation would be worse—since it was impossible to do away with the more liberal Spanish laws allowing the slaves to free themselves after seven years of labour.

Often, in the middle of these thoughts, the bells of the nearby Jesuit chapel would strike midnight; and this would set his train of thought on a different but related subject. The Jesuits had been expelled from Haiti in 1762 as being too liberal. The same *fear of a Black Republic* had inspired the decision. The Pedrosos had made some insinuations against the Jesuits in Havana already: the order had not been indifferent to the new and massive influx of slaves, insisting on their education and salvation. These doctrines were certainly irritating the powerful traders and planters. Worse still, the order had its own fleet and its own trading privileges with Spain.

The valuable cinchona from South America was handled exclusively by them—it was commonly referred to as *Jesuits' bark,* and fetched high prices on the black market in Havana, as it was a supposed remedy against the deadly tropical fevers of the summer months.

Bucarely sighed. He foresaw trouble. His orderly and timid soul sought refuge from all these temptations and ramifications of reality in the writing of a detailed report on the city's extension works, to be filed unread in the depths of the *Archives of the Indies* in Seville, amongst millions of other documents testifying to the vain attempts of entire generations to fight history with administration. But bearing witness, yes. Bearing witness.

CHAPTER 24

▼

This city of San Cristóbal De La Habana, then, where I lay on a straw mattress in a hovel in a mud alley called *El Hueco*—the Hole—behind the worst dance-hall in *El Fanguito* ...—this city was revealing its true character. Universal corruption was too simple a term to describe it. Having created an impossible mixture of ingredients, all *Habaneros* lived and breathed contradiction—some with natural grace, others with unstoppable greed or dark urges towards self-destruction.

During the occupation, the British had utterly failed to control the spirit of Havana. Their prejudices were enormous: against the mixing of the races, against the Cuban brand of Christianity and the overt sexuality oozing from even the walls of respectable palaces where mistresses and bastard children of counts and dukes lived alongside wives and heirs. Their moral indignation was expressed in some official reports, their military superiority was soon undermined by the contagious vices—and they left at the earliest pretext, preferring by far to retreat to Jamaica where the planters' whip, blessed by the Anglican Church, maintained order, segregation and all the pious hypocrisies of colonial family life.

The city already had me under its spell. Even as I lay in my lair, biding my time, I absorbed more and more of its fluid personality, its unique blend of generosity and degradation. I absorbed it from the distant sounds of the port and the shipping yard; from the yells, the laughter and the shouts from the construction site of the fort of *Atarés*; from the cracks of the whip; from the sharp voices of women gossiping and girls scheming; from the faraway but insistent African drums—church bells sometimes imitating their rhythmic patterns to convey deeply unchristian messages; from the crowing of roosters kept everywhere in preparation of ritual sacrifice.

This Havana then, intuitively reconstructed from its sounds, was timeless or eternal, a crossroads of oceans and displaced souls. And more and more, as I reconstructed a wholly subjective city in my own mind, the mysterious girl I was chasing in this dangerous labyrinth became a personification of the city itself.

Sometimes I would torture myself with images of the acrobatic sex acts she was no doubt engaging in with shady characters. The next moment, I would revel in her freedom, her good humour and her total availability for excitement and adventure.

CHAPTER 25

▼

This motionless search could have gone on for weeks. Sr. Serafín brought me a little food once in a while, and some rum and cigars every day. Women and girls came to check on me while I was half asleep. I don't know why the neighbourhood thus adopted me. Either they had a natural respect for crazy behaviour, or they understood that I had entered a *zone of vision* and were afraid to interfere with whatever spirits I was communicating with. I was too absorbed in the process to question it myself. The way I dreamed up the complexities of the city without moving around should maybe have alarmed me, but my mood during those days was so strange that I accepted my newly acquired second vision, my extra-lucid somnolence, as a given—even came to see it as a right.

Then one night, while the raucous fun was in full progress in *El Fanguito*, the door of the hovel opened slowly. I was in one of the strangest phases of the strange mood I'd been in for days. Even in the semi-darkness every colour was vivid, every shadow sharply drawn, every sound crystal clear. In this nigh painful acuity of my senses, I felt my body projecting an aura, I felt an almost impossible unity of purpose in all my thoughts and my most minute intuitions ... And suddenly there, freeing herself from the shadow of the door, was Epifania, the angel of this unnatural lucidity, in her cheerful incarnation, as I'd seen her first in *Calle de los Oficios*—dressed in off-white calico, narrow-waisted, proud-breasted, her long thin braids moving like a curtain in front of her incredibly lively eyes—and she smiled broadly with a wet and open mouth and kissed me and took my hand.

CHAPTER 26

▼

From then on, she took me under her wings. We left the hovel that very night. She guided me to a closed carriage drawn by two mules, waiting at the end of the *Alameda*. Inside the carriage, she was all of a sudden all over me—so I lost count of the streets we crossed and the neighbourhoods we traversed. When the carriage came to a stop, she was sitting half-naked astride of me. The cabdriver knocked on the roof. She dressed without haste and motioned me to follow her.

We were in a pitch-dark street somewhere on the outskirts of the city, I could not make out where. The street was lined with various constructions, mostly wooden houses of some size but with sagging roofs and verandas, like abandoned country cottages of the rich. In between were humbler shacks and stables. Above the roofs, moonlight was reflected off the gently swaying fronds of high royal palm trees. Torches and lanterns were burning on some of the balconies, sculpting deep shadows. There was laughter and the sound of quarrels. The air smelled of charcoal, of jerked meat and of mud. Epifania took off her high-heeled shoes to safe them from the dirt and running noiselessly on bare feet hustled me into an alley between a house and a shack, up a high flight of wooden stairs, into a dark passage and thence into a windowless room. She pushed me down on a hard bed, and finished making love to me. Afterwards, I fell into a trancelike sleep, vaguely aware of her body next to mine.

The next days I slowly recovered my senses. I was still too confused to ask questions. Epifania was always there, keeping me company or preventing me from checking my whereabouts—or both. She seemed to be on the run, yet she was happy and relaxed and full of jokes and laughter. She told me her story.

CHAPTER 27

▼

"I was fourteen when the English took the city; and soon they took me with it. It was going to happen anyway, I was of age. My mother, Caridad, was a free woman, having freed herself by *coartación* from a plantation in Las Tunas. My father was a newly arrived slave, a *bozal* named Callí. My mother wanted to make sure I was born within the Havana city walls, for she hoped this would entitle me to a less harsh life than she had known in the country. But my father could not free himself during the first seven years after his arrival. So my mother, pregnant with me, left him for the city. She took up work as a seamstress. Because she was a free woman, she could have me duly baptized in the convent of *Santa Catalina*. They wrote me up in their registers *de pardos y negros*, that's why I know I was fourteen when the city fell."

"My father never reappeared; but I keep on meeting sisters and brothers of mine leading the life like me in Havana, so I know he's well and seems to have a way with the *guajiras* out there. *Tremendo negrón!* Fourteen siblings I have found so far! I think I have more of his blood than my mother's. She is an excellent woman, but exceedingly obedient—and I am a free spirit. Already the year before the city fell, I had ran away from home once and stayed on the streets for some days, although I came back still a virgin. With the English it was different. They were ugly as devils with all that milky skin, the straw-like hair and those eyes so pale they looked fragile. And flabby asses! And bad teeth! *Por Dios*, were they ugly, brother! Probably finer ladies than we got to fuck the better looking ones. But even the ugly ones were still a novelty. We poor people didn't know of all the politics behind the war and the siege and we thought they were here to stay, so we adapted ..."

"They buried the dead, shipped the Spanish Captain-general and the bishop back to Cádiz—and the party started for good. With the Captain-general and the bishop gone, the whole city seemed to wake up. The cholera struck and thousands died; still we danced on. Yes, they were the enemy and we were not unaware of that. But they were the masters of the moment, and my Havana is a *tremenda puta*, proof thereof was now given once and forever. The soldiers fell on us little black girls with great gusto—since they had never seen a free African woman in their own lands. Nor heard one, I should add—for as you know this is a city of fast compliments and even quicker retorts. Within three months, every *puta* spoke enough English— *Bereguel! Sanavabiche! Guanti foqui!*—to find herself her own *yuma*, as we started to call them. It became a saying in every poor room and shack in the city, when money was low and food running scarce: '*Encuéntrate un yuma!*' Mothers cheerfully lived on their girls' prostitution. As I had tasted *la farándula*, the life, already, I was of course in over my ears. (She crossed herself) *Dios me cuide!* I don't know how I didn't catch every illness they brought with them. But no, I have my *aché* and my *iré*, as we call our spiritual protection, and my father's vigour and health ..."

At this point Epifania's tale became political. It was the first time I realised that her intelligence was not limited to her quick street-wit, but penetrated questions of principle as well. I also understood she wanted to impress me, because she knew I could read and write, she couldn't, and she was annoyed to admit any kind of superiority in a man.

"Men are always led to think that wars are about ideas. Some politician in a palace in London would have told us the English had come to liberate or enlighten us. Maybe he would even have believed it himself. But we girls from the streets of Havana see it different, for we know that every fight—be it on a street corner or a battlefield—is not about ideas but about *interests*: money, power, vanity—what have you: but never, never ever about those noble things you men call ideas or ideals."

"So we thought the English were going to stay and rule Cuba because we could not imagine why they would have come and taken us in the first place if such had not been their interest. See, that's the *limit of our superiority*: we're right in thinking that everything is done for some kind of profit or advantage, but mostly we only recognize *immediate* advantages. When the British packed up and left after merely a year of occupation, we were utterly lost and confused. Many lost a lover, many more the comforts of generalized whoring and dealing. But soon we found out that Havana had changed too, and was ready for the future."

I pressed her to know what precisely had happened during the *Noche de Reyes*. "Without you knowing, I made a deal with you. See: all your money and the stuff you carried was going to be stolen anyhow. It was all spoken for—even before you reached your lodgings. You were completely defenceless. So when the *Eleggua* child spotted you as a victim inside the Angola *solar*, I convinced Pompi to take the contraband and let you live, and to let me have the *guano* ... "

"The *what?*"

"The *guano*, the *barro—the cash!* See: that way everyone would benefit. I'm now your banker and your bodyguard. You keep me and I keep you. Otherwise, some really bad whore and her *chulo* would have had it all. But as for me, I work by myself, as you know. See again: I like you, you're cute. There's something in it for me as well, I won't deny that—but you are the main beneficiary ..."

"Show me the money, then."

"Easy now, brother. The money is safe, we'll take small amounts as we go."

"But you deliberately set me on a false trail when you came to see me in *Oficios*, speaking of the *Palenque* instead of the *Manglar* ... "

"I was testing your ingenuity, *asere!* And brilliantly you passed the test too ... My *yuma* is no fool! You understand this city, eh? You could be one of us ... Stop worrying, you're with me now."

But I kept on asking questions. She revealed some more details: the *Elegguá*-child was her spotter. Besides being already addicted to rum and smoke, the child was also an authentic visionary: he literally *saw through the victims*. She had four boys working with her to encircle victims and dance closer and closer to them. As soon as the goods were stolen they were tossed in turn to two other accomplices in the crowd, and everybody ran off in different directions. *Pompi el Palero*, as she called him, was the fence ...

"What does he look like?" I asked, hoping to find a link to a face I might remember from the *Noche de Reyes*, or even from *El Fanguito*. "He has gold teeth ... *and a small dick*," she answered, cracking up. And that was the extent of the description I got. Also, not once did she ask what the contraband had been, or where it had come from, etc. These questions were either superfluous to her, or she wanted to ignore them, or wanted me to think she was no longer interested in them. Thus, questions and doubts about her activities and her multiple personalities remained. When I tried to find out where she had lived before she joined me, the answer was always evasive—as if, indeed, the whole city had been her home, or she had lived on the streets—which her appearance contradicted, for she was always clean as driftwood. She often spoke of *Regla* as her true home.

The village of *Regla*—across the bay from Havana—was in fact a free territory of runaways, illegal migrants, smugglers, sorcerers and prostitutes. She told me she had many connections there. Apparently, during the British occupation, Regla had been her university or, as she put it: '*la escuela de la calle y de la noche.*' From what I understood now, when the British had taken the city, many of the colourful characters of the nightlife and '*la farándula*' or the demi-monde had fled to *Regla*. Most of them were free blacks—a class nonexistent under

British rule elsewhere—and feared to be reduced to slavery again. Thus *Regla* had become a haven for all kinds of irregulars, and would forever remain it, even though many of the refugees soon ventured into the city again. It was also in *Regla* that opium had become the fashionable drug.

The British had used some opium as a painkiller for the wounded during the 1762 battle of Havana, and some more to fight the cholera epidemic during their occupation. Sir George Pocock, the commanding admiral of the British fleet, had just returned from India and carried his own supply. The cholera, the yellow fever and the dysentery had so plagued the British already during their attack, that more men died of illness than in the fighting. Some of Pocock's opium was used, but reserved for noble officers only. The common soldier was of course left to die, or was amputated, without the solace of their *laudanum*. In the general confusion during the short occupation, the remaining opium disappeared on Havana's black market. Always quick to discover new fashions, The Habanera *hampa* or underworld had taken to the drug with delight. But the first drinkers of laudanum and the first smokers of opium paste had been cruelly disappointed when the British left, the frenetic whoring and dealing came to an abrupt end, and the supply of opium to Havana's night life all but dried up.

All of this Epifania must have witnessed if indeed she had been living in *Regla* in those days, but she seemed to avoid the topic. Still, through conversations such as these, I tried, slowly and delicately, to establish deeper confidence with her. Swapping stories was the best and most natural way. After she had told me about her early life I reciprocated with the tale of my youth in Antwerp, and how and why I had fled that city to wander the world. But she wanted to know more about the years between my flight and my arrival in Havana; and I obliged—*also to a certain point.*

CHAPTER 28

▼

In the spring of 1761, an opportunity offered itself for me to ship out as an inventory clerk on board a much grander vessel than the *Pigeon Voyageur.* This was the *Challenger,* out of Calais, a three-masted ship, slow but steady, plying the trade between its home port and various ports in the Mediterranean. Occasionally, and depending on the policies and alliances of the moment, the *Challenger* ventured out to Sicily and Malta. The captain was wary of those ports, though, as Berber corsairs were never far away and the ship carried but a few cannon for its defence.

Still, the sailing over wider distances, and out of sight of land, taught me a lot about navigation—for I observed the manoeuvres, and as the mate realised that I was a quick learner and could read & write well, he soon started to trust me with note-taking beyond my normal duties.

This brought me to the summer of the year 1763. I now had considerable sailing experience, and would qualify as a second navigator on an ocean-going vessel. The *Challenger* was detained in the port of Nantes for urgent repairs. I was offered twice to ship out on a slaver, plying the triangular trade between France, the Guinea Coast and Guadeloupe, but my instincts & judgement rejected this—although the pay was good, and a share in considerable profits was suggested. As I walked the streets of the town, aimlessly, for several weeks, I saw that the port was benefiting much from the slave trade. Entire new neighbourhoods were being laid out, and splendid new mansions of ship-owners and merchants were going up one next to the other, each one intended to outdo its neighbour with balconies and bow-windows and grand entrances.

I sat around plotting my future, trying to make my savings last by fasting and smoking, but then spending recklessly on wine and a girl on Sundays. (At this detail, Epifania almost suffocated with laughter.) In my idleness, I was tortured by thoughts about Antwerp and my mother. Again I felt how cruel and unnatural it was to have the city amputated of its port. I was now a full member of the sea-faring fraternity, and a ship would have brought me to my native city with relative safety. The absurdities of politics thus kept me separated from my duties as a son. (Epifania said to this that I was not honest with myself, and that I could have made contact with my mother by other means had I really wanted to.) This very argument I had debated with myself back then at Nantes whenever tobacco and an empty stomach made me light in the head. Even with myself, I never came to an honest conclusion. Maybe my newly gained sense of freedom made me fearful of moving backward. In the Mediterranean ports, I had sometimes felt an anticipation of the vivid colours and the smells and the sounds I had longed for as a child. But I was still unsatisfied, and convinced I had to go further in my *quest for intensity.* How far I would eventually go—and what I would discover there—I was not even able to imagine.

After more than a month in Nantes, unwilling to spend the winter in France, I got a berth on the *Dragon,* a fast and agile two-master bound for Africa. I shipped out on the third of September 1763. We left Nantes under ballast. In Bordeaux, we picked up our cargo. It consisted of wine—and glasses. The wine was cheap vintages in small kegs, demijohns and label-less bottles in straw-filled crates. It was sold in great quantities in every fort and trading post along the Guinea coast. The glasses were a side-trade, risky (there was always a lot of breakage) but lucrative, as the traders lost in the lugubrious slave forts desperately tried to maintain the fiction of being gentlemen and drinking in style.

While we were being loaded at Bordeaux, I found out that the ship had a reputation on the docks. They called it the *Drunken Dragon*. The master, Monsieur Dandélion, also owned the ship. He was a notorious drunkard himself, famous for flying his flags upside-down. I was apparently the only innocent having signed up to this ship without knowing these details. The crew were an odd lot indeed, a mixture of uncertain nationalities from Nordic and Baltic ports: pale, pink and stubborn men, of limited vocabulary when sober, sentimental and violent (in that order) when drunk; and fearless—for lack of imagination. Apart from the captain, there were no other Frenchmen on board. It seemed that Captain Dandélion, as a precaution, made sure to hire crews not interested in his cargo, for these men invariably got drunk on beer and rum only.

There were two Englishmen on board: a Mr. Trench, unremarkable-looking, short and wiry, with credentials as a second mate and stevedore; and Mr. Wingate, looking even more like a bureaucrat than his countryman (although illiterate by his own admission), signed as the boatswain. I did not establish confidence with anyone at first. My duties as a navigator and scribe set me somewhat apart and did not encourage easy friendships, which I avoided by temperament anyway, even—or especially—in the cramped conditions and enforced intimacies on shipboard. Mr. Trench and Mr. Wingate were polite to me, each in his way. This was the only apparent trait they shared. In spite of their common nationality, they seemed to avoid each other as much as possible (again, given the conditions on shipboard). I thought this odd at first, but as both men were obviously old salts, I said to myself that they must have their good reasons. Suspicious captains were often on the outlook for collusion between crew members of similar background.

We left Bordeaux for our fateful voyage on October 1st of the year 1763.

END OF BOOK I

BOOK II

SOLAR SARABANDA

CHAPTER 1

▼

Towards the summer of the year 1766, loiterers on the Havana quayside saw great quantities of timber being loaded on small boats and being ferried across the inner harbour. As always in Havana, speculations arose. Some whispered that a whole field of gallows was being erected to hang French spies or Dutch corsairs or English mercenaries. Others knew for a fact that a vast campaign was being mounted to rid the city of freemasons infiltrated from *St.Domingue*. Others still, invoking sources inside the government offices in the very *Castillo de la Fuerza*, confirmed that a massive influx of new slaves was expected, and that the government planned to keep them in camps outside the city so as to separate them from contacts with free Africans till they were dispatched to the plantations and the new sugar mills.

This last speculation seemed the least unlikely. It was a well-known fact that the sugar production was being expanded. All along the *muelle*, the same loiterers could see large pieces of cast-iron machinery being unloaded: tubes, furnaces, enormous cauldrons, grinding cylinders. It was obvious that new *ingenios* were under construction inland, and such new mills only made sense if more cane was to be grown; hence, more slaves.

Even the most professional loiterers, jaded in their appreciation of maritime commerce, acknowledged the exceptional size of the undertaking. Seeing the measures and the number of the cauldrons being unloaded, they whistled an admiring '*Muchacho!*' between their teeth, and spat tobacco juice with deep philosophy. If they happened to be black, the whisper became a loud '*Coño, asere!*'; and when occasionally a longshoreman was hurt or killed by a monstrous piece of cast-iron equipment falling off a faulty crane, both races shook their heads and agreed on the essence of such tragedies, in the most typical of Habaneros' comments on the vagaries of life: '*No es fácil!*'.

During the month of April, a minor act of piracy had occurred in Havana harbour. Three men who were later described as *enemies of the Crown* had captured one of the small ferry-boats linking Havana to *Regla*, menacing the helmsman with blunt knives and a rusty pistol. They pretended to escape to Florida. As a price for the retreat of the English, this colony had been given up by Spain, and rebellious subjects of the Empire now nursed the illusion of finding freedom there.

The inexperience of the pirates and the sailors' reluctance to assist them—once they had realized the pathetic arms were useless—stalled the boat a few miles past the lighthouse of *El Morro,* whence the runaways were retrieved by several fast brigantines of the Coast Guards, and brought back to the *Fuerza* in chains.

No one was killed or even hurt in the whole incident. Nevertheless the judges—urged on by the Pedroso brothers eager to set an example against future escapes by sea—showed themselves particularly merciless. The three were sentenced and executed within the week. In spite of the accusation—piracy—the men were not brought before an admiralty judge, but were instead court-martialed under the emergency decrees dating from the War. Nor were the executions public hangings. It seems the Pedrosos saw more advantage in secrecy, as the public whisperings about the executions would create even more fear than the simple view of corpses and the gallows.

The three were brought before a firing squad inside the *Morro* castle. Indeed the details got more sinister as the rumors were spreading. It was said that the condemned men were given a wake with their family members in a *capilla ardiente* normally reserved for dead bodies. One imagines the painful scenes of such a farewell. Next, the firing squad was timed to discharge at the same time as the 9 o'clock blank cannon shot from the fort announcing the curfew for slaves and the nightly closing of the city gates. These supposed precautions added again to the mystery, and hence to the climate of fear. A public hanging was always an entertainment. The bodies were there for all to see. Secret executions were far more sinister, and could go unchecked in great numbers.

Out on the streets of Havana, a few brave souls disapproved of the proceedings, as standing in no proportion to the crime committed. But everyone without exception understood that this was a warning from the Pedroso brothers that henceforth no dissidence or protest to their rule would be tolerated, as they moved to put into action their plans for accelerated slave imports, greatly expanded sugar production and aggressive free trade. The rumor that freedom was only ninety miles away in Florida, had to be wiped out. It has to be repeated that such freedom was inexistent anyway—the fugitives would merely have run into different and often harsher forms of slavery under protestant rule.

But one imagines the effects these events had on my fears. If one modest act of piracy met with such repression, my own fate if ever found out would leave no doubt. These uncertainties started to haunt me ever more. I still slept soundly enough, but each morning towards sunrise some mechanism in the depths of my soul prompted the release of an endless series of possible disasters in my imagination, growing in ever wider sequences, one leading to countless others, challenging me to take some kind of total responsibility; and I woke up feeling damned and exhausted, paralyzed by the demands of my own conscience. I became convinced that, if the hangman didn't get me, I would soon perish from nervous exhaustion.

Only Epifania's caresses could bring me back to some semblance of rest after these awful awakenings, and she faithfully assisted me. I came to understand later that she herself was given to extreme changes of mood, and that she perfectly understood the challenge of my mornings. But increasingly I took refuge in the night, when these tensions dissolved.

CHAPTER 2

▼

Our situation had changed regularly since my abduction. We moved from room to room, always under cover of the night. We remained mostly on the outskirts of the city. The rooms were in a wide variety of buildings, from semi-abandoned wooden summer cottages to elegant high-ceilinged ruins. It was easy enough to understand that, from her self-confessed activities as a *jinetera*, Epifania knew where to get to a bed fast and discreetly in most of the outer *barrios* of the city. Possessions didn't follow her around; yet she was always tidy and elegant, however loudly overdressed and bejeweled she would be at times: this was the habit of all Habaneras both vicious and virtuous. It was a small mystery how she organized herself in these practical matters, but I didn't ask any questions, preferring to respect the image of her light-footed availability.

But other habits developed as well. Frequently, Epifania disappeared from our room, mostly at night (but always after having made love with me). I could not distinguish a pattern in these absences, except that they seemed to become gradually longer as she became convinced that I was not going to leave her. The obvious explanation was that she was still working the streets at night. Fear of contagious disease apart, I had no reason to oppose this, as she had never pretended to be my woman exclusively. She said she knew how to protect herself, and showed me the devices, made of sheep's bladder, to slid over the man's cock. Making love unprotected or *a cappella* as the street called it, had become a rare and expensive vice in the nightlife since the English occupation, she explained—as the syphilis had been so rampant.

But I didn't fully believe that whoring was what she was out for. Yet she sometimes alluded to the fact that she was keeping me, and what money were we living on?—for there was always food and rum and cigars, wherever we were hiding.

The number and variety of her hideouts hinted at a vast network of connections and solidarities—serving what purpose? Was she observing me on someone's behalf, pacifying me with her caresses and then reporting back on my docility? But to whom? To the Authorities? To an agent of the *Vision Quest*? To the thieves of my contraband? The presence of Mr. Wingate in the city seemed to bear out one of these possibilities. As the tension in my nerves was growing day by day, I no longer doubted the veracity of my vision at the *Café Cantante*. It never once occurred to me, given as I was to fears and uncertainty, that even if Mr. Wingate was indeed in Havana, it could be for a variety of reasons, including some that were to my advantage.

My years on the run and my experiences on board the *Vision Quest* had shaped my soul in such a way that the worst had always to be certain. I would reflect on this in later life—yes, death is certain anyway in the end, so what reason for so-called optimism is there in the meantime? Probably my excessive immobility made me a poor philosopher—for deep thoughts are cheap and come easy to people of my disposition. From a Dutchman in the Orient I had once heard a quote from the Buddah: '*Questions about the origin of the universe are a housewife's diversions*' (or words to that effect). And a Chinaman once had laboriously translated for me a saying from Confucius' disciples, which the man had tattooed on the inside of his left forearm: '*The master refused to speak about prodigies, force, disorder and gods.*' I should have absorbed such practical wisdom and lived by the grace of the moment, but I could not.

Maybe, in the middle of my excessive thinking, Epifania's secret activities fascinated me because they were the very opposite of my idle and fearful speculations. Having been a warrior, I recognized her for one, and became only the more contemptuous of my own present confined and inactive condition.

However unsettled this way of life may seem, I somehow adapted to it. Ever since leaving Antwerp I had been immersed in intrigue and treachery. I cannot claim to have felt at home on any of the ships I'd sailed—least of all on the *Vision Quest*. But still, being on the run had become my natural condition, and I could no longer even imagine a strong attachment to a given place.

Havana must have been the most duplicitous city of all—what with the intrigues of politics and trade, the slavery question, the racial hypocrisies, and the battles of Commerce vs. Utopia. My poor soul was tossed to and fro in these currents, having long lost any sense of place, often even the sense of a recognizable and permanent Self. Adopting the form shaped by circumstances had become a virtue, or at any rate a condition for survival.

Thus Havana, with its inextricable treacheries, became as much a home to me as any other port would have been; and with rhythm, ecstasies and sex taken for granted in higher doses and intensities, it even had considerable advantages over more sedate berths.

CHAPTER 3

▼

This life went on unchanged through the heat and the extreme humidity of the summer months. As we had to stay indoors in hidden and airless spaces during the daytime, often we nearly suffocated.

Sometimes these circumstances, and the resulting necessity of permanent nakedness, made for a heightened, serpent-like sensuality, bathed in sweat and a profusion of all the spices and secretions of the body. Just like the buildings of Havana, built of coral, seemed to liquefy in the humidity, so our bodies as well carry in their atoms the secret nostalgia of sliding in primeval mud. But more often these circumstances were just unbearably annoying.

We spent the hottest months in a room on the edge of *El Vedado*, on the western outskirts of the city: a bleak zone of open chalk pits, dusty and unhealthy by day, by night utterly abandoned. At dusk I sometimes ventured out on the roof—in spite of Epifania's warnings—to breathe some fresher air.

One day, as I reached the roof, I saw two men working in one of the pits, raising high clouds of white dust which blew inland on the evening breeze. Looking the other way and stretching my neck, I could see the *Chorrera* fort, the mouth of the *Almendares* river and the sea far to the right. This set me musing about everything that had happened to me since I had crossed the *Almendares* to enter La Habana for the first time, so few weeks ago ... My own life seemed utterly unbelievable to me, what with the adventures, the challenges, the uncertainties. For a brief instant, taking in the balmy breeze from the seashore, I almost felt proud of myself in spite of all the quandaries I found myself in.

Just as I was basking in this satisfaction, by the merest coincidence I turned around to face *El Vedado* again—and now the presence of *three* men at the edge of the chalk pit struck me as somehow unusual. The two workers had laid down their pickaxes and had raised the masks they wore over their mouths. They were talking to a person of a more gentlemanlike appearance, dressed in breeches and a blue coat. It was the clothes I recognized first.

Mr. Wingate had kept them scrupulously neat and folded in his chest on board the *Vision Quest*, sometimes ridiculed by Captain Trench for this bourgeois precaution, but clearly anticipating the day on which he would have to give himself a respectable appearance in some port, either for his own or for the ship's sake. Even now, as he was talking to the two other men, he was constantly wiping the white dust off his sleeves and shoulders.

All my panic rose to the surface again, with a violent jolt of pain to my temples. I hid behind the water barrels standing in a small crowd on the roof, and observed the scene further.

Mr. Wingate was obviously asking his way around, or enquiring about persons living in the neighbourhood. The two workers, apart from being dusty and tired, were also wary to talk to a foreigner whose business they didn't know or trust. But now Mr. Wingate dug in his pockets and brought out some silver.

I hastened back to the room where Epifania was half asleep, and in a breathless voice told her that the pirates were catching up with me, and that we had to run again, the sooner the better. Mr. Wingate's turning up here could just not be yet another coincidence: he had obviously already located the *barrio* where I was staying, and it would be a matter of hours till he would also identify the building and the room, certainly if silver coins were changing hands in the process.

"Calm down, Rey," she said, sitting half up and her eyes thinking faster than ever, "Calm down. There is always a *last solution* ... "

In spite of my utter panic, I registered the fact that she accepted my problem as her own, and did not for one second—even when confronted so abruptly with the choice to make—consider the option to abandon me to my persecutors.

For whatever reason of her own, good or bad, for the time being I could still count on her connections.

"There is only one place left to go now, Reyito. Chased by the devil, you run to hell."

CHAPTER 4

▼

The village of *Regla,* situated on a thumb of land sticking out in the inner bay right across from the harbour, had grown around the church of the Black Virgin. This statue was a copy of the original in *Chipiona* near *Cádiz* as most mariners knew; but as this original statue was supposed to have come from Africa, the presence of its double at the far end of the African slave route was a poignant fact in its own right.

Behind the church, small shacks of fishermen, carpenters and coopers had interconnected and locked into labyrinths of rooms and courtyards. The *Solar Sarabanda* where Epifania and I found refuge, was such a human beehive situated between the church and a small sugar mill near the ferry landing. It was entered from the street through a narrow vaulted passageway about ten yards long and opening into a first courtyard called *Patio Blanco*. Circling this space was a number of individual rooms to the right, and a common kitchen and laundry area to the left.

These buildings and spaces constituted the visible settlement. In the *Patio Blanco*, children were always at play, laundry was drying, girls were sifting rice and beans, old women with heavy eyelids and tired legs sat smoking clay pipes or long cigars, men loudly played dominoes. Dogs, chickens and roosters were roaming free, shrill laughter or shriller fighting voices always rose from the kitchen.

Sometimes a child would come running out screaming, dripping wet from some practical joke of the washerwomen. At other times these women would chase each other with knives, threatening murder over some passing intrigue.

Wood and water were fetched constantly from outside the *Solar* on girls' heads, shaping their straight backs, the forceful arching of feet and calves under the weight, and thus sculpting the grace of their walk for generations to come.

The rooms on the right hand side of the *Patio Blanco* were mostly occupied by freedmen who had served in the auxiliary forces during the siege and the war, had lost eyes or limbs, had received grand certificates in His Majesty's Name on the cheapest parchment, and no pensions.

This lively urban village was the *Solar* as it was commonly acknowledged to exist. A whole different world lay beyond the walls of the kitchen area, the back end of the *Patio Blanco* and the veterans' quarters. This forbidden zone, where runaways, smugglers and secret migrants from the provinces and from other islands were hiding out, was also a spontaneous cathedral to African gods and spirits.

Regla had become a haven to the slaves' ancestral religions ever since the Black Virgin in the little church had been identified with the *Yoruba* ocean spirit *Yemayá*. Its incarnation had followed the Africans on their deadly journey of the Middle Passage; it was only normal that they sought solace from it here.

CHAPTER 5

▼

Such was the secret inner layout of the *Solar*.

To the south of the kitchen area there was a small *Obeah* yard, kept by a Jamaican calling himself *Ras Fasil*. Prolonging the axis of the *Patio Blanco* westward was the much smaller *Patio Carabalí*, the sacred enclosure of the *Yoruba* ancestors. Further west of this patio was the dark *Patio Congo*, home to sorcerers and men's secret societies, mentioned only in whispers even inside the *Solar*.

The *Patio Congo* was a dead end, but to the north of it a further extension, entered from the veterans' rooms, was a semi-covered space called *Houmfor Duchesse*, after the Haitian voudoun refugee Duchesse Malenfant who ruled over it.

It is on purpose that I refer to this secret world as a spontaneous cathedral. I became aware that the situation, even the orientation of the rooms and patios—however haphazard they may have looked to outsiders—responded to precise requirements and traditions. The main axis of the whole *Solar* was the East-West progression of the *Patio Blanco* leading to the *Patio Congo*. The *Obeah* yard and the *Houmfor Duchesse* formed wings on either side of the main axis. The third and deepest layer of the *Solar* were small, completely hidden rooms beyond the main axis and its wings. The most important of these hideouts, were the *Casa Tambor* and the *Casa Babalao* adjacent to the *Patio Carabalí*; and the *Cuarto Fambá* also called *Cuarto ñañigo,* attached to the *Patio Congo.* The last and deepest layer was the *Cuarto Sarabanda,* contents and secrets unknown even to most initiates, and entered only by very special *licencia.*

Duchesse's *Houmfor* was a special case: a mixture of covered room and open space, out of line with the other patios but itself organized around a mystical centre pole called *poteau mitan,* the private axis of Duchesse's world not just of spirits, but also of intense political intrigue, as I was to find out.

The fugitives and runaways mostly kept to the inner rooms of the *Solar* during the day, but at night everyone ventured out and socialized in and around the *Patio Blanco,* because it was so close to the kitchen.

CHAPTER 6

▼

I was living with Epifania in one of the hidden spaces wedged in between the *Obeah yard*, the *Casa Babalao* and the *Patio Carabalí*. It was a wooden platform about six feet above ground, reached by a ladder we'd retract up for privacy and added security. The space was like a ship's bunk between the bulkheads, but it was a distinct improvement over my former living quarters on board the *Vision Quest*. It was clean and snug, the floor covered with reed mats and a couple of old and lumpy cotton mattresses.

One had to lie down inside, as the improvised rafters of the roofing structure were only about four feet above the platform. But the intertwined palm fronds of the outer roof kept it dry even in the worst of downpours. The summer heat right under the roof, on the other hand, could become nearly unbearable. Also—countless mosquitoes almost constantly invaded the platform, though at night they were somewhat kept at bay by fumigating the nearby patios with smoldering dry coconut shells.

Epifania's extensive wardrobe and her wigs, shoes, hats and jewelry could obviously not be kept there. She had made a deal with Duchesse who rented out closet space in the anterooms of the *Houmfor*. This suited Epifania fine, as it always gave her a reason or a pretext to escape into the labyrinth when some intrigue, or the simple demands of her independence, made her restless. Duchesse for her part grandly played Mistress of the Wardrobe, as it gave her power over a young girl she obviously observed with a mixture of pride and jealousy.

CHAPTER 7

▼

After weeks on the run in the city, life in the *Solar* felt *good*. It was simple on the surface, revolving around questions of food and personal hygiene: finding, cooking and eating daily meals in spite of all the restrictions and rationings occupied most of our time. In the evenings, bathing was a cheerful routine. For most of these people were all remarkably and proudly *clean*. Maybe it was one of the reactions against slavery and the perfumed sloppiness of the masters.

Epifania would bathe twice a day, and to bathe with her soon became one of my most cherished pleasures. For me as well, this pleasure was made more intense by bad memories. Aboard the *Vision Quest*, bathing had of course been out of the question. For weeks on end, we would live with our own and our shipmates' stench of sweat, urine and excrement.

Epifania took a little girl's delight in being all wet and shiny, soaping her scalp thoroughly through the long woven-in tresses, or her own short wiry hair when she was in a mood for wigs.

Feeding the *Solar* was a cooperative effort of every day. Food was never taken for granted. Bags of rice would be smuggled in from the port—they were thrown into the *lanchas* from incoming ships, even before the customs men controlling the state monopolies could count the bags on shipboard. Beans, plantains, *yucca* and *malanga* could be bought directly from farmers at the outskirts of the village. This, too, was technically illegal, as the farmers were supposed to fill production quota and to sell their surplus produce only through the official markets inside the city limits. The government wanted to control all the food supplies under the pretext of rational and equal distribution to the people. What they had created, even in these simple matters, was a vast system of deception and subterfuge, forcing everyone into collective hypocrisies. For as I was soon to understand, the state monopolies created the black market, which in turn fed corrupt bureaucrats.

The meat of the official rationing system was the stuff of dreams. So the Solar kept its own animals. Apart from chickens there were also freely roaming piglets, to be slaughtered for occasional feasts when they would be gutted, impaled and pit-roasted filled with rice and beans. But sometimes a girl would choose one of the piglets for a pet, put a ribbon around its neck and forbid it being harmed; and even grown men hungry for pork would respect such play if the girl were pretty enough.

Harsh white rum drawn from dregs and molasses, straight from the distillery attached to the nearby *cachimbo* or small sugar mill, was always abundant. Tobacco, another state monopoly, had again to be smuggled in. Private *vegueros* in *Oriente* sold their snuff and cigars to clandestine traders and exporters, whereas the tobacco growers around Havana and in the western provinces were entirely controlled by the State and the Church. The *Solar* got its supply from runners who constantly traveled back and forth between *Bayamo* and Havana, braving highwaymen and customs officers alike.

CHAPTER 8

▼

And where, you will ask, was all the money to run the *Solar* coming from? A few of the inhabitants had legitimate businesses or trades. Some worked in the city as musicians or tailors or cobblers. Far more peddled black market tobacco or ran undercover pawn shops. Others sold tickets of the popular clandestine lotteries. Epifania was a self-confessed prostitute and thief. Few of the other *Solar* girls were as straightforward about their occupations, but no doubt many followed her example.

These girls collected cash and gifts—especially gold—from sailors, soldiers and visiting merchants, and the gold was inevitably sold or pawned after a few days, a few weeks at most.

All the *santeria* practitioners sold advice, charms and herbs, and made new initiates pay substantial sums of money for rituals.

Altogether these activities made a lot of cash. If the *Solar* still lived in poverty, it was due to the fact that most of the residents, like Epifania and myself, were given to reckless spending on whims and follies and had expensive drinking and smoking habits.

The way in which the money was shared inside the *Solar* represented nevertheless a peculiar mixture of generosity, calculation and envy.

Aboard the *Vision Quest*, in a purely masculine environment, the fictions of common purpose came to an abrupt end once loot had to be divided. The Articles spelled out the shares; yet quarrels after every prize was taken led to violence and mayhem on many a pirate ship, often to outright murder.

There were no such Articles inside the *Solar,* no fixed shares of loot. But it was in many respects a feminine environment. All of the young children had single mothers, and the women obviously ran the kitchen and thus controlled social life. Now I will not idealize any sex over any other. The women's approach to money was just different. Generosities straight from the heart would alternate with poisonous gossip and vindictiveness. Still, on the whole, these girls and women were convinced they had to protect each other from us males, as well as to protect us against ourselves, and this double purpose formed strong solidarities among them.

Whatever Epifania's own problems were, she would always share her last *Real* with another girl, and she would spoil any child within reach even if it meant going hungry herself. At the same time, she used her generosity to improve her status within the community. As she had supposedly given up whoring since moving to *Regla,* and yet never appeared short of cash, I began to suspect again that she had kept all of my missing contraband and was now living off it. In this way she could also maintain the fiction that *she* was keeping *me,* while selling off what she had stolen from me. But as I myself had stolen everything from Captain Trench, could I blame her? And had Trench's possession of the goods been any more legitimate? He had stolen everything from the ships we'd attacked. But had the goods belonged more rightfully even on those ships? Didn't they belong to the people who produced them in horrible conditions under harsh latitudes?

If Epifania had kept the goods, the use of the money she made off them remained mysterious. At times she hinted at expensive ceremonies she had to undergo in order to complete her initiation as *Hija de Ochún.* At other times, I heard suggestions that her *Cabildo* functioned as a mutual aid society, and financed the freeing of as many *Yoruba* slaves as possible.

This would of course have been an attractive proposition to Epifania: freeing her tribal sisters and brothers was an act of true philanthropy, but if she contributed substantially towards its financing it also increased her respect and her power inside the *Cabildo*. And there was nothing she yearned more for, than respect.

CHAPTER 9

▼

The *Solar* had its intellectual pursuits as well. The practitioners of the various rites were always busy interrogating the older freedmen or runaways about African words and concepts, as they wanted to establish vocabularies to preserve the languages. I offered to make notes but Duchesse—wise from her attempts at revolution in *St.Domingue*—warned against having anything whatsoever in writing. Her warnings were heeded, and hence long lists of words were committed to memory and passed on orally. There were epic discussions when various of the veterans and elders disagreed over the meaning or the pronunciation of a certain expression. Thus I got slowly immersed in the wet, pebble-like sounds of the *Yoruba* language—*Ifa, Ifé, Ilé, Iku* ... From remembering the words, the veterans would lapse into musings about herbal remedies or the composition of potions and spells, or their private theories about the causes and prevention of impotence, venereal disease, fevers and the cholera. I remember various of those traditions.

The gonorrhea was caught from standing barefoot on a cold floor after making love.

The belief was widespread that impotence is caused by nervousness, *debilidad cerebral, falta de fósforo en el cerebro, mucho esfuerzo cerebral* ... Maybe this indirectly revealed how much unhappiness this island and its forcibly displaced inhabitants, in spite of their visible feistiness and *alegría*, had really known since the coming of the Conquerors.

Plant remedies were respected. Impotence was best cured by *garañon*, more commonly referred to as *parapinga*.

One of the elders taught me a rhyme about it:

> *'El garañon es el palo*
> *De la vejez salvación*
> *Porque llevanta la pinga*
> *Y da fuerza de león.'*

But more than spices and herbs, magic was the universal remedy.

I had become extremely superstitious myself. How could it have been otherwise, my whole life and all my experiences having convinced me of the shallowness of pretended reason in human affairs?

I became firmly convinced that magic teaches the unreasonable means to counteract the unreasonable nature of the world and our lives. It's going with the flow—while pretended reason is the very height of delusion: because we are not in control of the inextricable mechanisms guiding the most crucial events of our existence.

Why would sticks and stones and certain seashells, thrown at random in a *sacred* space, reveal secret patterns of *order?* You may resist that belief. But your very reason, when dictating such resistance, is unreasonable. Real life doesn't unfold along neat lines of single causes and effects, but rather progresses chaotically—multiple and simultaneous causes continuously producing entire generations of consequences. How then to get a glimpse at these gratuitous yet fatal patterns, but through means equally gratuitous and fatal? Once immersed in the life of the *Solar*, I moved deeper and deeper into the sacred time of magic.

CHAPTER 10

▼

Whatever the advantages and the revelations of life in *Regla,* I was never so naïve as to let the sense of community, or Epifania's more relaxed spirits, make me believe that this was the end of the intrigues. On the contrary: the kind of well-balanced anarchy prevalent in the *Solar* had to be filled with new kinds of treachery, since the common interest had to be redefined daily, and strong personalities such as Duchesse Malenfant could impose their will without the open contradiction of established rules.

After not too many weeks, it became obvious to me that Duchesse was the mistress of most of the mysteries in the *Solar*—in spite of being a woman and a foreigner. Epifania became strongly attached to her, to the point where I felt pangs of jealousy I had never experienced when imagining my girlfriend in other men's arms during her nightly escapades.

I will relate Duchesse's story as it was gradually revealed to me. Some of the other protagonists were more accessible. Let me sketch their portraits first.

CHAPTER 11

▼

Bozal was a runaway slave. He had arrived at *Matanzas* only about a year earlier (by his own calculation), had been put to work on a sugar plantation in the *Yumurí* valley and had escaped in the middle of the *zafra*. He had eluded the bounty hunters and their bloodhounds thanks to a powerful protective spirit, his *Eleggúa*, who had confused men and dogs at every crossroads.

He was a man of medium height, taking considerable strength from his nervous energies rather than from his muscles. His eyes would often wander off to deep regions when he told of the horrors he had witnessed. He came from the *Yoruba* people in the old country and had been sold into slavery by *Fulani* traders. Towards the end of the crossing, the slaver had run into a British man-of-war. Rather than forfeiting his ship, the master had decided in cold blood to throw overboard all of his human cargo. *Bozal's* Spanish was rudimentary, but his strong emotions about these events spoke loudly where words would fail him. Once I saw even Epifania—who otherwise would pretend slavery did not concern her, since *she* had been born free—clinch her fists till her knuckles turned pale, and wipe tears from her trembling eyes when *Bozal* repeated his story with some previously unmentioned detail of cruelty.

Floating on some driftwood, he had been washed up the shore after countless hours on the surface of the deep, escaping sharks and madness. One of his brothers had been on the same ship. He had held on to him while the sharks were devouring him alive, and had ended up floating about holding his brother's agonizing torso. He had been thrown by a motherly wave upon the sharp reefs of the flat coastline between Havana and *Matanzas*. Much as the sea had spared him, the land had been cruel. The cliffs tore his flesh, mangled bodies of his less fortunate companions were strewn all around him—and he was captured by a gang of beachcombers even before he could find fresh water or any kind of nourishment.

They bound him hand and feet; and gagged him as he shouted his thanks to *Yemayá,* the *Orisha* of the ocean, and *Olokun,* the ruler of the Deep, for having spared his life. On the outskirts of *Matanzas,* they sold him to a trader dealing in such *goods,* adding his description to the cargo list of a slaver already in port, so as to avoid later claims by his captors or the master of the death-ship. All of this he had understood as being procedures of tradespeople; for he had himself been a merchant before the *Fulani* raided his town and captured him. At the slave auction, he had been given a Spanish name collectively with the others bought by the same master. He did not remember the name. The buyer had tossed a coin to a drunken priest who had sprinkled the whole group with some dirty water, declaring them henceforth to be immortal and bound for paradise, if obedient and respectful of the master.

It is easy to understand *Bozal's* importance to the life of the *Solar.* He was new to Cuba and spoke, thought and dreamed in *Yoruba.* He knew all the spirits of the old country and was a staunch believer in them, as one must be who has escaped such perils, naked as a child and surrounded by every impulse & system of inhumanity. It was entirely reasonable to believe that, but for the joint protection of *Yemayá* and *Eleggúa,* and but for the rare exception made by *Olokun* from claiming the lives of the shipwrecked, he would not have been among the living. Hence, when he instructed the others in chanting and dancing to the *Orishas,* his words and acts carried a conviction *not of this world.*

CHAPTER 12

▼

Ras Fasil was a Jamaican who pretended to be the son of a slave owner and an Ethiopian princess. He spoke a deep Creole *patois* and had extremely vague and contradictory notions about the geography of East Africa—which I did not correct, although I had been on the shores of Ethiopia with the *Vision Quest*, as I will later explain. *Ras Fasil* had made a vow not to cut his hair or shave his beard till he would return to Africa, where he had obviously never been. Most of his time he would sit on a rooftop, read the bible and smoke strong *ganja*, shouting his approval of the Book when the effects of the herb made him discover some deep meaning behind a simple quote of the Psalms or the Prophets (as he mostly disregarded the more descriptive Books). But he was also well-connected outside the *Solar*, for he kept it supplied with marijuana coming all the way from Oriente. Although *Fasil* had great difficulty in communicating with Duchesse, she seemed fascinated with his stories, and much interested in his outside connections.

CHAPTER 13

▼

Several of the young girls who had sought refuge in the *Solar* had interesting stories. One of them, a beautiful *mulata* calling herself Cecilia, was the illegitimate daughter of a slave master, raised in an orphanage and later by her grandmother, till she had fallen in love with a young white gentleman who turned out to be her half-brother. She showed a half-moon tattooed in blue ink on her back, the mark she had been identified by when she left the orphanage, and which had later revealed the ties of her blood. When the incest was consumed and discovered, one of her friends, secretly in love with her himself, had stabbed the young aristocrat. She had run from the city in despair, vowing revenge on her father's family. Her mood alternated between frantic preparations for elaborate schemes & plots— and weeklong melancholies. She had made friends with Mildrey, a fifteen-year old girl from *El Cerro* who was pregnant with the child of an Italian—there was a large contingent of Italian workers building the new fortifications of *Atarés* and *La Cabaña*.

The Italian had promised to take her to Milan but she hadn't believed him. Young as she was, she had made a point of reversing every notion of victimhood. She claimed that she had cheated the Italian into getting her pregnant so he would keep her, but having long decided that she wanted her child to be raised as a Cuban and not as a European. Her cheerfulness her and shamelessly admitted calculations had the best effects on Cecilia's melancholy.

A very discreet member of the *Solar* was an elderly Chinese man, called *el Chino Wong* or simple *El Chino*. He spoke nothing but Chinese, dressed in his ancestral clothes, and passed the time flying a kite from the roofs surrounding the *Patio Blanco*. He communicated with us by means of a series of lively colored prints which he kept in a red-lacquered chest in the veteran's quarters. From the chest I concluded he had once been a sailor. Several of the prints told the story of a female pirate captain commanding a whole fleet of junks in the South China Seas, others were about emperors and concubines and secret societies. Epifania got intrigued by the prints. She had *El Chino* show them to her contacts running the clandestine lottery, and these inventive souls came up with the idea to camouflage the game with Chinese images corresponding to the numbers. This became a huge success, and was soon referred to as *'la Charada china'.*

Some of the numbers and their corresponding images are etched in my memory: 50: *La Policia*; 67: A Stabbing; 63: Murderer; 84: Blood; 12: Evil Woman ... Conversely, the *Solar* started to use the numbers to refer to the ideas or actions illustrated by the drawings. When someone whispered or yelled *'Cinco Cero!'* soon everyone knew the police was around.

CHAPTER 14

▼

And now on to Duchesse Malenfant herself—undisputedly the strangest, deepest and most dangerous personality of the *Solar*. She was a survivor of the great *Macandal* uprising in *St. Domingue*—the slave revolution in the year 1757 which had had such deep effects throughout the West Indies, in facing the masters with the ultimate paradox of their own greed: the vaster the plantations, the greater the number of slaves, the greater the risk of revolt. Duchesse had lived the uprising passionately and—as one of Macandal's mistresses—intimately. Violence and fear had spread from plantation to plantation. Macandal was a great leader and a great sorcerer. He stirred the masses and poisoned the masters. His supernatural powers—including the ability to take the form of any animal—were taken for granted, even by many of the planters themselves.

When he was eventually caught, his execution had been a spectacular and protracted affair. Twice the very flames had refused to consume his body. In the end, his visible form had to be tied to a plank in order for the fire to do its work. But the assembled crowd knew for a fact that he had escaped by turning himself into an insect.

The revolt, however, failed—and the planters' revenge had been terrible. Part of the blame fell on the Jesuits for having insisted that the slaves had souls.

There was a considerable gap in Duchesse's life story between the time of Macandal's execution and her turning up in the *Solar* at *Regla,* a gap she preferred herself to fill only with the merest suggestions. But one thing was certain: while witnessing the painful struggle between Macandal's soul and the planters' pyre, Duchesse's hatred of the white man had become so violent and unredeemable that the years had only concentrated it in her heart and her mind. She had fled to Santiago with the help of the Jesuits, but this made her judgment of the Order no less severe, for she said that no more halfway positions were possible when it came to slavery; and added that the Jesuits' dream of *educated* slaves was merely pathetic.

The same contempt she showed for the British abolitionists, whose actions she saw as mere politics to disadvantage Cuba in the race among wealthy white nations & monarchs.

The most plausible explanation for the years missing between her escape from *St. Domingue* in the year 1757 and her turning up in *Regla* was that she had slowly worked her way westward, building up connections as she went, till she had reached the crossroads of all trade which was Havana, whence she could contact her agents and rule her network of revolutionaries without ever leaving the *Houmfor.* But to reconstitute her itinerary was nigh impossible, among other reasons because she rejected the Christian calendar and counted the years following a method entirely her own: the *Year of the Mongoose,* the *Year of the Snake,* the *Year of the Crocodile …* She had reached sacred time, and rejected the white man's astronomy altogether. The Revolution, she insisted, would create its own era.

Her system of communications was manifold and complex. She kept homing pigeons on the roof of the *Houmfor,* and these were constantly on the move. Sailors came and went, never carrying anything in writing but often relaying long, whispered messages haltingly memorized in strange tongues. Bell towers sometimes played a part in the transmission of urgent appeals over long distances, although this method had the disadvantage that priests or masters—when plantation bells were used—might discern unfamiliar patterns in the tolling and grow suspicious. Even *El Chino* was soon drawn into her system: she had him fly kites of different colors and forms on certain days, and we all understood that these silent signs were meant to be transmitted by other means over the distances inland.

To finance her network and its functioning, Duchesse needed great sums of money, which she made from various forms of contraband. Every single one of her agents was also a tobacco dealer or a gold smuggler or a rum trafficker etc. Opportunities were endless, and profits were good, as basically every form of private trade was forbidden.

CHAPTER 15

▼

Presently, whenever Epifania disappeared from my company for a few hours, it was mostly to seek out Duchesse. One night I followed her through the inner maze of the *Solar*, and spied on them while they were conversing near the entrance of the *Houmfor*—Duchesse sitting stiffly erect, dignified and dressed queen-like head to toe in colorful silks, and Epifania crouching at her feet, looking up with wide eyes and playing with her toes and her long braids, very much the feral child being tamed.

Not entirely to my surprise, they were talking about me.

Duchesse was asking: "Does he sleep with his hands open?"

"No. Fists clenched, always."

"Does he laugh in his sleep?"

"He talks. Sometimes he's jumpy, like a dreaming dog. He's restless because he's so intelligent. He knows *so* many things ..."

"He's stuck in the middle, child: just clever enough to impress a song-and-dance girl. If he were *very* intelligent, he'd be a happier person."

I retreated to our room, half proud at Epifania's praise, and half ashamed of my indiscretion.

Observing Duchesse's growing influence over Epifania raised new questions. The obvious reason was Epifania's admiration for a ripe woman who had organized her life in such a way as to command respect and even seduction well beyond the best years of her physical attractions. Although Epifania was never one to worry much about the future, I could well imagine that Duchesse's example made her think about her own later years. She loved power quite as much as the voodoun queen, and was used to exercise it over men and dogs alike through her sexiness and her liveliness.

Duchesse being such a commanding presence in middle age may have presented Epifania with hope and a challenge. I was still jealous but now I was also intrigued; and having overheard their conversation when they were discussing the revealing merits of my sleep, I tried to spy on them more often when they met in secret to exchange confidences. This devious procedure made me part of some of the strangest conversations imaginable. For, after some initial reluctance, Duchesse herself took up the challenge and seemed to find pleasure in educating the *jinetera.*

Their discussions—or, often, Duchesse's monologues—covered a wide range of subjects, from politics and religion to trade and finance, world history as seen from *St. Domingue,* the relations between the sexes and the races ... I found it easier now to justify my spying, since every aspect of my companionship with Epifania was based on the same mixture of attraction and distrust.

When questioned by Epifania about the sources of her information, Duchesse answered: "Words and ideas travel. The sea carries them. Sailors come and go. Some of them read and write (however dangerous that may be for them) but often the illiterate ones are more useful, for they pick up a reasoning or a thought and carry it in their minds unaltered, repeating it for me when I question them."

"Students and writers hang out in taverns and brothels with low-lifes. Thus the actively wicked and the uselessly clever drink the same wine and fuck the same girls. What I need to know about the state of the world, I gather from this traveling library written in whispers only. But very effective it is: the Censors and the Inquisition may eventually arrest *Monsieur Diderot* or *Monsieur Voltaire,* or may forbid the works of *Signor Beccaria* being printed—I know the contents and the ideas nonetheless—*and my books can't be burned.*"

"That's why I know, child, that a great and irreversible change is coming to the world, that our struggle in *St. Domingue* has not been in vain. That's why I teach that the gods and the spirits of the old country are not dead but just biding their time. That's why I believe that Europe is wallowing in its own slow corruption, swearing by a false religion which brings neither dance nor joy, and destroying countless souls in the name of Holy Profit …"

"*Pero señora, con permiso,*" said Epifania, more than a little frightened now by Duchesse's peroration, "*que tiene todo eso a ver con nuestras vidas?*"

"*Démons-là nous gouvernent, timoun!*"

Ras Fasil once asked Duchesse if she knew about the successful uprising of the Maroons in Jamaica. Of course, said Duchesse: Macandal in *St. Domingue* had been in contact with the Maroon leader colonel Cudjoe. But she disagreed as to the proclaimed success of the uprising. True, Cudjoe had been able to force the British army into signing a peace treaty with the Maroons. But, showing her mastery of detail, she enumerated three major flaws of the treaty. Cudjoe had settled for the control of a mere 1500 acres of land, out of the whole of Jamaica. Worse: while retaining political power, he had submitted to the colonial judiciary. And worse still: *the Maroons had agreed to return future runaways to the slave masters!* This was not just beneath contempt. As a matter of fact, the Maroons had become the most feared slave-hunters in every island, as the British lent them for missions abroad. For all these reasons, she said, the treaty was but a shameful compromise and certainly not an alternative to new and larger uprisings.

CHAPTER 16

▼

In Duchesse's masterful presence, Epifania was often reduced to a pleading and eager child. She didn't know that I ever saw her in that condition, and with me her manner was as feisty as ever. It was a strange and endearing reversal, that this hot street-cat should escape in the middle of the night from a male she easily dominated, to humiliate herself at the feet of a teacher.

But there still were different escapades as well; and since Epifania's wardrobe was kept in Duchesse's quarters, a stop at the *Houmfor* was often the first leg of some adventure. I became convinced that Epifania regularly returned to the city by herself—in spite of the fact that, by daylight, she accepted and shared my fears about the presence of Mr. Wingate in Havana. I was certain that she went to the city because she would dress elaborately on those occasions. Often I saw her put together her costume under Duchesse's watchful eye.

Epifania always took great care of her appearance and her clothes. Her concern about *good hair* led to a fascination with wigs and weaves, the higher and the brighter the better. From head to foot: her next big worry was—shoes. Most of Havana's streets were muddy and rutted, and a girl would often prefer to go barefoot or in simple *chancletas* rather than ruin her pumps. But the free *jineteras* were anxious lest bare feet identify them as slaves or *guajiras* and hence placed all of their self-respect in high-heeled shoes, the more extravagant the better, just like in the case of their wigs. The untainted *Carabalí* princesses among them possessed a natural grace and elegance in all their movements, which the loudness of their apparel somehow turned into bright promises of fun.

It's commonplace for sour and wise humanitarians to seek the sadness under our pleasures. But Havana was truly an exceptional place in that its frenzy of music and sex and forbidden substances rested on the very real ability to squeeze as much happiness as possible out of every day, and leave concerns behind. The city as a whole, and these girls as her most ardent torchbearers, had another kind of wisdom: *to shine as much and as long as possible—since mud and ashes would come anyhow.*

Epifania had the narrow waist, the round buttocks and the tight, high breasts of her West-African tribe. From her father, broad shoulders. But that was her only feature reminiscent of the muscular cane cutters. She had light bones and delicate, aristocratic hands with long fingers. Long legs as well, on the thin side of elegance; and unsmall feet. The fashions of the day sculpted her body even more, pushing buttocks outward, belly inward and breasts up. Or, as she would tease herself while being laced up: '*Callí, mete barriga y saca teta!*' She never powdered her face, unlike the light-skinned *mulatas* longing to be white. In private, she always preferred to be naked. But she never *slept* in the nude, her explanation being that a girl like herself always had to be ready to run: from the guards, from another woman, from another man. Fires, earthquakes and hurricanes also tend to strike at night, and one should always be ready to run. On the more general principle, human beings are just not allowed that much security. Nudity was for sex, and for the moments of brash confidence before it is consumed.

Novelty-hungry and fashion-conscious as Havana was, the lingering story of the girl pirates Ann Bonney and Mary Read had started quite a current of cross-dressing. The priests ranted against it, but couldn't stop any fashion since girls and younger women would only come to church if they had new clothes to show off. The concept of decency inside the churches was a very relative one: on Christmas and Easter eves, whoring was going on in very back of the main churches. Pretty girls were seen in taverns and dance halls dressed in wide, striped trousers gathered at the waist by big-buckled leather belts, white cheesecloth shirts worn without underwear and provocatively showing their breasts, just as in the engravings of the girl pirates sold at the printer's shop in *Calle Aguacate* and copied from Captain Johnson's famous book (well-known to me).

Epifania also loved men's clothes, although she was entirely against the fashionable lesbians referred to as *tortilleras* who often wore them. In her case, it was more the spirit of urban guerrilla which inspired her. I had seen real warrior girls in Angola, as I will report in due course, and I presumed they had existed in her ancestral lands as well. But talking about Africa always remained a delicate subject with her, for being reminded of her people's slavery would sometimes throw her into fits of rage. Her cheerfulness would always quickly gain the upper hand again, yet it was obvious that the invisible marks of slavery would go unforgiven for generations to come, and rightly so.

Thus Epifania's whole attitude—the way she used her body, her glittery clothes and bright wigs and vertiginous shoes—were as many acts of provocation and resistance, loud cries of freedom.

CHAPTER 17

▼

Whenever she discussed politics with Duchesse, the latter's idealism soon began to clash with Epifania's street wisdom. Duchesse's belief in salvation through the *Black Republic* was absolute—or she pretended it was, using it as the perfect reversal of the white masters' worst political fears. Epifania, for her part, maintained that power would be power, and was as just as likely to lead to abuse and corruption in African hands as it had been in the Europeans'. She argued respectfully: "*Con permiso señora, pero yo soy más negra que Ud.—y a mí me parece* ... It seems to me men will act the same, whatever their skin colour; I know men ..." But Duchesse said contemptuously: "You despise your own race, child: that's what the masters have done to you and your country."

Bozal was sitting nearby, working on a drum and explaining that afterwards he had to go through a ceremony *pa' da voz al tambol* (to give the drum its voice). He laughed and shook his head at the exchanges between Duchesse and Epifania. *Ras Fasil*, on the roof above us, was getting higher and higher and disappearing deeper and deeper into his imaginary Africa. A fly settled on Epifania's face. She chased it with an impatient movement of her hand, but the fly was of the insistent kind and settled on the girl's other cheek. She chased it yet again, and as the fly next landed on the drum being carved by

Bozal next to her, Epifania drew her handkerchief out of the décolleté of her dress, and positioned herself to slap the insect into oblivion.

But at that very moment, Duchesse saw the intended move and shrieked: "*Non! Non! Pas faire ça!*"

And she was suddenly on her feet, standing in front of *Bozal* and protecting the fly's retreat.

Epifania frowned. "*Dios mio, vecina, si Ud. pretende proteger a todas las moscas de Regla ...*"

"*Toi pas comprend', timoun,*" said Duchesse. Her face was at the same time harsh and vulnerable, as if she were fighting back tears of anger.

Only several days later did I fully understand the incident: the story went, that Macandal on the pyre had changed himself into a fly at the last moment to cheat his executioners. To this legend even the queenly Duchesse was clinging to remember her dead lover and the righteousness of her cause.

CHAPTER 18

▼

Duchesse never emitted an opinion about the activities Epifania was dressing up for. Her very silence made me uneasy. She must have known by now that I was observing them, because her extremely perceptive spirit—if not her supernatural abilities—surely warned her that the girl's lover would not simply accept these escapades as a given. But one of the major sources of power is having and not sharing information; and if ever a woman was power-conscious it was Duchesse. She may have raised her eyes obliquely towards the roof where I was hiding, so as to let me know that I had long been detected—but to Epifania not a word, not a sign about it.

Apart from motives of curiosity and jealousy, I had other reasons for wanting to return to Havana with her. My fate was still suspended. My contraband was still missing. How had things evolved in my absence? Was Mr. Wingate still there, or had he accomplished his mission, and moved on? These questions also reminded me of the danger of my going to the city; but as I was secretly convinced that Epifania also returned to Havana to court some private disaster, I wanted to live just as dangerously.

So one night, after her meeting with Duchesse, and when she was all dressed up to go out, I confronted her in the narrow passageway leading from the *Houmfor* to the patio Carabalí. She was wearing a long skirt made of some light, rustling fabric and a minuscule, tightly laced bodice. Her high wooden platform shoes made her look very tall. Her braided hair was done up and bound to look like a palm tree. She looked desirable enough to sink a ship or stop a war.

I simply said: "I'm coming with you."

Devil or angel, she smiled and answered: "But of course, Rey. Put on a clean shirt."

CHAPTER 19

▼

Under the vaulted passage leading from the *Solar* to the street, she stopped in the shade to take off her high-heeled shoes. Holding them in her left hand together with the hem of her skirt, so as to save both from the mud, she took my arm with her other hand and carefully looked around the corner.

Moonlight fell on the church of Regla some distance to the left. The space between the church and the bay was menacingly open. Uniformed guards were playing dominoes under a torch near the entrance of a warehouse. To our right, the street narrowed as it ran past the outer wall of the sugar mill.

Epifania whispered: "The safest way to the boat is going round by the *cachimbo*.... " She turned her head and faced me to complete the sentence, the moon giving an almost maniacal expression to her lively eyes: "*... But then, we don't do things the safe way*".

With this, she pulled me out onto the street. We ran in one breath across the open space, risking discovery by the guards, and jumped almost blindly into a skiff waiting below the *muelle*. A muscular man sitting ready at the oars immediately pushed us off.

Not till we were about twenty yards from the shore, approaching the forest of masts surrounding the city, did the man turn around to greet me, saying quietly: "*Volvemos a vernos, Señor Rey!*"—and I recognised Sr. Serafín from the Café Cantante. He displayed the same lack of surprise as Epifania herself, as if I had been fully expected to be part of this clandestine expedition.

Epifania, with a quiet efficiency somehow contradicting the sense of danger in her eyes, was checking on something she seemed to be carrying under her long skirt. But I also noticed that she was sweating, that her hands trembled slightly, and that her otherwise generous lips were unnaturally clenched.

Her eyes became thoughtful for a while—as she obviously had to adapt her plans to my presence—but whenever her glance met mine, she smiled confidently. Sr. Serafín rowed on in silence, with the serene indifference of the very strong. I was absorbed for a while by the different perspectives the city offered as seen from the middle of the inner bay—the crowded harbour to the west, then in succession the empty *Alameda*, the shipyard with its gigantic propped-up skeletons, the low mangroves with the lights of *El Fanguito* behind them; and at the far left, the construction site of the *Castillo de Atarés*.

Sr. Serafín took the shortest crossing, then veered off towards the mangroves, staying at some twenty yards distance from the shoreline. His rowing was regular and very silent. Obviously, he had crossed the bay in similar fashion many times before, and even the boat's oars were padded or otherwise adapted for discretion. At the end of the port channel, the *Morro* lighthouse sent its signal to desperate souls on the deep dark sea out there.

Suddenly another beam of light passed above our heads, as a brigantine of the coast guards surveyed the anchored ships. We came to a standstill and lay down on the benches. Someone on the brigantine shouted an order and we distinctly heard something falling in the water near one of the ships. The beam of the lantern passed over our heads a second time. Then the shouts were concentrated somewhere far to our right and the brigantine steered away. Some deal was in progress, or some contraband had been intercepted, or both. Pressed together on the bench, I felt Epifania's tension and her fast breathing. But our boat was low enough to escape notice.

We landed in the middle of the mangroves. Sr. Serafín stepped ashore and fastened the boat. He reached out and took Epifania's shoes. She hitched up her skirt again and stepped carefully over the side of the skiff, long legs searching balance, narrow, long-toed foot avoiding the mud and planting itself firmly on a protruding mangrove root.

The ease and the routine with which all these moves were performed confirmed once again that these outings were well rehearsed. But, subtle as always, Epifania took care to lean on my shoulder and hold my hand while she left the boat, so as to involve me in the procedures and make me feel part of the crew. The crossing must have afforded her time to adapt her plans. Sr. Serafín, for his part, displayed his usual innate diplomacy and betrayed doubt nor question.

We took a shortcut through the mangroves, avoiding the front of the dance halls in *El Fanguito* and emerging directly in the alley called *El Hueco*. There we went to the very room where I had been drugged, confined and observed for an unknown number of days before my abduction. Epifania got busy now.

CHAPTER 20

▼

With Sr. Serafín standing guard at the door, she cleaned her feet, stepped back in her high heels, untied the knot of her braids so as to let them hang loose, smoothened her bodice and pushed up her breasts. Next she reached under her skirt and brought out a long, narrow purse which she had carried high up between her legs, and laid it out on the bed.

When she undid the string, she took out a number of neatly folded brown paper packages—some square, some triangular, both forms of a size to fit discreetly in the palm of her hand. She counted them and looked at Sr. Serafín for confirmation, and he nodded his approval. While these procedures were in progress, the sounds of the rowdy nightlife in the *Café Cantante* and the other dance halls had steadily been growing noisier. Sr. Serafín handed out cigars and we smoked in silence till, above the din of the dancers and the drinkers at the other side of the wall, we heard the bells of the church of Paula tolling midnight.

"*Bueno, voy!*" Said Epifania with a half-sigh but with eyes all shiny. She asked for a quick kiss, and left the room. Sr. Serafín stayed by the door. Through its narrow opening, I got a steady view of all the traffics now developing between the bars, the backstreet and the room.

Epifania went back and forth—I heard her voice and her laugh, and caught glimpses of her as she brought victims to the backrooms:

luring sailors and soldiers out of the dance hall, handing them over to the very young prostitutes or to Sr. Serafín to buy ganja or snuff, or both transactions in succession, as the case might be.

There was more: Sr. Serafín was also selling cheap rum from his observation post, keeping count of the bottles as they were carefully handed back to him by the bartenders. Once in a while, when some thievery was committed, the loot in the form of a gold or silver chain or a well-worn purse would pass through Sr. Serafín's hands for a quick assessment, before being tossed to a runner who escaped with it to a safer location.

As I sat observing all this, two thoughts occurred to me. The first was gratefulness for being allowed this look into the workings of the real Havana: for it seemed to me that I was now privileged to see the clockworks of the street life I had discovered superficially during the *Noche de Reyes*.

The second thought developed naturally from the first: *everything being a racket here, surely Epifania's reasons for letting me in on her real life must also be part of a wider scheme.*

I tried to concentrate on extracting more information from the transactions in progress. The snuff must be Duchesse's main source of income, brought to the Solar by undercover traders from Bayamo subverting the Crown's tobacco monopoly.

The ganja surely came from Jamaica through Ras Fasil's connections—but with Duchesse probably assisting him in getting part of the profits back to the island where they might help finance slave revolts, Duchesse's ultimate aim.

On a smaller and probably far more efficient scale, these forbidden trades were similar to the vast networks of piracy—but also to the legitimate businesses conducted by respected traders in Havana; and as the slave trade was one of the latter—and hence legitimacy and morality utterly failed to coincide—the conclusion was self-evident, that business and government were little else but criminal rackets writ large and made respectable by the sheer forces of convention and repression.

I was, of course, reminded of the fiery speeches of the pirate Captain Bellamy which I had sold undercover in Antwerp at the beginning of my adventures. This brought me back to my own part in the scheme of things. The recovery of my contraband seemed as necessary as ever—even more so, as my own actions seemed more justified.

All this time, Sr. Serafín kept me supplied with cigars and shots of rum. My lucidity increased by those stimulants, I discovered new rackets being added to the ones already in progress. Wiry old sailors, too wise to be seduced themselves, came and collected fees for having directed their younger shipmates to the *Café Cantante* as being the ultimate in Havana's night life. Once in a while, when a dope buyer wanted a quantity obviously too large for his own consumption, Sr. Serafín sent off an informer to the police, so as to get rid of the interloper; and he collected from the police as well, for having helped them to fill their arrest quota and provided them with confiscated goods to be sold for their own profit.

The bells of Paula Church had long tolled two, three and the half-hours in between. At four o'clock, Epifania came in to check again with Sr. Serafín. All the snuff and dope had been sold. She entered the room looking both excited and exhausted, kissed me and threw herself down on the bed. Substantial amounts of money must have changed hands between her and Sr. Serafín, and presumably more of it was hidden on her person; but of that I saw no trace. She said she was calling it quits for the night. I thought we'd be returning to Regla but she said no, not by far yet: there was more business to attend to.

CHAPTER 21

▼

We said good night to Sr. Serafín and walked back cautiously all the way to the Alameda. Just beside the Paula Church, we woke up a coachman waiting for slumming *señoritos* to wash up from the *Manglar* and urgently in need of a discreet ride with their *negritas* and *mulatas*. We got into the cab and rode towards the city. Epifania's heart was still beating fast, as I felt through the flimsy fabric of her bodice, and her breasts were hard with excitement. Her eyes remained wide open and dangerously bright in the darkness, as we made our way along the old city wall.

Small fires, smelling of charred bone, were burning in dark corners sheltering beggars and street dogs. The chanting *serenos,* near every church and palace, kept on reassuring the good citizens that all was well.

This time Epifania made no attempt to distract my attention. We went through a maze of narrow streets heading west. There was a short stop to bribe the guards into letting us pass after the *toque de queda* or curfew. This was a swift operation, as it had a set price like everything in Havana.

Leaving behind the last lanterns and torches of the city, we crossed the Rio Almendares in El Vedado, the open chalk pits of this deserted neighbourhood a ghostly white in the night. The coachman had to be bribed by now to go on.

Next we entered successive zones of wood and shrubland, under a vast sky thick with stars, reviving my dormant navigational eye. I made out Cassiopeia and the Pleiades. Then we saw the glow of fires, and perceived the smells of a settlement. We came to a halt on the bank of a narrow river. "This is the *Rio Quibú*," said Epifania. "And over there, the *Palenque*. Wait here for me." And off she went again into the mysterious night. Left to my own devices, I took in the smells of mud and charcoal, of fire and tobacco and burnt bone, and of excrement carried downstream by the river.

The *Palenque*, a settlement of *cimarrones*—runaway slaves—and other fugitives, was protected from the surrounding countryside by a wooden stockade. In the glow of the fires I saw various men standing guard at the gates of the defences, armed with axes and machetes. They were muscular and fierce looking Africans, their eyes flashing when they caught the reflection of the fires, their posture dignified and disciplined as they incessantly surveyed the surroundings.

But to my utter amazement, I also saw two Indian warriors among the guards, shorter in stature but just as broad-shouldered and wide-chested, long black hair framing their high cheeckbones, in con-trast with the Africans' shaven heads. This, then, was the rural and more assertive form of our Regla hideout. In the open air, the oppres-sion of Havana fell away; for it is true that we were so absorbed by intrigue and deception that the beauty of the world outside of Havana's confined spaces seemed no longer relevant to our lives, how-ever young and eager we were.

Epifania stayed inside the stockade for some time. I saw her com-ing out talking to a short, wiry mulatto, who scrutinized the darkness in my direction, but could probably not make me out, while he him-self, standing next to a torch, was plainly visible to me. When he opened his mouth to say goodbye to her, the light flashed on his gold teeth—and I recognized him for *Pompi el Palero*, the man supposedly behind my attackers during the *Noche de Reyes*. He stood at the gate watching Epifania as she walked back in my direction.

I could only conclude that Pompi had been her lover or her pimp at some earlier stage of her career, and that she had remained in debt to him or, just as likely, bound by some fearful magic, when she had managed to become a more independent operator. His reappearance, after his being linked to the theft of my contraband, was certainly no coincidence. The fact that she faithfully came to pay him his share of her loot after a long night's work confirmed his power over her. But I could not help thinking that sooner or later Duchesse would take over his part. Epifania probably feared him, but towards Duchesse she felt *respect*, and in the long term she wanted to be like her. This could well turn out to be a more powerful force than fear.

It's often disconcerting for a man to find out what other men he's put in league with by the same girl. The glimpse I got of *Pompi el Palero* while Epifania was dealing with him showed him indeed—as she had described him to me—to be a skinny guy with gold teeth. Of the size of his dick I can't be a judge. I have no doubt that he was dangerous—for again, otherwise Epifania wouldn't have crossed the whole city in the dead of night to pay him his dues. But strictly as a man, I may be forgiven for thinking that I was a distinct improvement over him in her tastes.

C H A P T E R   22

▼

Now after paying off Pompi, Epifania felt a little less tense. From the outskirts of the *Palenque*, she ordered the driver to bring us to *Los Sitios*, an outlying area nearer to the city. Upon arrival there, she paid the fare and a generous tip for silence—the coachman muttering about these dangerous *barrios* where no Christian soul had any business—and we got out.

The neighbourhood we now found ourselves in formed a compact mass of rundown buildings. Epifania picked her way without hesitation, twice whispering a password to tall, very skinny men appearing under doorways. For convenience, she had taken off her shoes again, and walked swifly over fragments of broken pavement, but she no longer cared to protect her skirt from the mud now.

After a few minutes' walk, we entered a dark, square building several stories high, with remnants of elegant balconies overlooking the street.

Indoors, we walked up two flights of stairs of broken and chipped-off marble. On the second landing, Epifania knocked on a finely carved door of dark hardwood, set in colorless walls smeared with excrement. An elderly Chinese lady in a red silk nightgown embroidered with dragons answered the door and let us in.

She guided us to a back room faintly lit by two yellowish paper lanterns. The room was mostly occupied by a large divan. On a low table at the end of this bed were laid out the opium paraphernalia I had come to expect.

The flame in the burner was on. The long needles were burnt dark with use. In various ocean ports I had seen luxurious pipes fashioned from delicate bamboo and semi-translucent porcelain. This one was made from a crude length of lead pipe, flattened to form a mouthpiece at one end, and with a small pewter recipient soldered to the other extremity.

As soon as the lady had received her payment and had closed the door, Epifania sat down on the bed and unlaced her bodice with a deep sigh of satisfaction. Her breasts sprang out and forward like eager young animals. She scratched her belly passionately. Being with her in these moments when she abandoned the last semblance of elegance and seduction gave me a jolt of pride of ownership—a feeling she rarely allowed. Her night had been long and complicated. Intense and quick-witted as she was, she was sure to get at every potential customer. Moreover, she had obviously been under the influence of some powerful stimulant.

In one night, all these aspects of her life had been truthfully revealed to me, whatever her ulterior motives. Now, towards the end of the night, she drifted by my side, beautiful flesh carelessly exposed and the soul—for a short while—as touchable as the skin.

She prepared us a pipe, skilfully separating a dose of the paste with the needle and heating it above the flame. The paste became soft and bubbly, and the pungent smell rose with its danger and promise. She smeared the dose in the bowl of the pipe and handed it to me first, humbly playing the servant girl. I smoked, inhaling deeply. She followed the example, reclining on the cushions of the divan. Very soon, tension left her body, all the muscles of her face and her torso visibly relaxing. Her eyes lost the glimmer of excitement and became soft, half closed and trusting.

Warm and insidious well-being and intimacy pervaded my own body, as well as a feeling of *wholeness.* I felt incredibly united with the night, the world, my own body and the whole person of my companion. Sexual desire, however, became secondary, absorbed in a different kind of unity.

Expanding this unity to include my previous adventures, I now also saw the whole planet as a vast network of connections and secret trajectories. The paths of trade and piracy and contraband, spreading wealth and ecstacies on the skin of the world, were all one, morally indifferent, and geared towards states such as this one as the ultimate goal of consciousness.

I knew of the trajectories of the opium paste, from the remote mountain strongholds of the Pashtun and Uzbek warlords beyond India, to the factories in Bengal and hence over the oceans. But I was also reminded now of the prophesies of the santeria priests during the *Noche de Reyes*, and their warnings about dragons from afar bringing sweet and poisonous dreams ...

How had those sorcerers known about my trade? Even the mention of the dragons bringing the dreams referred to the original name of the ship on which I had participated in the taking of the opium ...

I experienced a universal community of souls, the real Truth behind truth. The primitive pipe was just as effective as the beautiful ones from China. As the implements were crude and the settings were depressing, the euphoria itself became even more invading and necessary, its windows and tunnels into global consciousness even more revealing as an escape from our own bodies and circumstances.

We needed no words for our communication now. Epifania was lying on her back, smiling with wet eyes. I quietly put my cheeck on her soft, tight belly and listened to the sounds inside her.

CHAPTER 23

▼

There came to the Solar a white sailor who had jumped ship. He was a Frenchmen from Toulon. He stood on the shaky rafters roofing the *Houmfor Duchesse* and watched as his ship—a brig called *La Tramontane*—set sail and disappeared around *El Morro* castle. Duchesse mistrusted him as a white man but was secretly enchanted with the opportunity to show off her high French. The sailor called himself Martin. He turned out to be a young philosopher on the run, full of new and subversive political ideas.

Something was stirring in France, he said. The people were fed up with the excesses and frivolities of royalty. A generous and spontaneous movement was growing everywhere and would lead to revolution, the abolishing of slavery and all other inequalities, the recognition of the rights of every soul, and government by the masses.

Duchesse was delighted to listen to Martin's words—and distressed about them coming from a white man. According to her, revolution could only spring from the most oppressed of all races: the African. That didn't stop her from hearing him out greedily. The man was obviously a novice with island women. He took her attentions personally and lost his head over Duchesse's mature beauty. She for her part said behind his back that he stank from the mouth and never bathed—true facts, it has to be admitted. When she had sucked him dry of ideas and news about impending revolution in France, she had him denounced as a deserter to the port captaincy and sent him on a foolish lover's errand on the *lancha*. It seems he was arrested as soon as he set foot in the city, for he was never seen again in the *Solar*.

Now it was Duchesse herself who became the undisputed announcer of revolution. The Solar quietly agreed with her machiavellism. But she took Martin for a messenger of fate none the less. It remained unconceivable to her that the great rebellion of the end of the century would break out elsewhere than in St. Domingue where the causes were so much graver and deeper than in France. Hence, she began to feel pressed for time and she started to devise a system to set up even more constant communication with her agents and trustees in Port-au-Prince and Cap Français. As a person connected with spirits and ghosts, she laughed at the distances. Even her whispered words would travel far enough, island to island, to stir the right minds, she often boasted.

I do not rule out the possibility for the moods and visions of powerful souls to act directly and over great distances upon occurrences in the material world. But Duchesse was also an eminently practical woman, and with stubborn energy set up a network of couriers, runners and mariners bringing messages from Havana to Santiago, and hence to Port au Prince by passing ships releasing pigeons.

The great-house masters and plantation owners in St. Domingue would never know where the recipes for poison and the auspicious dates for revolt had come from.

CHAPTER 24

▼

But it was not only in Regla and the Caribbean that new ideas were spreading. Duchesse was right: those were crucial years for the future of the world.

In Paris, the installments of Monsieur Diderot's *Encyclopédie* were selling like hot cakes. In the American Colonies, the arrogance and incompetence of the Colonial Government, illustrated by such arbitrary laws as the *Sugar Act* and the *Stamp Act*, were spreading revolutionary ideas even faster than subversive intellectuals could do it. Everywhere from Boston and Philadelphia to Paris and Milan, and in the West Indies from the Guyanas and Trinidad to St. Domingue, so-called *Societies of Philanthropists* were being set up. These brotherhoods met in secret to prepare a future world, giving free rein to their Utopias. They assembled men of very different backgrounds and dispositions: for in the beginning at least, they were authentically Democratic clubs.

But soon enough the various temperaments would clash. Some opposed, some advocated violence. Some intellectuals thought the new ideas should benefit slave and free man alike. Others, who owned businesses and plantations, saw a more limited concept of responsible and tax-paying citizenship. Women were generally excluded. Religion was either seen as a civic duty, or as a superstition to be abolished by decree.

The Spanish court and the Council of the Indies in Seville remained a world removed from these ideas and discussions. But in Havana, the Pedroso brothers and their henchmen were all too well aware of them.

Now their position was delicate. Inasmuch as Revolution in the British Americas would greatly benefit their sugar and rum exports, they hoped for it; but they also feared that the new ideas would be fatal to their own class, and might bring about the ever-feared Black Republic in Cuba.

Moreover, even if not all Philanthropists were against slavery as such, Revolution would surely create a shortage of labor on the plantations, and would further complicate the slave trade.

If that came to happen, they would lose immediately the advantages of Free Trade with the Americas, since they would simply be unable to fill the demand.

The Court in Madrid, for its part, even though the present monarch called himself *Enlightened* for reasons of fashion and to be taken seriously in Paris, was stuck in another age and considered the Monarchy, and the Colonies, and slavery itself as god-given and eternal. Any suspicion of disloyalty or even the consideration of separate interests of a colony such as Cuba, would be a capital crime.

Faced with such dilemmas, the Pedrosos and Arrango steered a middle course. Through Bucarely's reports, they let it be known to Seville and Madrid that in no other Colony was there a more effective repression of subversion and staunch defense of the Church than in Cuba. In secret, they met with the more conservative Philanthropists in Havana, and encouraged them to encourage the American revolts. Large amounts of money changed hands. Trusted captains of fast ships running the British blockade enforcing the Sugar Act brought oral messages back and forth from Havana to Charleston, Savannah and New York. As always, double-dealing was a virtue for Cuba's real interests. When Bucarely got a confidential report back from Seville, under Royal Seal, informing of the impending expulsion of the Jesuits from the Spanish Empire—as being subversives themselves—the

Pedroso brothers came up with an immediate proposal to illustrate Havana's loyalty to the Crown: they offered to regroup the expelled Jesuits in a camp in Havana.

The proposal was accepted as fast as two Atlantic crossings could be effected.

CHAPTER 25

▼

On an early morning in October just before dawn, three shabby-looking frigates presented themselves before the *Morro* lighthouse. They were escorted into the port channel by two brigantines of the Port Captaincy. Against all custom and expectation, they were piloted to a berth opposite the *Muelle de Paula,* on the Regla side of the bay. We always had a watch on duty on the roofs of the *Solar,* to keep whores, dealers and traders informed of the shipping news, so this strange occurrence did not go unnoticed. Soon as the ship had docked, our spies were on the move. This is what they saw:

Hundreds of men, many in rags and with bleeding feet, were escorted from the ships and marched to the new barracks, built on the Regla side supposedly to house the new influx of slaves. But they were not common convicts or deportees: many faces were aristocratic and ascetic, and they underwent their plight with patient dignity. The crowd marched to its doom in solemn silence, which was unthinkable with your common chain-gangs.

At the same time, it struck our spies that the bell-tower of the Jesuit chapel on the city side was muted. We were always attentive to the bells, as many of the city's bell-ringers were members of the *cabildos* and used their office to communicate secret messages by ringing the bells in certain patterns and rhythms.

A little later, various boats coming from the city crossed into Regla. To their astonishment, people on the regular ferry-boat between both sides of the bay, saw that the boats were filled with the Jesuit priests, friars and novices from the school and the convent. These too, upon landing, were marched off to the camp, and disappeared through its well-defended iron gates.

People started to talk about the event. The Jesuits, it was said, had been too sympathetic towards the Africans. They had even learned the Kikongo and Yoruba languages to be able to teach the newly arrived slaves. But not only that: the Jesuits had made many enemies in the colonial establishment by openly accusing the defenders of Havana in 1762 of cowardice during the British invasion. One of them—an Irishman—had written to the King in Madrid criticizing the widespread collaboration during the occupation. This letter had been widely publicized and discussed. To even greater dishonor of the defenders of the city, a group of Cuban ladies led by the Marquesa Jústiz de Santa Ana had subscribed to the Jesuit's critics in a Memorial to the King, affirming that Havana had not been lost in battle but simply handed over: '*estimaron como conquista lo que en realidad fue cesión.*' Worse still, those distinguished ladies had praised the courage of the African slaves fighting with machetes while the Spanish troops ran for their lives.

Inside the *Solar,* Duchesse commented that the Jesuits had already been expelled from St. Domingue in 1762, as being too zealous in making the slaves true Christians. This the planters resented: for who could justify the infliction of the cruelties of slavery, if the Africans were true souls and not some kind of lower creature?

The Jesuits deported to Regla came from all parts of the Spanish' American empire: from the high mountains and dense jungles of the viceroyalties of Lima and Mexico; from the vast plains and the river lands and marshes of the South Atlantic territories. Seeing them together in chains, many of them with faces of character and determination, and in such vast numbers, gave us an idea of the hidden power they had wielded.

CHAPTER 26

▼

The power wielded by the Pedroso brothers was growing insidiously. Under what pretexts did they rule? Life on board the *Vision Quest*, which I will relate in great detail in due course, had accustomed me to the semblances of Democracy. Yes, all the crew's decisions were taken by a vote under the Articles. Yes, this was mostly a sham: intrigue and manipulation were, if not the base, certainly the main *consequences* of Democracy. '

But as the Pedrosos were increasing their power, and gradually rendering it more absolute, in retrospect the decision-making process on the *Vision Quest* came to look noble, almost idyllic; and yet, life on the ship had been a deep and multi-layered system of betrayals, as the reader will soon find out.

This is how the Pedroso brothers proceeded. First, they had to convince a whole social class—the planters and slave-owners—that their interests were the interests of the island as a whole. Next, that those interests were best represented—and next, represented exclusively—by them, the Pedrosos.

Once these tenets were firmly established, they could move deeper into the collective consciousness and manipulate it more freely. The defense of National Interest now also demanded unanimity of opinion. The Spanish Crown had tolerated little enough freedom in the past—but the old system of Government had nevertheless contained its own checks & balances. In the name of *national unity*, these were now subtly undermined, discredited and done away with. The printing presses were reduced to produce fashion magazines, announcements of slave auctions, and the scores of popular drinking songs and *guarachas*. As the Havana *hampa* or underworld could not be exterminated, it was co-opted into social controls: vice is the eternal accomplice of a strong police force.

All of this was done gradually and skillfully, under loud protests of loyalty to the Crown. The erosion of each public freedom was carefully compensated for: with public works, free drinks, a colorful parade.

Habaneros would wake up one morning and find themselves living under a full-fledged dictatorship and would wonder what had gone so wrong, and when?

But I could no longer believe that the so-called Pirate Utopias showed a better use of power. For one thing, none of those Ideal Republics, established in Madagascar or elsewhere, had lasted more than a few years at most. Second, when established, they had merely imitated, on a smaller scale, the very mistakes, vanities and absurdities of Power in the real world—concentrating on titles and uniforms, formalities of Privilege and Respect, and fast enrichment by a few at the expense of the majority. I now began to understand another aspect of Captain Johnson's *History of the Pyrates*, one I had failed to see when we were printing our illegal copies back in Antwerp. Just as the minute descriptions of the pirate trials and hangings compensated for the glorification of their adventures, so the detailed account of their political failures had corrected the grand speeches on the beauties of Anarchy.

CHAPTER 27

▼

Duchesse, of course, laughed at the official statements about the Jesuits' intrigues and the reasons for their expulsion. She gave us her own version of the true motives for the Order's downfall. She assured us that this, the true story, was based upon information from her most solid contacts. It went as follows:

The Cuban plantation owners, in their greed for more hands to cut the sugarcane but also fearful of the Black Republic, had resorted to import Maya Indian laborers from the Yucatán and elsewhere on the mainland. The scheme had proved a failure, because the Indians escaped in even greater numbers than the Africans, and joined the runaway communities all over the island.

Now among them were guardians of ancient secrets from cities still hidden deep in the jungles of Mexico and Guatemala, connected with brotherly tribes everywhere from the Spanish Main to the mountains of the Inca. Whereas the Maya in their own lands were maintaining the visionary rites of the sacred mushroom, their brothers of the Amazon and the Andes were ancient cultivators of the coca leaf.

The dried coca plant had always been known in Havana: it grew in the same regions whence the Jesuits exported and commercialized the red cinchona bark. Some in Havana had tried to chew the leaf and had liked it as a mild stimulant, but mostly came to the conclusion that strong coffee had a more lasting effect.

One plantation owner experimented with the leaf to make his cane cutters work even longer days, on an even more empty stomach. But this led to nothing, as the Jesuits could or would not ship the leaf in great enough quantities to Cuba to sustain its commercial use.

Now about five years ago, there was a certain Jesuit in Santa Fé de Bogotá who was somewhat of a physician, but also a botanist and a chemist. He was trying to concentrate the essence of the cinchona bark into a purer and stronger substance as a febrifuge medicine. Being momentarily unsuccessful, and driven by an obstinate character unable to admit failure, he used the same method trying to achieve similar results from the coca leaf.

He produced a substance, but was at first disappointed as to the effects when he drank it dissolved in water. He would have abandoned the search, were it not that another Jesuit, freshly rescued from a tribe of cannibals on the Rio Orinoco, and resting for some months in the same convent, mentioned the rites he had witnessed at a tribal invocation of the ancestors or the guiding spirits, during which the shaman had taken a drug *through the nose.*

The chemist tried this method of taking his newly developed substance—and immediately got so scared of the effects on himself that he destroyed the formula, convinced that he had initiated a dialogue with a devilish soul hiding in the essence of the plant. His Indian assistant, however, had observed and memorized all the stages of the process. Improving it with ancient traditions still known to his cousins living in the wilds, he soon produced a crystalline powder of the highest quality and concentration.

The Indians started to manufacture it in increasing quantities, setting up simple but very effective laboratories in their remote hideouts. They soon discovered that their Spanish masters could not resist the drug, and when addicted to it increased both in cruelty and in foolishness, the latter gaining the upper hand.

They saw the advantage in this for slowly and fatally subverting the colonial order and they spread the production ever more widely. The drug secretly traveled from garrison to garrison, till recently some

Yucatecan Maya Indians had brought it to Havana. Here it remained a rare and expensive commodity, as we were far removed from the clandestine laboratories, and as shipping was hazardous. But as the powder formed part of the revenge of ancestral spirits over foreign oppression, its course was set and would continue.

There was a whispered panic about the effects of the substance all over the vice-royalties of Mexico and Peru. Somehow the origin of the problem got traced back to the Jesuits: who else was engaged in botanical research and drugs trade in the colonies? But the Crown found it also an excellent pretext to do away with the last obstacle to its commercial monopolies, as the Jesuits and their autonomous trading fleet had become far too powerful anyway.

CHAPTER 28

▼

After the opium night, I found myself in an even more difficult situation. Epifania's behaviour amounted to a confession to a double cycle of addiction. *Pompi el Palero* kept her supplied with the coca-powder, so as to allow her to keep working the *Fanguito* with frantic energy. From these highs, she could only come down with opium.

Like so many users, she had started out as a drinker of laudanum, mixing the opium with sweet Canary wine, spicing it with cinnamon cloves and saffron. But as the craving for ever greater raptures is built into our brains, and demands to be satisfied in the name of curiosity and challenge, she had soon graduated to the full-blown smoking habit.

She still refused to reveal where the opium stolen from me during the *Noche de Reyes* had gone. I could conclude with a degree of certainty that she had simply sold it to the lady running the den in *Los Sitios* for quick cash to buy coca—so that now she had to pay to smoke my contraband and the product of her own thievery—but such is the logic of the addicted mind.

I also started to suspect that her very frankness in the early days of our companionship, the ever cheerful manner, the quick brightness of her eyes—had all been the effects of the constant consumption of the powerful stimulant.

All of this I could analyze. But her comportment could also be seen as a cry for help, the complete sincerity of which I did not want to accept firsthand, not to become a victim again of yet another scheme.

I sounded out the reactions of the other inhabitants of the Solar. Duchesse Malenfant maintained a sibylline attitude when confronted with the problem. Maybe she had seen the girl only as a prop for her own self-esteem, or else as an expandable pawn in her dealings to finance the Revolution. Ras Fasil's response was far more sympathetic, if hardly more helpful: he suggested that all evil came from taking drugs, and that Epifania should smoke, and stick to, his ganja. From sounding out our younger companions, I came away with the distinct impression that they envied our lifestyle, and would greedily try the drugs themselves if given an opportunity. Whenever you're in dire need of help, and humiliate yourself into asking advice, somehow the people you turn to end up simply revealing their own needs and ego's.

All the while, Epifania repeated: "All my cards are on the table now, Reyito. If you reject me now, I'm lost." Her pleading was heartbreaking, but I would not abandon all my defenses. She added: "We are too bright, *mi Reyito*, way too bright, and too light, and too hot for these bodies of ours. There *is* no remedy for us but to shoot all our guns and burn all our candles at once." Another time she said: "We're the butterflies in a world of frogs."

As I could not make up my mind to believe her completely, her reaction was to run head on towards her own destruction. For days and nights on end, she would disappear in the labyrinths of low life. Her snorting and smoking binges became longer—two, three days without interruption now—and upon her return she tried to escape even my worried enquiries. She seemed determined to reach her own ruin fast, and reach it on her own broken wings, alone and unattached.

Such, then, was my dilemma. The greatest risk to my survival was that she was still lying and scheming. But the greater risk to my soul was that she was sincere, genuinely needed my help and was going to be turned away by me for selfish reasons. How would I face myself, having refused such an appeal?

Then one night she came back to the room, dirty and disheveled, the shadow of her former elegant self and she simply cried: "*Sálvame de esta mierda, sálvame!*"

I calmed her down, and decided then and there to take the risk to trust her. This promised to be a slow and difficult process, as I knew not all the force of the substances and circumstances I was up against. Again, the best way to establish this new confidence was to talk. As a first step, I asked her what exactly had happened during my stay in the hovel in *El Hueco*. She dried her tears and answered that Sr. Serafín had fed me laudanum made with my own opium in the rum he had given me that night, so as to test the quality before they sold it. This answer seemed to be a good start.

Swapping stories once again, I confided to her the early part of my real seagoing adventures, thinking that maybe the revelation of my own dangerous quest for intensity could help her find her way back to herself. Also, going over these vast spaces if only through words, made us temporarily escape again the narrow walls of our hideout, and the sense of inevitable doom they had come to carry.

CHAPTER 29

▼

After leaving Bordeaux, the *Dragon* sailed due south. We called at Cádiz and saw the Havana fleet at anchor there—an early omen for my later destination. Having bought cheap Port and Jerez wines to supplement our cargo (but also the apothecary's chest, port being a favorite seaman's medicine), we sailed on through the dangerous currents off the Gibraltar Straits. Dolphins started to escort us, and for the first time I felt the blessings of the great, open North Sea or Atlantic.

Now we followed a well-established sea-lane, passing in between the African coast and the Canary Islands first, next leaving the Cabo Verde Islands to our west as we entered the Gulf of Guinea in a wide sweep. We sighted various outbound ships of the Dutch East India Company—as this was their traditional route to Batavia, called the *'Wagenspoor'* for being constantly plowed by majestic three-masters.

I now recall catching Mr. Trench staring at those grand and rich ships with an unfathomable expression in his eyes. Mr. Wingate for his part made a comment on their slow progress, comparing it with our own swiftness.

We sailed along the Ivory Coast and the Gold Coast, entering the Bight of Benin and from then on making trading stops at all forts: Elmina, Accra, Keta, Jakin, Wydah, Porto Novo, Badagri ... and at many meaner locations in between. In all these ports we sold cheap wine for good money, discarded broken glasses from every box, and sold the remainder at an even better gain than the one made from the wine.

These were the Dragon's routines. Relations on board hadn't developed much, either. The Nordics and the Baltics stuck to their sober and drunken habits. Mr. Trench and Mr. Wingate remained aloof and strangely (I thought) apart from each other. They didn't touch any liquor. Captain Dandélion himself remained reasonably sober when at sea, but as soon as we were moored he started drinking and mostly continued till we left our berth.

Mr. Trench seemed to profit from this situation to increase his influence on board, for he had commercial talents, and someone had to negotiate the prices and the deliveries.

Moreover, many of the slave traders were British themselves and preferred to deal with a countryman. Monsieur Dandélion, like most Frenchmen, was impervious to other languages, holding his native tongue to be universal, spoken as a matter of course by God & Devil, understood by women and tavern-keepers anywhere. Mr. Trench for his part even spoke some Portuguese and a few words of Dutch. I might have assisted him with the latter language but I chose to remain strictly neutral in these matters, sticking to my own duties and routines. Maybe I had already started to abdicate my critical faculties, ignoring signs and omens, or maybe I was simply too busy with my own thoughts.

My quest for intensity remained unfulfilled, even now on the African coast. There were strong moments of anticipation, stronger by various degrees than whatever I had experienced on board the *Challenger* in the Mediterranean. The light, the colors, the smells and the sounds were more satisfying. But witnessing the abject conditions in the slave forts, one became aware that the Europeans had girt the coast of Africa with a belt of shame.

This discovery poisoned the quest. Maybe not *every* bestiality lurking in the dregs of our consciousness was committed upon these countless naked women, men and children—for the young and healthy ones were considered a valuable commodity after all. But I became aware of a very disturbing truth, namely that the search for intensity was deeply amoral, and that maybe the worst overseer living in a slave port on a routine of drink and rape before the fevers took him, probably felt that his short and brutish life had satisfied basic and legitimate instincts.

At Elmina we spent a few days for repairs. This was a slaving post originally built by the Portuguese but later taken over by the Dutch. And proudly so: the monogram of William of Orange and his coat of arms were worked into the iron railings of the balconies of the Resident's quarters, facing the courtyard and the slave barracks.

Now in the Antwerp of my youth, foolish and ignorant idealists had revered the Oranges as being the Champions of Freedom. Here they shamelessly lent their name to the worst and most degrading form of oppression.

Epifania's reactions to these details of the slave trade were unpredictable. She knew for a fact that her father had been brought from Africa. She knew he was a *Carabalí* slave. He must have come from those very lands, must have passed through those very forts. Everything else apart, these discussions greatly benefited her recovery, for she entirely forgot her miseries when we talked about this subject. She would get angry or cynical, sometimes blaming the slaves for not fighting back or for not preferring to die rather than surrender. At other moments, she considered herself as coming from victimized blood, and swore she would only bear children whiter than herself— *'pa' mejorar la sangre"*. At yet other moments, her old and happy devil-may-care attitude would prevail and she would revel in her own freedom and say wisely: *'Esos negros son trágicos'*.

CHAPTER 30

▼

As I have already indicated, the working procedures of the *Dragon*—the captain being mostly useless for our trade—had steadily increased Mr. Trench's influence on board. Now after we completed the round of the slave forts, Monsieur Dandélion counted the money and, somewhat to his own surprise, came to the conclusion that we had flourished under Mr. Trench's management, and that profits had been exceptionally good. Here Mr. Trench stepped in with a bold suggestion.

Rather than return to Bordeaux and Nantes with the cash, why not invest it in a further venture at sea? The Dragon was doing well after the repairs at Elmira, the crew was competent. Mr. Trench proposed to push further south, stop at the Cape for food and go on to Madagascar, there to buy spices and vanilla, known to bring enormous profits in any European port.

Monsieur Dandélion hesitated, as he was a man of habits, had never gone beyond the Guinea Coast, and seemed to doubt his own seamanship in unknown waters.

These objections Mr. Trench calmly, slowly and subtly argued against: cited me as an asset for safe navigation and bookkeeping, Mr. Wingate as the champion of order and discipline on board, etc.—not once mentioning his own qualities or advantages. Most of the crew remained passive in this discussion. As long as they were paid their wages and allowed their rations of drink, they would go with the ship. Monsieur Dandélion was not the person to call assemblies and make speeches. Mr. Trench and Mr. Wingate, on the other hand, remained entirely respectful of his authority, however theoretical it was becoming.

In private, Monsieur Dandélion raised two objections. In order to push on to Madagascar, we needed supplies for the ship—some of which were not to be found on the Slave Coast. Navigation to the Cape was notoriously treacherous and through unhealthy waters. If we were becalmed for weeks—as was not uncommon around the Equator—we would face starvation and deadly illness, the dreaded scurvy becoming unavoidable under those circumstances.

The fact that he made these objections proved that Monsieur Dandélion, when sober, was anything but a fool. But it also illustrated that he had come halfway to accept a dialogue on these *proposals,* and such a first step towards compromise with doom is often already fatal.

I again thought that all these circumstances came together for the benefit of my own experience—much as I had seen world politics as a child in Antwerp.

Now Mr. Trench's reaction to the objections raised by the captain was remarkable. He convinced Monsieur Dandélion to order a thorough cleaning of the ship with great quantities of water in which he dissolved entire pitchers of lemon-juice. The same treatment was inflicted upon the crew—and provoked near mutiny, as the Nordics were extremely averse to bathing.

Rats fled the hold by the hundreds during these procedures, and jumped ship in despair. Much against protests of the crew, any stores touched by the rats were thrown overboard after them.

Leaving the ship clean, Mr. Wingate talked Monsieur Dandélion into suspending all shore leaves. He went, however, to the markets himself and brought back great quantities of yams, mangoes and more lemons.

We stood in wonder as he washed his shoes in lemon juice before coming on board. The same was done with the supplies before they were stored away. Now the crew wondered aloud where their salt pork and hard-tack biscuit was going to come from.

Sealed casks of lemon juice, protected from fermentation by a layer of olive-oil, were also brought on board by Mr. Trench. A daily ration of the juice was mixed in the grog, over the objections of the Nordics who loathed the bitter taste.

While still in Europe, Mr. Wingate had spent part of his hard-earned money on a supply of *Ward's Pill & Drop*, a laxative reputed to cure the scurvy. Now Mr. Trench scornfully threw the pills overboard, saying that they did no good—were in fact worse than no cure at all. While vinegar & vitriol were merely ineffective, he maintained, the laxative, through its debilitating consequences, made the scurvy worse, apart from adding to the already problematic hygiene in a ship's sick-ward through the further excess of excrement sloshing to and fro.

To nobody's understanding, Mr. Trench now declared the ship ready to withstand the scurvy, even if becalmed for weeks. We never found out where he had gotten these notions of salutary hygiene, so different from all accepted habits at sea.

Monsieur Dandélion's other objection—the one about navigation—was even more difficult to deal with. In this matter, Mr. Trench set a masterly course. As he did not want to let on too much navigating experience for himself, he skillfully co-opted me into his plans, provoking my pride and my desire to prove myself where my skills were still blatantly insufficient. Yes, I said, I could take latitudes anywhere, I had learned my procedures for dead reckoning well enough by now. Still, to have the entire ship's fate in my hands frightened me. Mr. Trench very cleverly turned this fear into a challenge—till I swore before an increasingly bewildered Monsieur Dandélion, increasingly confined to his cabin, that I would get the ship safely to Madagascar and back.

CHAPTER 31

▼

As the Dragon's scribe and navigator, I distinctly remember the entries I made in the ship's log as we approached the Cape. I will not refer to the Cape with its full name, as to call it a place of good tidings now seems utterly perverted to me.

These were the signs of our approaching land, after venturing out considerably into the South Atlantic to avoid the equatorial doldrums: white birds with black-tipped wings came wheeling around the ship in great numbers. Mr. Wingate, perhaps betraying an earlier passage through these waters, told me (but nobody else) that they were a species of gannet, called 'velvet sleeves' by the Dutch.

Two days later, entire mats of broken, trumpet-shaped reeds were floating around us. Next, shells of dead cuttlefish began bobbing on the waves. These signs extended to about thirty miles offshore, as I later calculated for myself.

Whenever the crew got restive about the voyage to Madagascar, Mr. Trench spread rumors blaming the invisible Monsieur Dandélion for this enterprise; and whenever the favorable prospects for the ship came under discussion, he himself took credit for them.

This policy seemed so crude I often wondered why the crew swallowed it all. But the manipulation worked—because the men were either so ignorant or so unwilling to take responsibility for their own fates that they preferred to follow blindly where even the most questionable leader took them.

The Cape was the ideal place to supplement our stores. The local Dutch traders, working for the East India Company, were a despicable lot. There was no slave trade here, but the Company had set up a system to deceive the local people with wholly inadequate terms of trade, buying sheep and oxen for a few metal trinkets, and treating the harmless nomads with utter contempt as if they were animals themselves, citing their habits of going naked and eating raw meat. Again I witnessed how, under their philosophical pretexts, the Free Traders were but universal exporters of contempt and exploitation.

Shore leave was granted here, and—urged on by Mr. Trench—the crew hunted penguins and sea-lions for fresh meat. Having brought the ship this far, I had effectively joined the cabal formed by Mr. Trench and Mr. Wingate. I was proud of my navigation skills, yet at the same time could not avoid the suspicion that these skills were likely being used for some unspoken purpose. One imagines the conflicts this created in my soul.

But as the Cape was also a busy naval crossroads, the Atlantic meeting the Indian Ocean trade, and as we were spending time ashore, I also heard many rumors and completed my education.

CHAPTER 32

▼

Word about the opium trade was spreading port to port, ship to ship. The East India Companies—especially the British—were setting up a perfect network of profit, carefully wrapped in politics of deception. The Portuguese were said to control the poppy plantations in Goa. The opium was processed in ever greater quantities in private, even clandestine, laboratories, the authorities turning a blind eye. It was sold anonymously at auctions in Calcutta, the British East India Company abjuring all responsibility. Hence, it was exported to China and sold for hard silver in the southern ports, making up for the huge British trade deficit caused by London's addiction to Chinese teas and silks.

All of this illustrated that the opium trade was not an incident or a side-profit, but resulted from a grand and indeed imperial design to exploit, to subvert and to subdue in the name of Free Commerce.

Weaker peoples and their states were left defenseless before the onslaught of pale-eyed merchants and their mercenaries. When I told these stories now inside the *Solar Sarabanda*, Duchesse Malenfant—fully aware of all these events from her own maritime information networks—said that the worst of her predictions were coming true, and that only revolution would save the world now.

When she sat up late at night in her *Houmfor*, Duchesse would often smoke Ras Fasil's herb and meditate herself into a deep trance, and then she would prophecy about the future state of the world—seeing an endless multiplication of crimes as vast and unpunished as slavery itself, committed by mean little men acting as Emperors, assisted by faithful servants invoking Laws the simplest judgment would know to be a codification of the worst instincts of dehumanized minds.

Two hundred years of war between Power and Power she predicted; carnage on scales unimagined and unimaginable to our minds unaware of mechanical warfare; deportation of souls by the millions, as in slavery but towards even worse fates; whole countries destroyed by incredibly powerful explosions; every horseman of the Apocalypse multiplied to form his own cavalry. And even after such horrors, the dawning of a better age was doubtful.

The logic of White Power, Duchesse maintained, *is deadly in itself.* This Power accumulates and needs an enemy outside the gates or outside the borders to justify the privileges of the powerful. Hence, wars are inevitable, and will be so till the common interests of mankind are recognized. But this may never happen—because even our best and most generous instincts are all too often poisoned by greed and envy.

Accompanying these wars, said Duchesse, there would be endless speeches—millions and millions of words, shouted from platforms to armies and crowds passive or festive, printed on entire planets of paper, carried through the airs and the ether by devices as yet unknown to us, but sure to exist in the future. Millions upon millions of words, numerous as ant colonies on the move—and often as blindly destructive.

Here in Havana, she prophesized, a single man of a million words would come from the mountains and rule, cherishing the island and the city as if they were his mistresses, and treating them with the corresponding possessiveness and obsessive jealousy.

As for the present slavery—oh yes, it would be abolished on paper sooner or later—but in reality it would only change face and become even vaster. Africans toiling in bright light on plantations would be replaced by infinite numbers of colorless souls toiling in darkness and

steam, their brains poisoned and their lives controlled by unimagin-
ably complicated machines.

In the end, only the return to Sacred Time would save us all.
Towards this, the Black Republic would only be the first but necessary step.

C H A P T E R   33

▼

It often seemed preposterous to myself that I had undertaken Epifania's *salvation*. At times I had flattered myself with the thought that I
was quite a womanizer. I fact, I knew little of women: I had known
my mother and my grandmother, and I had known whores on three
continents. Epifania was my first real experience in *living* with a
woman, and thus in exploring their longer-term motives and tactics.

While Epifania no doubt enjoyed sexual intercourse under certain
circumstances, her whoring days had made her immune to the simple
charms of love. What she really enjoyed was the exercise of power
over men. I had gradually discovered the double source of this incli-
nation. First, as a prostitute she would have seen so many men under
degrading circumstances that she could hardly still respect us as a species. Knowing our vulnerabilities, she knew how to dominate us.

At the same time, she must have been humiliated countless times,
even by those pathetic creatures she knew males to be. Thus, she
wanted also to take her revenge.

Reproductive urges naturally drive most young women, and determine the security they seek and the males they attach themselves to in
order to gain that security. But Epifania was also a warrior girl as I
had seen them on the Luanda coast (as I will relate further), and often
her womanhood seemed to take second place to her desire for free-

dom and independence, and to the battles she was prepared to wage to secure that freedom and not to depend on any man.

The only woman she really admired was Duchesse, because the St. Domingue voodoun queen had gained a power able to subsist and even to increase beyond her best years of physical beauty and seduction. For generation upon generation, European women of the better classes had been bred towards the institution of marriage and its inevitable failures. This had turned most of them into quite pathetic creatures, often helpless parasites, unable to give a sense of purpose or direction to their own lives. In the world of warrior girls and single mothers I was now living in, things were deeply different. Women ruled.

My relationship with Epifania thus responded to complex laws. Of course my vanity was much involved, in being with the prettiest, the loudest and the most reckless of Havana's *jineteras,* and ending the nights inside her after she had provoked every man within reach with her sexual bravado, to test her powers.

She, for her part, never completely abandoned her whore's logic, in that she extracted pay for every kindness—not just in a material sense: every emotional favor came also at an emotional prize. But this gradually evolved. As she became truly attached to me, she had to *force herself* to maintain high prices, as it were. It was a kind of discipline to her, to reaffirm her freedom by disappearing for various nights after we had had truly intimate and rewarding sex. Punishing herself for her affection, she also paid a high price for her own attachments.

Coming down from such high defenses to place her fate in my inexperienced hands—as she had done when she had cried out for help that one night—must have been very difficult for her. But I had my own second thoughts as well. I never wanted to be a saint, could not be one. As long as I was wild, I was sincere. I didn't want to change Epifania from a butterfly into a frog. The holy fires of intensity I had admired in her were still what I craved for myself too.

Our private demons were at work just as much as the demons of power and profit in the world out there, spanning oceans and continents with their crimes that would go forever unpunished. But maybe our inner demons were more respectable, because we always had to take responsibility for them, at the highest risk—whereas our leaders living in palaces always put ramparts of stones and lies between themselves and their consciences.

CHAPTER 34

▼

Dark and luminous energies pulse blindly in Duchesse's blood: her personal revenge, the hope she wants to represent for oppressed millions. Carried by such invisible currents or waves, her messages travel the distances from Havana: over and through the vast plains of the interior, where sugar cane fields stretching for many *cabalerias* around the new mills alternate with equally enormous and equally monotonous tracts of wasteland; over the mosquito-and-crocodile infested marshes of the south coast where aquatic hunters—amphibian mutants themselves—eke out a miserably wet and muddy living; through the *Valle de los Ingenios* around deceptively trim Trinidad, cruel mistress to thousands of slaves, but made an accomplice to subversion by the secret signals from her bell-towers; and further east still, over the coffee plantations of the Sierra Escambray, over lonely beaches invaded by millions of crabs in the mating season, forming marching armies of armored warfare, proving the might of numbers; on and on, past sierras and copper mines in the deeper back lands of Oriente, along beaches and reefs, past coral keys lying like lost jewels in crystalline seas.

Not even the most serene, most dazzling beauties of sky or ocean or landscape will detain Duchesse's signals or slow down the progress of her appeals.

All along the way, panting and sweating runaways hiding from the *rancheadores* and their blood-hounds in ditches or caves feel the breeze of revolt, passing over their dark fate for a brief moment, and receive *hope* like a draught of fresh water, even as the hounds are upon them; and the groups of Africans and Indians in their well-protected *Palenques*, agents of a free future, hear from the faraway drums or the conch-shells blown at a nearby beach the confirmation that time is running its inevitable course against the arrogance and the ignorance of the present masters of the shackle and the whip.

Thus the messages reach Santiago de Cuba, ancient capital of the *hidalgos* from Extremadura, driven by ambition and poverty and blind faith, their honest impulses soon poisoned by greed and deception as they conquered and murdered and gave wrong names to lands and rivers long existing in other worlds, words and memories .

From Santiago the messages become maritime, first on skiffs and barges of ship-chandlers, next on coastal traders and fast frigates and majestic ships.

By now the messages, safely memorized and encoded, concentrated and intensified by the distances traveled, have become insistent whispers and are carried to Port-au-Prince and Cap-Français with more care and precision than the jewels in the captain's strong-box.

Meanwhile in Regla, Duchesse—sitting in trance—oversees the whole trajectory and falls down exhausted when the message has reached St. Domingue. Epifania, admiring her as ever, sits faithfully by her side till she recovers.

CHAPTER 35

▼

At other moments, when Duchesse was holding court and expanding even further her vast and visionary monologues, Ras Fasil, high as ever, commented: *"Man no mek 'istory. Is 'istory mek man ..."*

"Coño, asere, you see right through everything, eh?" said Epifania teasingly. "We're right to be afraid of you Jamaicans."

She was doing better after staying away from her drugs for several weeks, not letting on any tension during the days (as her pride forbade her to acknowledge any problem in public), but passing the nights sweating, taking cold baths and biting a string of leather to dominate her urges. And me holding her hand, till her long nails drew blood.

Taking advantage of the better circumstances, I asked her again to explain all I had seen during the *Noche de Reyes.*

"Much of it cannot be explained, Rey: it comes from the old country."

"I know more of Africa than you do."

"It travels *in the blood alone.*"

"I know your blood."

She considered that for a while, then said proudly:

"Yo no soy ninguna negrita cocotimba. I'm Yoruba. We're city people. *We were merchants and traders and administrators. We were never, ever meant to cut sugar cane!* So we have to resist as best we can. We are

organized. We trade. We buy and sell. You're not one of *them*, Reyito; but that doesn't make you one of us, either."

"I'm nobody and I'm nowhere. I'm just living here and now. I am what I make myself. You're part of me."

"You never abandoned me, Reyito. I love you, yes I do. I've been two handfuls of flesh to too many men for way too long. It's you I want to be with. *El cuerpo no me pide más.* But still there are things not meant for you. *La Religión* is a great and secret thing."

"If it's great enough, can it not belong to all? If it's deep enough, *doesn't* it belong to everyone? Surely then it can't be the property of one people?"

"Right now it is, Rey—for it's all we have left."

CHAPTER 36

▼

Sleep is an unknown ocean and even the best navigator is set adrift on it. Beset by dangers and fears, we discover reefs and islands: our dreams. Increasingly, not just the present and my uncertain future, but also my past started to haunt me in those dreams. Regrets and remorse about my mother, questions about what may have happened to Inky back in Antwerp … And a new concern, which had hardly ever bothered me before: what about my father? Who had he really been, what was his legacy?

As far as the mysteries of the blood were concerned, I was abandoned on an open crossroads. I knew my mother, yes, but what about the other half of the blood—which in my case probably carried the currents of danger and adventure? I envied Epifania for knowing which such assurance who she was and where she belonged.

The mystery of my father: he must have been one of the adventurers carrying their names and their claims to ancient nobility as their only luggage, as they set out to conquer. The results of their deeds were all around me, much as I had switched sides. Not that I wanted in any way to redeem a form of guilt I didn't feel. It wasn't me, nor even my generation, who had made the Colonies and invented slavery. But neither could I escape certain of the urges inherited from my father's blood, of which the secret allure of violence was the strongest. Moreover, I was left with direct questions. If my father had left

Antwerp to come to the Colonies, had he not been in Havana at a certain point in time? *Was he maybe still there?*

From Sra. Marisél's reaction when I had signed her guest-book, I remembered that my uncommon name had seemed somehow familiar to her. Havana was the crossroads of the Spanish Empire. Any adventurer was bound to pass it sooner or later. Hadn't my own trajectories, however haphazard, finally attracted me to it?

It's easy to understand, then, that often my dreams carried wild fantasies about meeting my father in Havana, discovering his true character, and having to come to terms with such revelations.

CHAPTER 37

▼

For weeks on end now, I had been thinking about escape routes. For myself alone, there may have been a few. But as I now included Epifania in the question, the choices became severely limited.

The most obvious escape—to join the *Palenque* of the *Rio Quibú*—was forbidden because of Pompi el Palero. Ras Fasil suggested that we try to reach Maroon country in Jamaica, but Duchesse's knowledge of the Maroon Treaty had warned me that those independent former slaves were now committed to return new runaways to the masters.

I knew that Mr. Trench had intended to sail to New Orleans and even on to Charleston in the Carolinas. New Orleans had fallen to the Spanish after the war. Possibly free black persons would be recognized there. But this was all but certain, as established custom is slower to adapt than the law of faraway new sovereigns.

The American colonies were excluded, since Epifania would surely have been enslaved there. Moreover, I had heard on shipboard about the horrors of those lands—the harsh winters, the endless brownish marshlands and bleak pine barrens surrounding the cotton fields stretching from horizon to flat horizon; and the rule by protestant puritans, seen in Havana as a hundred times more hypocritical in their self-righteousness than the worst Catholics. Did we really have to bide our time till Duchesse's Republic would come about in St. Domingue?

The feeling of being trapped in Havana became ever stronger. The more difficult the escape would be, the more I needed to be sure of Epifania's trust. I had reconstructed with her help most of the events after the *Noche de Reyes*; but the missing opium was not the whole story, as the reader will come to understand.

The one but last piece of the puzzle I brought up with her as delicately as possible:

"The way things are now, little sister, we are both as good as lost. There is no more time for lies—so tell me: when you stole my packages, and you checked the contents, did you find anything *inside?*"

"Inside? You know what was inside, Reyito."

"I mean *in the paste, pressed into it.*"

I studied her expression with desperate attention, as this was a vital question. If she still held back, I was the ultimate fool to throw in my fate with hers. Together, with my knowledge of the world and her resourcefulness maybe we still had a small chance to escape: from Mr. Wingate and Captain Trench, from Pompi el Palero and his henchmen. But this required full confidence.

Her answer came naturally and with the deepest appearance of sincerity: "Reyito, we cut up the shit that same night, to hide it in different places. I was there all the time, I cut up one of the packages myself. *There was nothing, absolutely nothing inside.*"

Did I believe her? Could I trust her?

END OF BOOK II

BOOK III

A PIRATE'S PROGRESS

CHAPTER 1

▼

From the Cape, we pushed on to Madagascar in February of the year 1764. The isle of Madagascar occupied a very special place in sailors' lore, next only to the remote Spice Islands as the source of fabulous natural riches, inhabited by peoples of mysterious race and origin, and moreover the seat of Rogues' Republics described in whispers in every port.

It was said that in those Anarchist States, a man could do as he pleased, could own five women for his comfort and pleasure, and need not work a single day of his life, as bread was growing on the trees, wild pigs were so tame they waited for the knife, and intoxicating liquors flowed from hidden sources in the woods.

Absurd though these tales were, it was not unlikely that the Nordic crew of the *Dragon* had accepted to follow Mr. Trench and Mr. Wingate so far beyond the limits of the foreseen voyage because they could just not resist the belief in such a paradise, even against their slow and solid common sense.

We had indeed so far exceeded the boundaries of our original venture that Captain Dandélion had been as good as forgotten. The vessel was run by Mr. Trench, Mr. Wingate and myself. I was still aware, in spite of my successes so far, of the limits of my navigation skills. Hence, after we successfully rounded the Cape, I chose to guide the Dragon towards the northeast following the coastal route.

This, as I later found out, was a common mistake among inexperienced navigators: the dangers and challenges of the Mozambique Channel were far greater than the ones of the open Indian Ocean. A strong adverse—southern—current forced us to sail close to the coast, where it was obvious from observing the surf that numerous bars and reefs lay close under the surface. We constantly had to throw out the lead for soundings, and the fathoms had to be read speedily.

Staying within view of the shoreline, we spied various Portuguese settlements and forts. But being occupied on deck all the time, I found it difficult to jut down even the mere soundings on a slate, the more so since I still had to perform the dead reckoning procedures in the meantime to keep an approximate idea of our longitudinal progress. After two days and nights on the watch, we found a sheltered berth at about 14° 50' S and 41° E—the longitude being my best estimate, given the circumstances.

I slept for a few hours, then sat down to bring the log-book up to date. While I was doing so, the ship was gently rocking at anchor. Except for the watch, the crew had been dismissed and the deck was eerily quiet under the early morning sun. As I was in a meditative mood after the rigors of the last days, I opened the logbook from the very beginning and studied the history of the ship. I was reminded that she had been built in the year of Our Lord 1751 at Port Royal, Jamaica, by Mrs Wray & Nephew, master shipbuilders. Moving on to the opening page of the present voyage, I read in my own hand: *Bordeaux ..., Monsieur Zénobe Dandélion, Owner & Master*. Those last words stood in sharp contrast with Monsieur Dandélion's invisibility during the hardships of the past days and nights.

With time on my hands to think things over, it now struck me as completely out of the ordinary that the captain had not even appeared on deck during the manoeuvring—for however useless a drunk he was when at anchor, his seamanship was still sound, and our difficult navigation would have provided him an opportunity to reassert his command.

One thing leading to another in my head—as random thoughts will do—I started wondering how the decision to sail up the Mozambique Channel had come about. My own doubts about navigating the wide-open ocean had certainly been one of the reasons. But had not Mr. Trench quietly and subtly nudged me towards that choice, every time the topic had been discussed at the Cape?

My thoughts again changed course. If the Dragon had been built in Jamaica, how had she ended up in France, and under Monsieur Dandélion's ownership? Probably she had changed hands during the war, captured at sea or confiscated in port. Surely she had already quite a story to tell, imperfectly recorded in her books but doubtlessly remembered by her planks and joints. Down in the hold, where I often spent time between the bulkheads when making or checking inventories, names and dates were carved into the ship's bones, sometimes a message of loneliness and yearning, more often one of defiance or sex. One such carving, hidden deep in the narrowing compartments around the base of the foremast, had struck my attention: *NO GOD NO KING ...*

Steps resounded overhead, interrupting my musings. Mr. Wingate appeared at the bottom of the stairs. After congratulating me on our safe arrival at berth, he said, in a cursory way: "Maybe the time is right, when you finish, to bring the books to Captain Dandélion for his approval." He went up the stairs again. I thought he was right, finished my copying, dried the ink, took the logbook under my arm and went to the captain's quarters.

CHAPTER 2

▼

I knocked and waited. The silence was even deeper in the aft section of the ship. Only the subtle sighs of her woodwork and ropes reacting to the gentle surf gave rhythm to the quiet. I waited some more, and when no answer came I knocked again, and again counted silent seconds. "Captain! *Capitaine!*" I called—presuming the man to be in his cups and, in such a state, even more exclusively given to his native tongue. "*Capitaine, c'est moi, vous m'entendez?*" With still no answer forthcoming, I quietly opened the door.

The cabin smelled stale. The table held remnants of an unfinished meal: some broken and crumbled hard-tack; a lump of cheese; an open jar of marmalade with a fly caught in the sticky mass buzzing desperately, adding yet another dimension to the silence. Monsieur Dandélion was not a tidy man. Clothes were also strewn about on the floor and the furniture. On top of a pile of dirty linen, a book lay open which I discovered to be an anonymous pamphlet, purportedly translated from the German, and titled *Candide.* The captain had marked a passage with a pencil stroke. It ran thus:

> '*Ils se mirent tous à genoux et demandèrent au corsaire une absolution In Articulo Mortis.*'
> '*They all kneeled down and asked the pirate's blessing in the hour of death....*'

On the floor next to the clothes and the book, I found Monsieur Dandélion's pocket-watch. The hands stood at ten minutes to three. Holding the watch to my ear, I found it not to be ticking.

I did not touch anything further and resolved, by instinct, not to reveal the details of my discoveries to anyone. I turned my heels, closed the door as quietly as possible and went upstairs. On deck, I told the lone sailor on duty that the captain did not answer his door, and asked him to assist me. Caught unprepared for such a responsibility, he spat tobacco juice and deeply scratched his beard. I had good reason not to raise the alarm by myself, as I did not want to take sides or reveal an immediate involvement with whomever was going to exercise authority under these unforeseen circumstances. I had been a sailor long enough to know that intrigues were always rife on and below decks. It was better to play the innocent for a while.

But the sailor on duty, looking for the easiest way out of his bafflement, and betraying where the crew already thought that real authority rested, went and fetched Mr. Trench. I repeated my story to him. As I was still holding the logbook under my arm, I thought it was convincing enough.

So it was that no one knew that I had entered the captain's room, had seen the traces of an interrupted meal, his watch stopped at least six hours earlier, and a hint that some deadly fear had been on his mind (as the passage marked in his *Candide* seemed to indicate. Mr. Trench, also taking precautions at this point, said he would open the captain's door in the presence of two witnesses. He added that it was a happy coincidence that I was one of these, as I could give a written statement of the procedure, if the need arose. So he led the way to the captain's quarters, the sailor and myself following close upon his heels.

I was thinking fast at that point. Mr. Trench's attitude had been strange to say the least: for he overreacted by implying right away that something serious was amiss. For all he *should have known*, Monsieur Dandélion might simply have been in a state of drunken stupor. Moreover, his formality in making me a witness to the events indicated that he was already thinking in terms of a succession somehow to be legitimized. Now he went through the motions, knocking at the door, calling Monsieur Dandélion's name and getting no reply. Next I was invited to do the same in French yet again. No result being obtained, Mr. Trench said with a certain solemnity that he would now proceed to open the door and that we were his witnesses to whatever would be found inside. The sailor cursed, and crossed himself. I nodded. Trench opened the door.

At first glance, the scene was exactly as I had seen it shortly before, except that the fly in the marmalade had been silenced upon being mummified in its sugary grave. I caught myself thinking that this eliminated the only *true* witness of what had happened in the cabin.

"There's no one here," said Mr. Trench. This statement of the obvious was again meant in a procedural way. "Room in some disorder. Some drinking been going on." Drinking? Yes, that was a fair assumption, knowing the captain's habits; but was I mistaken, *or had two empty bottles been added to the table's inventory?*

Now as I surveyed the room in greater detail, to my astonishment I saw that *the open book was no longer on top of the pile of clothes.* Mr. Trench, standing with his back towards me, retrieved the captain's watch, looked at it, held it to his ear and nodded. "Watch ticking and reading the exact hour," he said, turning slowly around and facing us. Addressing the sailor he said abruptly: "The captain's missing! Raise the alarm!" The man scrambled upstairs and rang the bell insistently.

Trench now stood facing me, man to man, for a few long heartbeats, his expression at first questioning, then slowly turning to quiet triumph as he realized that I knew what he had done, yet would not protest or resist. And so I missed once again an opportunity to assert myself. Physically, Trench could not stand up to me, if I choose to attack him. Wiry he was, and alert; but I was twenty years his junior, and in perfect health. If I had felt enough indignation or disgust, I would have beaten him easily—and would have changed the course of my own life and many others' in the process.

Fact is, though, I did not. I allowed him to subdue me. His eyes, now more and more provocative, told his story almost word for word: I know that you know that I came here in the dead of night and strangled the man and tossed him overboard. I will be the new captain and you will go along, wherever I take you.

CHAPTER 3

▼

So it happened that Mr. Trench took over the ship, on March 20, 1764, without a shot being fired. He insisted that his authority was provisional, but his command was tacitly acknowledged by all—because it had been anticipated since weeks anyhow. I was probably the only person in a position to resist, but that faculty I had abdicated by not reacting immediately.

We sailed northeast the next morning, and he directed us towards a sheltered careening area on the small island of *Nosy Boraha*. I now began to suspect that he was familiar with these latitudes, although he pretended to have spotted the berth by sheer luck.

While at anchor there, Trench consolidated his rule. His first accomplice was Mr. Wingate, who had obviously been involved in plotting and executing Monsieur Dandélion's disappearance. I guessed now that it was Mr. Wingate who had visited the captain's quarters after my own investigation, and had taken advantage of the short time I had spent on deck raising the alarm, to put the empty bottles on the table, make the *Candide* disappear, and to set and rewind Monsieur Dandélion's watch.

As soon as Trench had taken command, he established a pirate democracy. He had Articles voted by the crew and had himself duly elected under those. The next few weeks he spent in subtly subverting these newly established rules, while scrupulously respecting their letter.

He made sure of three things: *First,* that several officers were always competing to be second in command; *next,* that grand titles were void of substance and reduced to mere gratifications of vanity—the monetary rewards being dissociated from them; *and lastly,* that the common crew member always felt blind loyalty towards the Leader, while distrusting the middle layers of command.

I was far too young and inexperienced at the time to realize what an instinctive genius the man was in these matters—for, being purportedly illiterate and without formal education, while at anchor in a forlorn cove off Madagascar, he reinvented the very essence of dictatorial politics with the exact intuitions of a Caesar or Alexander.

Trench also renamed the ship, in spite of many a sailor's superstitious aversion towards such changes. The name he gave her was a mystery in its own right: *Vision Quest.* But this name strangely appealed *to me*—since it reminded me of my search for a colorful and intense life, brought home the fact that I was now living just such a life, and left me with the question why then did I still feel unsatisfied? Besides, I pondered what vision Mr. Trench was after in his own quest. But I could not deny that the man must have unexplored depths and complexities.

As for my own feelings upon turning pirate—I was caught in a deep contradiction. I had not resisted or fought back, although I now realized that since Trench needed me as a navigator, I would probably have been spared anyhow. Hence, my attitude went even beyond tacit approval. But I postponed to judge myself, much like the rest of the crew, I suppose, who took the changes with the same resignation they showed toward foul weather. One thing I made clear to myself, though: *Mr. Trench had wanted me to see through his plot.* It would have been easy enough for him to have the captain's cabin *fully* arranged for the supposed disappearance of Monsieur Dandélion while drunk and disoriented, *before* he had Mr. Wingate suggest I go down with the logbooks. Instead of which, they had chosen to let me draw my own conclusions, so as to make the effrontery of their actions even more shameless. But why? I could not solve this riddle now, and concentrated instead on my duties.

Although not far removed from major shipping lanes, our berth looked deserted. When spotting the cove from afar, we had seen some movement on the beach. The people disappeared when we approached. I guessed they were wreckers or beach-cumbers, and lost interest in us the moment they saw us anchoring in good shape.

While at anchor on Nosy Boraha (or *Sainte Marie* as it was called on Monsieur Dandélion's French *de Vaugondy* maps), the ship was not just renamed but also adapted to Trench's future undertakings. The *Dragon* had already been a swift vessel and easy to handle, but she was still a trader. Mr. Wingate was commissioned to oversee changes ordered from the carpenter to turn her into a small warship. In general structure, although somewhat altered at various stages, the *Dragon* was a snow. The great advantage of this type of vessel was that its main deck was flush and unobstructed, the masts wide apart, offering a clean platform. Also, the snow was a common type of vessel both for trading and for war, and was thus easily converted. The last remaining obstacles on the main deck were now cut away. Mr. Trench also insisted on improving the ventilation of the hold as an additional sanitary measure. This led me to interrogate him about his extraordinary measures to prevent the scurvy. He answered curtly at first that these beneficial measures were well known to practiced captains, but that the Admiralty and the traders choose to ignore them for the simple reason that seafaring lives were far cheaper than an adequate supply of lemons. Elaborating on the theme, and becoming agitated over it, he used it at length to expose the hypocrisies of the Establishment—yea, even their ignorance of their own better interest, as the loss of so many lives at sea doubtlessly affected success both in Commerce and at War. I heard him out in silence, impressed by his reasoning as a further proof of his leadership qualities.

Mr. Wingate also ordered the bulkheads of the cargo spaces removed as much as possible, and had twelve gun-ports cut on either

side. With these changes, the Vision Quest became a fast and potentially formidable fighting machine.

I say potentially because the ship was as yet poorly armed. As was
common in ocean-going trading vessels, she carried a few cannon and
swivel guns for protection. But this was clearly insufficient for our
new purpose. Besides, the guns we had on board were in bad condition for lack of maintenance, and there was hardly any ammunition
to speak of.

Mr. Trench and Mr. Wingate deliberated and came up with a
solution. We broke up the beach camp, extinguished the fires and
rowed all the equipment back to the ship. We left a crate of the late
Monsieur Dandélion's own wine in evidence on the beach, and
retreated for the night.

In the morning, the crate was gone. The exact spot where we had
left it was occupied by a pile of coconuts, bananas, mangoes and other
fruit. This invisible trade was carried on for two more nights. Mr.
Trench, in a rare show of humour, boasted about his *miracles*: changing wine into mangoes.

On the third night, we left a small fire burning next to the offer-
ings, and left the great lantern in the stern of the ship alight, with Mr.
Wingate sitting under it, smoking. The idea was that both sides
would now reveal themselves.

The next morning, contact was established with the Invisibles.
Their aspect should have warned me against this and any Utopia.
They were lean and mean, of uncertain race, tanned and toothless,
and carried on their trade with a bitter obstinacy, while looking as
good as starving in the middle of tropical abundance. From the *patois*
they spoke, we understood they were survivors of shipwrecks, pirate
republics and doomed settlements, seduced for a short while by the
smooth skin of local girls, but soon sunken in dreadful routines and
isolation.

They knew, however, of every ship run aground here since the days
of Captain Kidd, and let us know they had *salvaged 'beaucoup
merveille'* or 'many marvellous things'. Including guns? Mr. Trench

enquired. The answer was in the affirmative. A mission to accompany the wreckers to their hideout was trusted to Mr. Wingate and myself.

Mr. Trench asked for a hostage for our safe return and was promptly brought a naked brown girl of about fifteen with taut upward-pointed breasts, smooth yellowish hair and slanted Chinese eyes of a vivid green, wearing one ankle iron as if to stress her nakedness. Her behaviour was uncommonly confident, to the point of arrogance. I was somehow flattered to be temporarily exchanged for such a strange jewel. But I also understood that Trench was deepening my involvement, as active participation in fitting the ship for piracy did away with my last claim of acting under duress or necessity.

We were blindfolded and led along the beach and later through the bush for about an hour. I got bored and started to fantasize about the hostage—I hadn't been with a girl for months. In my wild imagination, she was a special breed created out of a careful blend of various races by some Asian secret society for use in the Sheiks' and Sultans' harems, fallen in the hands of these marooned wreckers by some unfortunate incident, and exercising all her natural provocation even under these diminished circumstances.

The thought, once it had taken root, seemed natural enough: given the fact that sex is always in demand by the very rich, and that desire constantly has to be reinvented by new stimuli against boredom of the senses, was not such an experiment entirely predictable? Often I had used such daydreams to keep my own recurrent abstinence exciting. I found that it made sex so much the richer when it was then finally performed—as excitement stems from the brain just as much as from the lower belly. But given to these thoughts, I neglected to concentrate on our course.

Blindfolded as we were, and kept apart (for I had tried to exchange a few words with Mr. Wingate, and had gotten no reply), I had to rely on such information as was afforded by ears, nose and skin. We had left the beach a good while ago, and even the sound of the surf was no longer audible. The smells were more acrid now—of the sticky resins of tangled under-bush, I thought—and a man ahead of our little column was furiously hacking away with a machete. The humidity was worse, and bugs and mosquitoes were constantly attacking my arms, neck and ankles. Also the terrain had been rising, at first slowly, then more abruptly, and I had to be held by a man on either side not to slip.

We followed the course of a fast-flowing river for a while. Then I had the impression we crossed into a closed space, for the sounds became even more remote. The humidity became stronger, but different, and the smells more musty. Finally we came to a halt. The blindfold was taken off.

We were standing in a deep cave, the entrance camouflaged by tangled vines and creepers. A torch was lit, and revealed the wreckers' treasure.

They had accumulated a most wondrous assortment of loot. Every item ever carried on shipboard was stashed in inextricable arrays— broken, discolored, mildewed, melted into a mass of fabrics, porcelain, glass, wood and metal, making the cave look like an allegoric painting of the Vanities of the World.

After the blindfold and under the torchlight, it took the eye a while to distinguish individual objects: stools, chests, draperies, pewter plates, lanterns, candlesticks, chains … To have accumulated this much junk, the wreckers must have been here longer than I'd thought, and have more manpower than we'd seen so far. Probably also, the cave was close to the beach, and we'd just been taken around in circles to make it look farther away.

I was confirmed in these beliefs when the wreckers took us deeper into the cave, through a narrow passage leading to a second chamber, where their arms cache was laid out in far greater order than the household items. They had guns and swords of every description; and against the far wall, the most neatly arrayed, twenty or more cannon. Inspecting them closely, we saw that all the foundry marks had been filed off. Now it became even more obvious that these beach-cumbers indeed had considerable manpower—for to haul up these cannon from the wrecks was no small undertaking.

Mr. Wingate made a selection, and the price was debated at length. After this we were blindfolded again and escorted back to the beach. Deliveries would be made during the night.

All the way back, my mind was again on the beautiful hostage. Mr. Trench had not touched the girl. She had been kept in full view all the time, even to the point where she herself showed some signs of doubt: she was trained to seduce, and when a whole crew of rogues did not fall for her, her assets seemed to become questionable in her own eyes.

But Mr. Trench was too much of a politician by now to cede to such an obvious stratagem. Marc Anthony had fallen for Cleopatra— but not the shrewder Octavian. Had Mr. Trench or anyone of the crew even laid a finger on the hostage, the wreckers would have used this as a pretext to raise their prices, or to attack us, or to send us off empty-handed after the agreed price had been paid. This again should have warned me against our new captain: for if he made such a strong impulse as the sexual one subordinate to a vaster scheme, that scheme had of necessity to be deep and far-reaching. In other words, he was looking for more dangerous satisfactions than the wildest embrace on offer in the Indian Ocean. Being young and healthy, I would have given up any philosophical or monetary pursuit for an hour with the girl; but this only goes to show how utterly naïve I still was.

The next morning, we found the cannon lined up on the beach. The agreed price was paid out of Monsieur Dandélion's honest profits from the wine-and-glass trade on the Guinea Coast. With great difficulty, we transferred the guns to the ship. The wreckers and their sublime hostage disappeared in the bush, erasing their footmarks on the beach with palm fronds as they went.

CHAPTER 4

▼

Sailing up the Swahili coast was Trench's first proposal as a pirate captain. It was also the first occasion to illustrate the workings of the democracy initiated under the Articles of Regulation. Since hardly anybody on board understood the new rules, and since the vote was preceded by extra rations of rum, the proposal was carried unanimously.

Whatever the circumstances of this approval, taken on its own merits the proposal made eminent sense. Trench wanted to test his crew's abilities at their new trade. This could best be done within easy reach of land. Also, the East African coast was relatively safe for us, as there were hardly any European powers established there. Likewise, to choose light and unarmed Arab shipping for the first stage of our apprenticeship was an act of good governance. Over and again, I would come to appreciate that Trench possessed excellent qualities of management and foresight, whatever his ultimate motives and his deeper drives.

We sailed up the coast without troubles, but also without loot. The only shipping we encountered was *dhows* carrying slaves, and Trench chose not to interfere. We had no interest in the slave trade, and moreover we didn't want to provoke the Sultan of Zanzibar, the only coastal ruler of some importance. Both Mr. Wingate and Mr. Trench were still upholding the pretence that they'd never sailed these seas before, but given their knowledge of not just the coastline but even the politics of the region, this became more and more doubtful.

After several weeks, we passed the cross erected at Malindi by the Portuguese during their first circumnavigations. A week later we landed briefly near Mogadiscio to fetch water. The land was arid, the people warlike, proud and beautiful. We had to pay for every drop.

It was the month of July of the Christian year 1764. The monsoons were blowing landward, passing the coastal deserts and carrying heavy rains to the highlands of Abyssinia. North of Mogadiscio, we entered a busy and ancient trade route. But there seemed to be no one clearly established coastal ruler here, and the Somalis were active pirates themselves, as we soon understood. This amounted to a general license to raid. We attacked dhows carrying coffee from Mocha, and took their cargo without resistance. We found out that the Yemeni mariners were well armed, with curved daggers called *jambiya* and with old muskets. But when attacked in the heat of the afternoon, entire crews were helpless from chewing a narcotic leaf called *khat*, of which they also carried great quantities on their ships. The best khat was said to grow in Abyssinia, and to fetch high prices at Mocha.

We did a brisk business for about two months, taking the khat and other goods from every dhow we encountered, selling the leaf on small markets across the straits from Zeila, and retreating to a hidden berth were we could rest and count our growing loot of coffee, ivory, incense and silver Austrian Thalers.

Traders on this side of the straits relayed rumours of war in Abyssinia, where a new emperor was said to be fighting rebellious tribesmen. The wars encouraged the slave trade. The Ethiopian slave girls we saw in the traders' encampments were haughty and splendid, undefiled by their chains and openly contemptuous of their Arab masters, spitting them in the face at the slightest insult and daring them to harm their beauty.

The heat was extreme. We sat on arid beaches in the early evening and watched enormous fleets of cloud move from the ocean to the mysterious mountains, and silently absorbed the messengers' tales. Abyssinia's secrets appeared impenetrable. The stories of vast underground cathedrals and hidden cities in the highlands, although testing our disbelief, seemed possible.

I saw Trench deep in thought. I surmised that he dreamt himself a conqueror of such fabled kingdoms, like Cortès and Pizarro in the Americas. Was he tempted to cloak his ambitions and his lust for cruelty under some respectable political purpose—as those illustrious and murderous Spaniards, my own ancestors, had done? But ever after these meditations he turned his back to the interior and faced the sea again, recognizing the borderless territories where his true fate would be accomplished.

The crew had no real combat training so far, the Yemeni prizes being so easy to take on account of the *khat*. Trench spoke with the leader of a caravan encamped near our berth, and reached a strange agreement.

The caravan was about to execute by decapitation a guard who had stolen gold and ivory. Trench negotiated our crew's participation after the execution, every man having to stab the headless body at least once. This was again a deep stratagem: stabbing a dead and headless body was certainly gory, and conveyed to the perpetrator all the moral *transgression* of murder. But guilt could still be evaded, since the man was dead already. Trench exempted Mr. Wingate and myself from this duty—for reasons only to become clear to me much later.

The violent and messy business was carried out under an acacia tree some hundred paces from our camp. I looked out over the sea, but could hear the terrible noises. Afterward, Trench declared himself satisfied. Some of the men showed some revulsion, but they were told the victim was a criminal, and they had merely participated in an act of justice. Thus he neutralized whatever resistance against the use of violence our sullen crew might still have felt.

He allowed some time to lapse. The deed had to sink in, and be absorbed in *normalcy*. Next time our sailors were given swords and sabres, they would kill for real without hesitation. The use of firearms, being so much more distant and neutral than the acts of cutting and stabbing, would come even easier.

Mr. Wingate, now grandly called *First Quartermaster*, was ordered to organize some military drills. Grumbling about these was overcome with the first sharing of loot, according to the Articles, and again with extra ladles of rum. Shortly after this, in December of the year 1764, Trench called an assembly and pronounced the ship fit for heavier duties. He proposed we enter the ocean to attack ships of the East India Companies. This was a fateful decision, as it would turn us into real pirates in the eyes of the European Powers.

Like waves breaking on a beach, the enormous weight of these decisions sometimes overwhelmed my thoughts, sometimes receded.

Whoever went into the pirate business, raised a black or red flag or the skull-and-bones banner over a ship's company, set out on a path of destruction. Some did so under the pretext of politics, with *Letters of Marque* making them temporary mercenaries in this or that war. Some even retired in comfort and honour, like Captain Morgan in Jamaica. But the only true ones, the ones most interesting for my tale, were the ones who simply went with their urges and instincts, loved the chase and the kill and the spoils, loved the gold and the rum and the blood and the rape.

True, some of the men on pirate ships were only trying to escape the rigors of the merchant navy, whose mariners were so often mistreated by tyrant captains under orders of impatient ship-owners and traders in remote ports. A merchant vessel on the high seas might look like an orderly society from afar, but more often than not it was a floating penal colony, a smoldering fire of hatred turned inward.

Under the pirate flag, all the evil was directed outward, towards the random prizes crossing our random paths on nameless waves. This unity of purpose was similar to the hunting techniques of wolves or other such animals. It has been called noble by some, arguing that only within such narrow tribes can there be solidarity and brotherhood. I will not debate the point here, reserving for later my final opinion on Mr. Trench's moral progress—and my own, in his wake.

But there were other and simpler factors having formed Trench's character as a pirate, as I found out from overhearing his conversations with Mr. Wingate, and from an occasional confidence. His grandfather—a civilian supplier to the Navy—had belonged to the middle class ruined by the Peace Treaties of 1713. Trench blamed the downfall of his family, first on the hypocrisy of politics—hollow pretences of international reconciliation following close upon the whipped-up patriotism and rhetoric of war times—and next on the evil of peace itself, as being contrary to our instincts and interests.

Following the Peace of 1743, Trench himself had lost any hope of pursuing an honest career in the Navy. Twice in two generations, the absence of war had struck fatal blows at a Trench's good fortunes. Having become an enemy of peace, Trench had carried on with his own personal wars and, bringing them to the vastness of the oceans, had tried to give them relevance and a dignity of sorts.

CHAPTER 5

▼

As the ship's scribe, I was normally exempt from combat duty.

This was even stipulated in the Articles, as it was supposedly in the crew's higher interest to keep the only literate person on board alive. Navigation would become impossible without me, as no one else could keep the logbook. Although unable to check on it, and in spite of the fact that it would appear unwise to leave written proof of the trajectories of pirate wanderings, Trench was peculiar about keeping the logbook.

Maybe this was a remnant of respectable seamanship as a former member of the merchant navy. But there was a more practical purpose. Cruising the vast expanses of the oceans, we were in far more need of positioning ourselves by dead reckoning than other pirates who were satisfied with the easier distances of the Caribbean or the New England coast. Every glass—twice every hour that is, roughly—Captain Trench ran the logs and checked the winds. I had to make notes on a slate, and in the evenings of every other day I filled out in pen and ink the six columns of the tables: date, course, distance sailed from noon to noon, corrections to the course as it differed from a straight line, latitude either by observation or by dead reckoning, and prevailing winds. As I said, the captain laid great store by this ritual, as if his conscience were engaged in registering the exact frame within which his cruelty could run amok.

Another reason for my supposed importance was that inventories of the goods taken from the prizes also depended on my literacy. But this pretence was also a part of Captain Trench's hidden purposes, as I would come to understand. The crew, on the other hand, accepted only with great difficulty that one like myself was considered superior to them, while avoiding the risks and rigours of battle. I now think that Trench's purpose was to simulate respect for my exemption, while constantly testing my loyalty, observing how I would weather the violence and the crew's contempt, and patiently poisoning my soul in the process.

As far as sharing the loot taken from the prizes was concerned, the Articles of Regulation of the *Vision Quest* stipulated as follows:

The captain was given a share 'for the ship', and six shares for himself. The mate received two shares. The carpenter and the surgeon were entitled to fixed amounts in coin, set at 150 and 200 Pieces of Eight respectively. The other crew members were entitled to one share each.

It was also part of my duties to determine the value of one share after a prize was taken. This was by no means an easy task. It was relatively straightforward reckoning when the takings consisted of money or other valuables, or prized commodities such as spices, oils, cotton, indigo, tobacco, rum, sugar, tea or coffee.

But sometimes the takings were limited to household goods—candles, lamp-oil, salt—or to sail-cloth, rope and tools; or we took charts, maps and instruments; or foodstuffs.

How did a set of admiralty charts of the Straits of Malacca relate in value to twenty boxes of candles? Some of the goods were precious to a captain or a navigator, but quite useless to the common mariner. Thus there was always an element of the arbitrary in my calculations and this, together with the other objections against my person and my role on board, certainly contributed to the ill-feeling of the crew.

The Articles also spelled out the compensations for injuries received in battle. The loss of a right arm was worth 600 Pieces of

Eight; a left arm was valued at 500; losing the left leg was paid 400; an eye or a finger brought a 100.

CHAPTER 6

▼

On July 4th, 1765, heading east into the Indian Ocean against the monsoons, we spotted a promising prize. It was three glasses into the first afternoon watch. I had been busy with my usual duties helping Trench to take latitudes. As the day was cloudy and rainy, we were into the procedures for dead reckoning. I stood by with the slate, as the quartermaster held the small hourglass and the first mate ran the log. The glass emptied in about 28 seconds. Hauling in the log, the mate counted seven knots in the rope. I made a note. We were flying no colours, as it was part of Trench's concept of honour to either go anonymous or identify himself for what he was, and not to use friendly flags for easier approaches.

The watch spied a sail on the windward side and Trench left his station on the quarterdeck and stood on the roomy spot between the masts with his looking glass and scrutinized the horizon. A slow, deadly grin grew around his closed left eye and the left corner of his thin mouth as he made out the ship in the distance.

He handed the glass to the quartermaster, who confirmed the sighting: "Three-masted ship, square-rigged, on a south-west course, captain."

"Shall we give chase, Mr. Wingate?" The captain asked, ever desiring to appear respectful of procedure. "I recommend that we do."

"Affirmative, captain," said Wingate.

Trench gave orders for all hands to stand by on deck, and we adapted our own course and gave chase.

Protocol for engaging another vessel was very precise under Captain Trench. As soon as the chase was on, the sealskin covers protecting the cannon from moisture were removed. The gun-ports were opened. All fighting hands were ordered to check the readiness of their firearms. The men handling the grappling hooks were ordered to crouch at ready behind the gunwales. Two flags were hoisted: the well-known skull-and-bones banner, and a blood-red signal understood by all sailors to mean that no quarter would be given once the battle was on.

The sighted vessel had reversed her course and was under full sail trying to get away from us. But she was broad in the beam and heavy and probably (and in our piratical prayers) fully stocked. Hence she was no match for the swift and agile *Vision Quest*. As we were catching up with her, soon I was able to make out her name, written in fanciful gold lettering under the aft cabin windows: *SULTANA*. I reported this name to Captain Trench and he nodded in approval at the idea of such a regal prey. We were now close in the Sultana's wake. She was revealed to be a substantial, stately East Indiaman. Trench quietly gave his orders to overtake her on the windward side. Mr. Wingate shouted the commands. We overshot her. Her sails flapped. We slowed down. The gunners were told to stand by to fire a broadside.

But at the very last moment, when the other vessel's defences were expecting us alongside according to the traditional rules of battle, Mr. Trench ordered a sudden manoeuvre that brought us at right angles, and fired all our starboard guns dead-on into the bow of the Sultana.

This tactical move threw the defences of the Indiaman into total confusion. Standing close to Trench and Wingate, I felt all the anticipation and the anxieties of battle. We moved closer and closer alongside now. Trench drew his sword and shouted the order to fire again.

The Indiaman was now so close by that we could see the terror-stricken faces of her crew above the gunwales. I participated in the ancient and elementary satisfaction of inflicting such fear: for maybe a male in his deepest secrets seeks only this kind of respect, to see himself feared in the eyes of other men.

Captain Trench, standing on the quarterdeck, had started shouting rallying cries while we were coming alongside the already damaged ship. Presently, just before the battle was on, and above the roar of the cannon, he embarked on a series of loud and pagan imprecations which will forever remain etched in my memory:

> *'Let us praise great men! Let us praise bold deeds! Let us tear up bibles and charters and praise the strength of arms, the barrels of guns, the blades of swords! Let us praise the energy of evil, called evil because of its energies! For there is no god but gold! There is no prayer but blood! Let us praise the tightness of young whores, and the generous breasts of their mothers! Let us praise rum and smoke! Let us praise death as we inflict it! Let us praise victory! If we fail, let us praise the hangman's rope, and the chains prepared for our bodies rotting in the wind!*

The grappling hooks were thrown at the same time a second broadside was fired by all cannon, this time doubly loaded with balls and shrapnel so as to maim bodies aboveboard as well as inflict maximum damage on the ship itself and its masts and rigging.

When the smoke of this volley cleared, the confusion on the decks of the Indiaman was extreme. In one second, a proud symbol of commerce and enterprise had been turned into a writhing allegory of human disaster. Broken and splintered beams, torn sailcloth and loose rigging framed bloody bodies and torn-off limbs. Courage and cowardice were both on display as some of the sailors took a last stand on the quarterdeck and others jumped overboard in despair on the leeside of the Sultana—both attitudes being equally fruitless against our onslaught. And all the time, Trench was shouting and ranting on, his words ever louder and darker, perfectly fitting the gradual blinding of our prudence and humanity by the primitive impulses of the blood. You must also consider that these imprecations were shouted under grandiose and forlorn skies in mid-ocean. The vast indifference of nature made the battle seem even more cruel and fatal.

CHAPTER 7

▼

With the battle over, and the dead bodies thrown overboard, Captain
Trench resumed the formalities of command. The almost administrative behaviour he displayed on such occasions again seemed to compensate for the demands of his cruelty. The shaken and distraught
captain of the Sultana was received with honors, sat down in the
cabin and offered a glass of Madeira wine. The survivors of the Sultana's crew were disarmed and regrouped under armed guard on their
own quarterdeck, but otherwise treated better than prisoners of war in
a real conflict. This unpredictable behaviour on Trench's side, however *he* intended it to be seen, actually made him look even more dangerous.

Meanwhile, Mr. Wingate and myself were dispatched to take
inventory of the Sultana's cargo. Trench felt no pressure of time, as
we were in lonely seas and the risk of any interference was minimal. I
descended into the hold with my clipboard and the ship's manifesto,
Mr. Wingate leading the way with a lantern.

Since the rebuilding of the *Vision Quest* as a pirate vessel, with lots
of open space below decks, I had grown unaccustomed to the many
partitions inside the bones of a trading ship. While these existed for
practical and even structural purposes, it now felt as if they merely
multiplied secrets and hiding places.

The ship was well-stocked: the forecastle was full of foodstuffs, teas and silks filled the lazarette. The manifesto gave a large shipment of rice, carried in square woven baskets, as the main cargo in the hold. Mr. Wingate shone the lantern over the cargo, and asked me to read out the quantities mentioned on the manifesto. I did so, and he shone the lantern on the endless rows of baskets again, and seemed lost in thought for a brief moment. He asked me to check something above-board and he remained alone in the hold for a short time. When I joined him again, he seemed agitated and was wiping his forehead constantly. His behaviour looked strange, but he said nothing. We finished the inspection and went back to the *Vision Quest* to report.

While we were about to climb over the gunwales, Mr. Wingate held my arm and now seemed about to say something—but then he shook his head, let go of my arm and followed me.

In the meantime the captain of the Sultana had been promised release if he undertook on his honour to return to Bombay. Trench would even leave the crew with enough materials for basic repairs to keep the ship seaworthy till she reached port. I overheard the end of the conversation. Trench was trying to act the statesman, or he was testing the power of honorable blackmail. I thought this was a silly exercise, but little could I suspect at that point how good Trench was at such games. The Sultana was to hand over such portions of her cargo as were of interest to us, and also a set of new admiralty charts of West Africa, found in the captain's cabin. While the humiliated master pondered this, his hand still shaking around the glass of sweet wine, Trench stepped outside to hear our report. Before he let Mr. Wingate speak, Trench's quick eyes made sure none of the crew were in the passageway to listen in. This detail struck me, especially after Mr. Wingate's strange behaviour on board the Sultana. And indeed, Mr. Wingate too looked over his shoulder now. Next, Mr. Trench looked at me and—again very much like Mr. Wingate before him— seemed about to send me off, but then changed his mind and shrugged his shoulders. Some strange contamination or poison was at work.

Wingate made his report. Trench decided to submit to the crew that we take all of the silk and the tea, and part of the rice—as we could not possibly carry the whole shipment. But I felt that these routines were merely a charade now, and that a different issue was at stake. Finally, Mr. Wingate spoke up: captain, let's go back to the Sultana. Trench nodded, and we crossed over.

Inside the hold, Wingate again held his silence for a while and shone the lantern over the baskets of rice. But I had come to a conclusion about the meaning of all this, and so apparently had Captain Trench. Without great enthusiasm, Wingate drew our attention to what we already knew: the quantities of rice mentioned in the manifesto could not possibly correspond to the number of baskets we saw on the surface, multiplied by the depth of the hold. Hence, a great quantity of a *different* product had to be hidden underneath and behind the rice. The novelty of all this was elsewhere. I now understood that, whatever the hidden merchandise, Mr. Wingate had first been tempted to keep it for himself, and had next come to the conclusion that this was impossible; had considered for a brief moment to share the secret and the profits with me only; had concluded that this too was impracticable; and finally had resigned himself to involve the captain. Mr. Trench's reactions had followed a similar course: he had immediately felt that Mr. Wingate had made a discovery; had considered the option to cheat the whole crew, or to share the secret with the discoverer only, but had accepted my involvement as unavoidable. What was thus revealed by these short glances and hesitations, was a whole latent system of treachery at work, led by powerful instincts and making a mockery of the pretence of solidarity and equality contained in the piracy Articles.

At a nod of the captain, I started to remove the baskets of rice from the surface of the cargo. Two rows deep, I came upon an alignment of wooden chests without outer markings, but obviously of Indian craftsmanship. I lifted one of the chests out of the row with great difficulty. It weighed certainly more than a hundred lbs. I pushed and dragged the chest to the captain's feet. He pried it open with his pocket-knife. Inside were smaller square boxes, in rows of three, made of tin and wrapped in semi-transparent paper marked with two Chinese characters:

"What say you, Mr. Wingate?" Trench asked.

"It's obvious, captain. That's the way it's always packed. And a great deal of it, too."

Trench addressed me: "Do you read Chinese as well, Rey?"

He was mocking me, of course. I said no, I did not. I carefully copied the two characters stamped on the wrappers, so as to find out later what they meant.

The word was not spoken once. But I knew for a fact that we had discovered—*a fabulous shipment of opium!*

CHAPTER 8

▼

While I was thus getting to the core of my piracy adventures in my conversations with Epifania, the questions and doubts in my own mind became increasingly focused on the enigma of my father's personality.

Although the situation in Havana proper had become ever more dangerous for us because of the increased controls and searches, I wanted to return to Calle Oficios and interrogate Sra. Marisél—for I had never forgotten the strange look in her eyes when she had deciphered my name in her lodging register. I had come to believe that my father must have been in Havana at some point in his own wanderings, as the city was the great funnel for all drifters of the Empire, and more so if they had impressive names to hide their true souls and intentions.

Even as this last thought formulated itself, I felt that it applied in equal fashion to my father and myself; and I had to recognize that the blood—even when unknown—carries these fatal similarities.

But to return to the city, even on such a limited and relatively innocent errand, now looked like a deadly risk. As Epifania was curing herself gradually of the use of stimulants, her earlier recklessness also evaporated. This I observed without ever commenting on it, of course—but I wondered for myself how this would affect the high-strung intensity without which she would no longer be herself.

For a while she showed signs of associating herself with Duchesse's political intrigues, but I knew these would soon disappoint her, as her experiences with raw power in the nightlife and the drug business forbade her to believe in any kind of idealism. At the same time, just as in my own case, those very experiences also rendered it impossible to seek refuge in ignorant routines of respectable middle-class life. I knew the Roman emperors had often succeeded in turning warriors into settlers—but not our kind of warriors, who'd had to discover true selves and deepest urges without the orderly pretexts of military life, and had found our revelations in chaos, destruction and self-destruction.

After diving so deep, how could we ever quietly swim the surface, as society expects and commands? My own way forward thus remained doubtful. Epifania, for her part, now seemed to find it in the rites of her ancestral religion. The *tambores* or *toquesantos* became the physical outlets for her intensity. The night-long drum sessions with their intoxicating and syncopated rhythms became her surrogate addiction. She often danced herself into trances; and as her competitive and fighting self was present even in her subconscious mind when truly entranced, her possession by the *orishas* summoned by the drums was just deeper, longer and more convincing than any other woman's. While a thief and a *jinetera,* she had practiced the *Regla de Ocha* out of the mere superstitions always associated with living dangerously. Now, it seemed, she went deeper into its essence and emerged with greater tranquillity. This road remained closed to me, since Epifania's earlier refusal to initiate me into the real core of the African mysteries.

Hence, for a long time, in my idleness and fears, I was sinking ever deeper in the male's morass, scratching and bleeding the sore spots instead of letting them heal. But while threatened by the unavoidable madness which must spring from total consciousness—*hearing the blood flow, feeling the organs function, aware of the planets turning*—I also descended very far into a naked soul, and sometimes, by the grace of a moment, found myself in territories much older than the ones explored by the Bible. If I went *deep enough* into the core of things, maybe I'd go *beyond* the pleasure of destruction and the pain inflicted by self-consciousness. If such could be my own path to serenity, maybe I was able to catch up with Epifania—for now I felt that she had the advantage over me. Such, then, were the *spiritual* circumstances under which I finally convinced Epifania to undertake a visit to Sra. Marisél's house.

CHAPTER 9

▼

We choose the most innocent time of day to cross the bay, hoping to blend in with the crowd of workers being ferried to the shipyards and the Arsenal. To achieve this, we dressed as anonymously as possible, but still decently enough to be taken for self-respecting free laborers. Epifania in a colorless long skirt, a close-necked bodice, a handkerchief tied over her hair, looked a far cry from the flamboyant character of her earlier life.

My own story, if interrogated, was that I was one of the foreign workers employed on the Atarés construction site, and that I was living with my Cuban common-law wife in Regla. I needed such a story, for in spite of my dark skin, eyes and hair, Cubans had an uncanny ability to spot a foreigner, even one so well adapted to their life as myself.

Epifania's only problem were her shoes. Well could she dress like a quiet working-girl—her vast collection of high-heeled pumps just cried out 'jinetera'. Going barefoot, on the other hand, exposed a girl to the suspicion of being a runaway slave from Oriente. The reader may find these worries tiresome. But one has to understand that under the increasingly stringent rule of the Pedroso brothers, Havana was becoming a city of endless controls and restrictions. Paradoxically, as long as we'd been part of the illegal night-life, we had moved in those shady borders of tolerance where crime and police meet for their mutual benefit. But to venture out in daylight and try to be an orderly citizen exposed one to the worst whims of unchecked authority.

Luck was on our side, though: while standing in queue for the ferry, Epifania spotted an elderly man she knew from the neighbourhood. Striking up a conversation with him, it turned out that he was a carpenter at the shipyard. He had a permit written on a slip of paper, and he quickly agreed to vouch for us, explaining to the guardsmen controlling access to the ferry that Epifania was his cousin, that she was looking for work at the shipyard and that he had promised to introduce and recommend her to his foreman.

"What kind of work?" The guard asked as our turn came.

"As a cook," said our man without the slightest hesitation; "Nobody makes a *congri* like this here girl, just like her mother taken by the fevers, *que en paz descanse.*"

The guard, acting important, holding the permit upside down and obviously illiterate, looked down at Epifania's bare feet, then pointed at me and asked: "And this here comrade—a foreigner?" "Works at the Atarés castle, you know? One of them *yumas* brought in for the building sites. And a good man too, taking care of my cousin and all. Doesn't beat her up much, drinks on Sundays only. I's telling her she better hang on to a catch like that ..." Our respective virtues & talents thus vouched for, we made it to the *lancha.*

It was the first time ever I got to cross the bay in daytime, and in the company of a large group of working people. Some looked cheerful and ready for work, others were visibly dejected and suffering under the oppression of routine. Most were clean and tidy within their means, but some had obviously given up on self-respect, were dressed in rags and smoking stubs of cigars retrieved from the gutter. Such was the small shipload of humanity in which' company we crossed to the city. Needless to say, I did not see myself readily accepting this kind of life, having belonged to the aristocracy of crime. Looking about me I felt a vague appreciation for the people, knowing full well that they were the ones baking our bread and producing our candles. But to be honest, I also felt a vague revulsion at their submission. For a short while I acknowledged the temptations of an orderly life in settled company. But almost immediately it felt like a treason, and I came face to face again with the fundamental question of how to deal with my own intensity.

We had to queue up again to step from the *lancha* on the city side, as it was moored along the *Alameda de Paula*. There were more guards checking all ferry passengers, but these excessive controls were all but efficient, as it was even more obvious here that most of the guardsmen were new recruits, fresh from their provinces, mostly illiterate and no match for the wit of Habaneros. We got through on the same story, telling it even more convincingly now as its first success had increased its credibility even in our own eyes.

From the ferry landing to Sra. Marisél's house in *Oficios* was only a short walk; but as the customs' warehouse and the *Muelle San Francisco* were nearby, the increased presence of the guardsmen was visible everywhere. It seemed as if the Authorities wanted to get the better of all the secret dealings of the port—stowaways, contraband ... But knowing the real soul of Havana, I thought the very stones of the buildings had absorbed so many duplicities, the city would have to be razed to the ground to exterminate its alleged corruption.

Plus—what right had its rulers to proclaim virtue? Razing the city, striving for the decency of the Void could be the appeal of some crazy and blinded Prophet, self-righteous even unto suicide. But were our actual rulers more righteous than their own city? And wasn't normal human life, ordered by Nature, this heat generated by survival through every form of invention, copulation and dealing?

Sra. Marisél received our visit with visible annoyance. Her mouth had grown even more bitter than I remembered it. She could not blame me for anything as, in fact, I had disappeared from her house before even enjoying the full week of lodging I had paid for in advance. Recognizing me instantly, she took a defensive attitude. I realized she thought that I came to claim a refund.

"Don't look for any money here," she said, "I've lost my *patente.*"

"How did that happen?" I asked, trying to sound sympathetic.

"Because of one sailor and one *jinetera,*" she answered.

Whether this was an allusion to myself and my companion or not, I caught her eyes examining Epifania's feet. Like me, she probably noticed traces of nail polish and a recent pedicure, not very compatible with the humble and modest outfit.

"Lost my licence, got a fine of two hundred and fifty pesos, and a threat to confiscate my house."

"*Ay, señora, qué desgracia!*" exclaimed Epifania, straight from the heart—for whatever her morals in other regards, she held property rights as sacred.

Sra. Marisél thawed a bit at this show of solidarity and the absence of claims for a refund. Taking advantage of the moment, I asked her the question which had been on my mind for weeks: "Señora, when I wrote my name in your register, what did you think?"

Again she gave Epifania's telltale feet a quick look; and then she answered: "I was reminded of the English occupation."

This was as strange a train of thought as I'd ever heard. Epifania frowned and hid her feet under the hem of her skirt. Sra. Marisél asked her : "*Joven,* do you remember the name of the Captain-general who lost the city to the English? But no, you were too young ..."

Epifania raised one eyebrow and answered without any hesitation (for she took pride in her excellent memory): "*Juan de Prado.*"

"His *full* name," Sra. Marisel insisted.

"I never knew his *segundo apellido,*" Epifania conceded.

"He was Juan de Prado *Portocarrero.* I knew all about him because at that time my sister Alicia, rest her soul, was working as a laundress at the *Castillo de la Fuerza.* She died of the cholera under the occupation.*"

"So you thought ..."

"It crossed my mind that you were a relative of the Captain-general, come to retrieve money or possessions left behind here after his disgrace in Spain."

Epifania sighed, clearly reminded of the careless carousing *she* associated with the occupation. But Sra. Marisél, whose memories of the same times were certainly very different, snapped:

"You know, *Joven*, what we *decent* women said about all the sleeping with the enemy that was going on:

> *Las muchachas de La Habana*
> *No tienen temor a Dios*
> *Y van con sus Ingleses*
> *Entre bocoyes de arroz.* "

"*Cállate, lengua,* " Epifania hissed between her teeth. I saw that a fight between the two women would only ruin my prospect of getting more information from Sra. Marisél. So I quickly steered the conversation back to my questions: "Since you thought I was on a secret mission here, señora, did the police find out about me?"

This was just a polite way of asking if she had informed on me. She sighed deeply. Grabbing the easy way out I handed her, she said: "They find out anyway, as you know. But I had nothing against you." This was an admission, I thought—and a troublesome one at that. Epifania was getting nervous too—the floor was getting hot under her feet in more than one sense now. "Let's split. This is *not good!*" she whispered.

We beat a hasty retreat towards the *lancha*—only to find out that the ferry-landing was now being policed by several guards of the Special Brigades, wearing distinctive blue hats. They were from a new and well-trained unit, blindly loyal to the Pedroso brothers, and a far cry from the illiterate ordinary guardsmen, easily outwitted and often 'imperfect'—this being a current euphemism to describe corruption. With our friend the carpenter no longer available to back up our stories, there was no chance to board the *lancha* now. That left us with two choices: find Sr. Serafín and wait till after dark so he could row us back in his boat; or else, return overland, going around the bay and the inner harbour. This was a long and dusty trek, especially for a girl with no shoes. But Epifania seemed reluctant now to sit out the day on the city side, and even to ask favors of Sr. Serafín. After all she'd been through, her life was ruled by a complex diplomacy and a constant keeping of accounts about who owed whom. Maybe she was also putting distance between herself and her various night-time careers. I reserved my opinion, concentrating on the immediate problem.

We set out and crossed the city limit through the barrio of *El Cerro*, where I knew Epifania had had many connections during her *jinetera* days. On this side too, the city was bursting through the old fortifications. There were numerous secret passages to avoid the guards. Epifania pointed out the wooden building where we had taken refuge on the first night after our escape from *El Hueco*. Seen by daylight, and no longer embedded in drug-induced mystery and excitement, the place looked merely shabby and depressing.

From the outermost layer of the makeshift constructions piercing the walls, we surveyed the dusty road called the *Via Blanca*, now our only possible route back to safety. Beyond the road, a series of low hills cut off the view. These were the sparsely populated suburbs of Lacret and Santos Suarez, Epifania explained. On the other side of the hills lay a wide stretch of woods and shrub-land, through which many runaway slaves sought their way to freedom.

There were no guards in view on the segment of the Via Blanca we were able to survey from our hideout, but of course there never was a guarantee against patrols. The road looked muddy and much rutted from traffic, and mean-looking outcrops of sharp white rock dotted its surface, a bad omen for a girl's bare feet.

"How far is it to Regla?" I asked, always the navigator.

"On my feet ... *or on your back?*" She quipped playfully—and with that she grabbed my shoulders, jumped and immediately found a comfortable position with me as her beast of burden.

And so we set off, me carrying allegorically and in the flesh, the weight of two lost souls circumnavigating the backside of Havana harbour.

CHAPTER 10

▼

Carrying Epifania on my back, I counted my steps and tried to go half a mile at a time before resting. She teased, and sang—her repertory of songs was inexhaustible. We must have offered quite a show—a wandering circus act to be sure: the stranded sailor mounted by the singing prostitute. But we were our own public, as the road was mostly deserted, and we found no traffic at all going our way.

I was proud of my strength. The ride was a sensuous one too—the girl's crotch rubbing against my backbone, her breasts resting on my shoulders and her long, bare legs dangling alongside.

As Epifania readied herself to jump on my back again after the second rest, there appeared, from behind a cluster of poinciana trees, a dangerous-looking group of men on muleback. Epifania shivered and grabbed my arm. I'd never seen her so deadly scared. "*Dios me cuide, son los rancheadores!*" she whispered.

The front man now rode forward to face us, leather whip in hand. His four followers together held eight or ten blood-hounds on long leashes. The men were all armed with machetes dangling from their belts, with silver-handled daggers, and with the unavoidable whips. Under their wide-brimmed hats, their weathered faces held the arrogance of officialdom combined with the sanguinary expressions of highwaymen. They moved in a cloud of dust and fear. The lean, shiny dogs were still held back, but they were sniffing furiously, yelping and looking up nervously at their masters for signs of approval, or the order to attack.

Frozen with fright, Epifania displayed none of her usual seducing powers towards these dogs. The mule of the headman though, approaching her, touched her shoulder with its nostrils, sensing her sympathies; but the rider rudely pulled the reins, cutting short the animal's instinctive diplomacy.

Now the man addressed us:

"I am Don Francisco Estévez, deputized with my *cuadrilla* to retrieve maroons and runaways." And to Epifania:

"*P'a donde tu corres, negra?*"

Epifania was still too scared to talk. I stepped forward and said: "*Con su licencia*, señor; but she's not running. I'm carrying her."

"And who be you, boy?"

"My name is Rey Portocarrero. I'm her nephew, sir."

"Why you carrying her?"

"Someone stole her shoes."

"Who would do a thing like that?"

One of the other *rancheadores* spat tobacco juice and said: "Some other nigger, no doubt. Where you say that happen, boy?"

"Calle Oficios, Señor. Near the *muelle*."

"And what business did you have there?"

"My aunt lives there."

Francisco Estevez cracked his whip in disdain. The dogs bayed and stood ready to jump.

"This story stinks, boy. You're escaping with this here bitch in the middle of nowhere. Expect me to believe you went on a fucking *family visit*?"

Meanwhile, though, the other *rancheadores* seemed to be getting nervous. "We're losing precious time, Don Francisco. *El Caimán* is making it into Santos Suarez and beyond. He'll soon be with the *apalencados* in the hills. Besides ..."

"Besides *what?*"

"There's no word of a juicy bitch like this one here running away,'s far as we know. And yet another thing-—look at her feet …"

"I'm looking at all of her, Taladrid," (which he was indeed, undressing her with his piercing eyes).

"Her feet are too soft and too clean," said Taladrid. "So the boy's story rings true."

"You're talking like the fool you are, Taladrid: some of those house bitches are kept richer than Persian cats … What if she's someone's toy girl running off with lover boy here, and left her shoes beside the bed when they were caught in the act …"

"You're right, Don Francisco," said one of the others. "*Dále cuero a la perra*—whip the bitch!"

But in spite of these objections, it became clear that Don Francisco Estevez didn't want to lose the *cimarrón* he had been commissioned to chase, for such a doubtful catch as Epifania. He took aim with great precision and cracked his whip again, hitting her on the shoulder. Then he whistled to his dogs, spurred his mule and led his party towards the hills.

And so, after nearly being her ruin in the city, Epifania's pedicured feet saved her from a worse fate on the wide open Via Blanca. As the cloud of dust stirred up by the slave hunters drifted away, she started sobbing. Blood was soaking through the thin cotton of her blouse, where the whip had touched her.

CHAPTER 11

▼

I could have saved Epifania ten times over from coca and opium—
having saved her from the slave-hunters meant infinitely more to her.
My own actions had not seemed particularly heroic to me—I had
merely had a somewhat tense conversation with the *rancheadores*—
but that was because I did not have even the remotest idea of the fear
Don Francisco Estévez and his *cuadrilla* or posse inspired in Epifania's people.

Not only was everyone of African descent fair game in their eyes—
they were trained to seek out and recognize the Yoruba people among
all other runaways, since they had the reputation of being headstrong
and rebellious and of never giving up on their ancestral beliefs. For
myself, I was convinced that Epifania had been saved by Estévez'
eagerness to catch the runaway they called *El Caimán;* maybe in part
by my aristocratic name, inasmuch as they had believed me. But from
the girl's perspective, only my person and my resolve had shielded her
from a terrible fate. If left undisturbed, she said, the posse would have
gang-raped her before throwing her to their dogs. Such occurrences
were common. Her being free-born made her even an easier bounty,
since her degradation and death would not have to be explained or
justified to any master. And who could ever prove what had happened
to her on a deserted road outside the city?

The lash of the *cuero* on her left shoulder she healed with a tobacco leaf drenched in urine and salt. Still, it left a long, raised scar on her skin from the shoulder down to her breast—a reminder of the encounter and a warning for the future. She had never been whipped. Her often indifferent attitude about the slavery of her people was forever changed. But another development affected me more. After this day, she abandoned herself body and soul to me. She handed me the responsibility for our escape. At the same time, she could no longer refuse to initiate me into the African mysteries. Now she promised to answer all my questions about the rites of the *Noche de Reyes.*

But before I took her up on that promise, and since in my earlier pleadings I had boasted of knowing more of the *real* Africa than she did, I completed to her the story of my experiences on that continent during the *Vision Quest*'s westward wanderings.

CHAPTER 12

▼

We reached the Congo coast in September 1765. Soundings had been taken, and we had found the hull and keel of the *Vision Quest* to be in a very bad condition, entirely covered in barnacles and sturdy sea-weeds, and the fillings leaking heavily below the water line. Sheltered from the monsoons, and out of the way of Atlantic hurricanes, the Congo coast offered good beaches for careening the ship. Moreover, the Portuguese who were supposedly in control left real authority to local chiefs and kinglets, as long as they contributed to the slave trade. These warlords commanding armies of child soldiers practiced their various trades with brutal honesty, as well as the efficiency of total corruption.

By mid-September, the *Vision Quest* had been towed ashore and stood majestically on the beach, propped up on all sides with heavy logwood beams, slanted eastward with the wind. The beach was sheltered at the bottom of a cove about two hundred yards deep. A sweet-water river flowed out of the bush into the sea towards the north of our berth. The water was surprisingly cold when we bathed in it, and several men fell ill from drinking it the first day.

The warlord controlling the beach called himself Jonathan Savemba and lived with his guards, wives and children in a stockaded compound on a low hill half a mile inland, flying a yellow flag. When Captain Trench had negotiated the careening privilege on Savemba's territory, the latter's manner had been smooth and suave, with the quiet assumption of absolute power. Of course, once the ship was grounded, his prices went up tremendously. But as such practices were entirely predictable, Captain Trench had fully taken them into account when making initial offers.

During the first few days, the carpenter was busy examining the extent of the damage, ordering wood and hemp and handing out tasks to the crew. This we took with ill grace, as seamen naturally see time on shore as fit for relaxation only. As I was new to this work, I was given menial tasks. I learned to make oakum, unravelling tired ropes to recuperate the hemp, and mixing it with tar to calk the ship's leaking seams. Needless to say, I hated the work, especially getting the pitch all over my hands and being unable to get it off for days, as washing in the sea only hardened it. I had not envisaged these aspects of piracy, turning salty warriors into cleaners and scrubbers. Many of the men made fun of me, getting even for the frequent occasions when the privileges of my being literate had made them feel inferior.

The ship was found to be in a reasonable condition after the hull had been scraped. As she had been built of red hardwood in Jamaica, she was immune to the dreaded *teredo* worm. Captain Trench had been dreaming all along to command a larger and more prestigious vessel; now however he congratulated himself on the qualities and the resistance of his ship.

There were some incidents on the second and third days on the beach, as an enterprising carpenter's apprentice tried to chat up some naked girls washing their loincloths in the river. Savemba sent a warning to stay away from his women, and offering slave girls for sale instead. The apprentice was whipped ceremoniously in view of Savemba to set an example. But later he told a shipmate that the girls had warned him not to drink the river water. He was a very fair-skinned and blond boy from Gdansk, and all along our voyages in the Tropics women had been interested in him, constantly touching his hair and his skin.

Trench got suspicious, as men kept on falling ill with cramps from drinking, and as the supply of fresh water had been part of the negotiated deal. 'The rascal is poisoning me', he was heard to mutter. With the ship grounded, and the drinking water carried in barrels from Madagascar running out, this was a very serious concern.

After a whole day of pondering his suspicions and his interests, Captain Trench went up to Savemba's compound one afternoon under a flag of truce. I was one of three crew members chosen to accompany him. Savemba's people made a great show of protocol when receiving us, as if to impress us with formalities of power once we entered his *palace*. There were various antechambers or waiting-rooms, the walls of mud painted ochre, the dirt floors carefully swept in circles, furniture consisting of jars and calabashes in the corners. But there was no show of sorcery or hocus-pocus as we might have anticipated: the rooms exuded the rationality of trade, authority and management. I started to have a different opinion about Savemba.

Muscular boy soldiers wearing Savemba's colors around their waists and as headbands stood guard. Among them there were also several girls of about sixteen, bare-breasted, armed with spears like their male companions, their faces impassive and harsh.

As always when I was ashore, the smells of the building caught my attention. The rooms exuded a rich mixture of dry straw, grains, young bodies' sweat, milk, oil and mud. The latter ingredient, I suppose, from the walls, indicating that the buildings were as new as they looked. Either Savemba had moved camp recently, or his prosperity was of recent origin. This intrigued me—for if his fortunes were linked to the slave trade he must have made his money since long; but why then should he have moved closer to the coast or deeper inland only a short time ago?

Savemba was seated in state in the innermost circular room. His throne was an intricately carved three-legged stool, standing on a leopard skin. Savemba was dressed in a saffron-colored wrap, gathered at his waist by a wide belt of gold and caurie shells. Above his bare feet he wore tight leggings entirely made of caurie shells as well; and similar coverings on both his forearms. Above those, bracelets of neatly cut white straw circled with a solid gold band. His right hand held a fly-whisk made of long greyish hair. Around his neck there was a collar of golden disks and caurie shells, wide enough to reach down to his shoulders as a kind of mantle. It rustled at his every move, the caurie shells clicking against the gold with a curious metallic whisper. Savemba wore a short beard. On his head was a kind of tiara made of felt or skin, with a feather ornament in the back and a row of gold beads in front.

Savemba's immediate escort consisted of a serious-looking counsellor standing on his left, dressed in a simpler version of Savemba's own costume, and a drunken-looking jester at his right side, wearing a black Dutch hat with a white feather.

Savemba was a man of substance, so much was obvious from the whole set-up, but even more from his face and his expression. Any local potentate, tolerated by the Portuguese and the Dutch as long as he served their purposes, might have put on a show of regalia. Savemba, however, radiated a strong character through and above his costume and his court. I have since learned that any fool can be dressed up as a king; but in men of natural authority, the presence permeates the uniform. Savemba's face—like the rooms of his compound—expressed real power, and the cunning of how to preserve and use it. I particularly admired the touch of facing us with the drunken jester dressed up as a European. The warning was infinitely subtle, as the jester was also acting as the translator.

I was curious to see how Captain Trench, who prided himself on being a politician, would handle this situation. Trench stated his case well enough. He said he was grateful for the facilities Savemba had granted him, and that he was paying fair prices for them. He said watering rights had been included in the deal. He asked for the complete deal to be respected.

Savemba smiled, nodded and spoke four or five words. The translator translated: did Captain Trench want to buy girls? I failed to understand the train of thought. Maybe the incident with the girls in the river had been reported to Savemba, and some confusing logic had developed around it in his head. Trench, mounting his high horses, answered: "I'm a libertarian, sir, I don't engage in such degrading practices ..."

Savemba's expression, while this was being translated, was full of mockery—his red eyes cynical, his lips smiling. But Trench was not going to miss such an opportunity to give free rein to his chosen character of pirate philosopher, and he ranted on and on: He said he respected Savemba because he was not somebody's pawn, not a governor or an administrator, but had taken power for himself and his own purposes instead. Yes, he respected that. Power was a necessary evil, but at least some men had the courage to seek it for themselves and not as crawling underlings ...

"As *what?*" the translator interrupted, anxiously looking from Trench's tense face to Savemba's puzzled malaria eyes ...

"As underlings. Subordinates ..."

This didn't help, but my two shipmates became more and more impressed with their captain's vocabulary.

"As *servants,*" said Trench. "As slaves to kings."

Now Savemba's expression became angry, the liquid border of his eyes growing almost purple, a vein throbbing in his left temple. "You call me a king's slave?" He shouted, and even the translator's voice rose as he decoded the message. It was Trench's turn to look utterly puzzled. "Quite the opposite, sir, quite the opposite," he responded.

I was looking at the guards. They were still standing motionless, but I couldn't help but noticing that as the voices grew louder, their muscles seemed to twitch right beneath the surface of their smooth skin, as if they were expecting an order to attack us any moment now. Captain Trench was learning diplomacy the hard way. Communication between separate universes is always wrought with misunderstanding. Savemba had apparently not understood one word of Trench's policy statement, but had picked up two familiar words—

king, slave—and had unconsciously reconstructed them around his private concerns.

The incident was solved peacefully, but we returned to the ship none the wiser. In his tent, Trench examined D'Anville's recent map of the African coast. This map was one of his prized possessions, taken from the *Sultana* together with admiralty charts and navigation tables. The interior of the Congo and the Angola was relatively well known to cartographers, as was apparent from the amount of detail shown on the map—next to the blankness both south and north of the Congo River basin. Trench determined that the river next to our berth was a tributary or a seasonal overflow of the Cuanza. But this still made him none the wiser. Then the overheard the ship's surgeon, quite by coincidence, mention the fact that the sick men *appeared to have symptoms of mercury poisoning.* I was standing nearby, and saw Trench's face first come to a strange quiet; next his eyes lit up and then, under control of his strong will, resumed an indifferent expression. It was obvious to me, who knew his moods well, that something of great importance had occurred to him, but that he didn't want to let on.

The routines of the careening continued unchanged the next day. I spent hours fluffing rope, heating pitch and mixing these ingredients with caulking moss. The older hands were still joking about my work, referring in unsubtle ways to the utter uselessness of intellectuals. But I was learning the tricks, and observing the use of the caulking irons and the mallets, as I was hoping to graduate soon to the more substantial and manly part of the repair tasks. Mr. Wingate came to fetch me early afternoon, saying the captain wanted to see me. I wiped my hands and went over to Trench's encampment.

He received me alone, contrary to his habits and policies. Normally he made sure there were witnesses to every conversation, so as to avoid accusations of planning fraud. This exceptional circumstance should have alarmed me then and there to Trench's real intentions as far as I was concerned; but I was worlds removed from such an understanding.

"What did you see yesterday, when we discussed the watering problems?" He asked in a confidential, almost fatherly voice.

"Your face betrayed a sudden insight, sir," I responded truthfully; "And next you wanted nobody to notice."

"Can you think of any specific reason?"

"It has to do with Savemba's secret, sir; and with something the surgeon mentioned about mercury poisoning."

"Very well so far, Rey. What more?"

"When we were at Savemba's, sir, it struck me that all his buildings were brand new; so it appears he had only recently moved to that compound."

"For what reason?"

"He wanted no foreigners near his original settlement, deeper inland."

"And why not?"

"That's precisely what the mercury in the river told you, sir."

"In other words?"

"The mercury is used to wash gold. Savemba has discovered a gold mine inland, and the runoff has poisoned the water. He's moved half-way to the coast to keep intruders away from the mine. That's his secret."

You see what a clever fellow I thought I was, and how I was out to prove it to my captain! To this day I curse this tendency I had to ingratiate myself with Trench. I should have kept silent, or kept the secret to myself; my future would have been different. But I stood there at a disadvantage, with dirty hands and none too sure if I had any friends on board. The urge to show off was stronger than my intelligence.

Now Trench could follow two courses of action. He could kill me or have me killed; or he could keep the secret between the two of us, and try to extract such gain from it as Savemba would concede. If he planned to keep the rest of the crew ignorant of his discovery, he would still have to involve me somehow in the potential gains. Fraud and diplomacy were to be the only weapons, though, as confronting the whole of Savemba's following with the ship unable to sail was out of the question.

Later that night, I was half asleep in my makeshift tent under the ship, my mind being too busy to allow me much rest. Outside, a rising full moon illuminated the dramatic setting: the *Vision Quest* lying aslant against the light, deep shadow projected on the white beach, the bulk of the ship and the length of its masts hugely magnified by the projection; the river a moving band of mercury carrying its poison in deadly silence; the ocean beyond, glittering and beautiful in its eternal indifference—its huge mass of formless yet all-powerful waters the best illustration of the divine.

I heard my name whispered outside, insistently. There was Captain Trench, all by himself, dressed in black, merged into the dramatic shadows, his eyes wide and intense, his cruel mouth clenched. "Come with me, Rey," he whispered. I followed without hesitating or asking questions. Trench leading the way, we moved quickly into the shade of the trees overhanging the poisoned river. "We want to see that gold mine, Rey," Trench said in a matter-of-fact way once we were on the bank of the river. "Let's just follow the river upstream. The night is perfect with this moon, and we have a few hours before us."

The river ran an erratic course through dry, thorny bushland. Our progress was slow, and the thorns mutilated our ankles. At certain moments, the bush reached up to our breasts, tearing our shirts and filling our nostrils with the acrid smells of sticky resins. We spoke little as we struggled through these obstacles.

The river seemed to be narrowing down. The terrain was rising moderately, and a few low hills stood out on the opposite bank. The moon was high now, and the landscape had absorbed its own shadows. The river was running faster as the ground rose. It occurred to me that the mine must be a considerable one if the mercury was used in such quantities as to poison a whole stream. Suddenly there was a yellowish glow behind a low hill in front of us. The area seemed to have been cleared of the sticky undergrowth. The light was shimmering *and rising from the ground.*

We took cover on the crest of the hill, and surveyed the other side. Little were we prepared for the sight revealed to us. About a hundred yards away from the riverbank, the light of a thousand torches rose from a deep, terraced excavation looking like a man-made volcano. The river had been dammed and diverted so as not to flood the pit. The hellish glow from below met the silvery light of the moon on the surface. In the strangely contrasting illuminations, what seemed like ten thousand naked men, women and children were toiling, climbing down long ladders into the pit, or struggling back to the surface with heavy loads of mud and gravel, carried on their heads or shoulders in leaky baskets. An ominous silence pervaded the whole scene. On the river's bank, where the mud was being washed, guards armed with whips and machetes surveyed the operation. Yet, as all the workers were absolutely naked, it was difficult to conceive how they could abscond any findings, except maybe the small quantities to be hidden in body cavities. But even that the clever Savemba had foreseen. Trench pointed out a station of the guards a little further upstream, where those workers who were allowed some rest were examined mouth, back and front, the girls and women more thoroughly than the men. Also, the punishment meted out for any concealment was obvious. Just behind the guards' station two girls hung crucified on X-shaped crosses, naked as they had been caught, their forced-open bodies still tense with life & agony.

The size of the whole undertaking was titanic. I thought I had still underestimated Savemba. From the security and the modalities of the mine, we had to abandon any hope of robbery. And another question arose in my mind: was he mining only gold, or—as the form of the excavations seemed to indicate—also diamonds? Trench motioned me to move back, and we made a toilsome retreat to the ship. Trench swore me to secrecy before I re-entered my tent. I could now consider myself in a position to harm him—for the crew would not forgive his silence on such a discovery. At the same time his ascendancy over me increased, as loyalty bound me to his private plans & calculations.

The issue of the water supply was resolved the next day, as Savemba accepted to give us access to the well supplying his compound. Trench paid the additional price with much apparent disgust, but helping to maintain (in both sides' treacherous interest) the fiction that Savemba needed the money.

As we finished careening the ship, I was at a loss to understand the profit Trench could possibly draw from his knowledge about the mine. The day before the ship was brought afloat again, Trench spent a long time by himself visiting Savemba's compound. Mr. Wingate, the mate, and the rest of the crew were less suspicious now of underhand dealings by the captain, as our stay was nearly over and everyone was eager to sail.

The ship was launched. Trench was rowed on board. At the very last moment, a messenger from Savemba appeared. The way I later reconstructed the events, Trench had quietly been blackmailing Savemba, menacing to reveal his secret to the Dutch or the Portuguese; and at the last moment, when Savemba couldn't stop him anymore, Trench had extracted from Savemba the price of his silence. As he had insisted on a *very high price,* given the size of the operation we had discovered, and on *the smallest volume for value,* Savemba had paid him in diamonds. This was the origin of Trench's second—and wholly private—treasure.

CHAPTER 13

▼

Such were the circumstances under which we undertook our Atlantic voyage, sailing to the northwest after leaving Savemba's coast, to effect the shortest crossing. On board we now had the considerable shipment of opium taken from the *Sultana*, besides the more traditional goods. We were doing well. Our forecastle was stocked with chandler's goods. We had a cargo of rice, indigo, tea and silks, fair amounts of Yemeni coffee, and of cardamon, nutmeg, vanilla and benzoin. There was about £ 500 in various gold and silver coin. Above all this—but unknown to the crew—came Trench's diamonds.

The stated purpose for the Atlantic crossing was to sell the opium at Havana through a third party to be identified on land. Havana was famous for its tolerance of all kinds of illicit trade, given the strictness of its government and hence the unavoidable corruption of its poorly paid officials.

Captain Trench's main line of argument was dead simple: if the British could sell opium to the Chinese—force it upon them, really—and build colossal fortunes and a complete Asian empire in the process, why then was he, Trench, not allowed to do likewise, on a smaller scale and with a more modest purpose? Was the trading in drugs sanctioned by divine right to the British East India Company, her vessels, captains, traders and administrators? This was clearly absurd. Even without going deeper into the political argument, the Free Trading principle alone could be invoked.

Trench's grand design was to enter the opium trade on a regular basis, use the gains of this first voyage to finance various other ships, and open a route from Bombay to Havana. I say this was the *avowed* purpose. It bound many of the crew to captain Trench, because of the long-term vision of enormous profits, even of an ultimate respectability once the trade had become vast enough to command political acceptance.

But I am now convinced, with hindsight, that this plan was a delusion. Possibly Trench's own character operated best when such deception was in place to mask deeper and more fatal intentions. There is no doubt for me that, underneath his building of a commercial empire, Trench was courting destruction and self-destruction, and would drag down ships and crews with him into his own abyss. This, then, was the great fraud underlying his declarations and all the pretexts of good management: he represented some organizing principle gone deeply wrong, even to the point of madness. With the possible exception of Mr. Wingate, the crew could not comprehend this. Apart from those who were tempted by Trench's grand plan, there were many simpler souls on board, living day by day and unable to grasp even the concept of a commercial enterprise. They were the eternal followers, the ones who would forever give their vote to a captain who kept them fed and clothed and guaranteed their rations of rum. They were the ones pleading not guilty at piracy trials anywhere in the world, alleging they had been pressed into service and had only followed orders. But neither category could see Trench for what he really was. This doubtful privilege fell to me, because of Trench' special intentions regarding my person.

CHAPTER 14

▼

After our Angola adventures, Trench started to adopt a fatherly tone with me. I had never told anyone about the circumstances of my youth, but my own behaviour may have given him occasion to think that I needed manly guidance. As we were often standing together side by side during navigational procedures, he took advantage of those private moments to impart his views. He did so mostly with his eyes fixed on the wide horizon of the open sea. This gave his words even more impact, as they seemed to come from the very elements we were seeking to chart for our survival.

Once he said this, word for word:

"Like childbirth turns a girl into a real woman, so the first kill initiates a man into his own ultimate power. The violence lives in all of us; to let it lie dormant poisons a man's seed. If he *but once* commits the ultimate, he liberates those energies. Otherwise, the temptation goes unexplored and he will forever doubt his own courage and ignore the territories which lie *beyond the transgression.*"

Another time:

"For killing and for dying, *the fear is so much worse than the fact.*"

On yet another occasion:

"When you are a warrior, the worst is not to kill or even to die. The worst is to accept the unacceptable. *And a warrior you are:* it's in your eyes, it must be in your blood, even if you choose to ignore it."

This time I reacted:

"And what, pray, is *the unacceptable?*"

"Only you can define that for yourself: the lies of priests and kings, a life too narrow, the company of the wrong woman …"

While I was being so instructed, and lending more ear to these thoughts than I admitted to myself at first, the *Vision Quest* was again following the so-called *Wagenspoor* of the Dutch East India vessels along the coast of West-Africa and into the mid-Atlantic. This was the safest route to the shortest crossing. It also put us in the way of the richest ships on earth, both in and outbound. On their way to the Spice Islands, the Dutch East Indiamen would normally travel in escorted convoys, to protect traders and passengers—and the great amounts of coin they carried on the long and dangerous outbound voyage to Batavia. But occasionally, these convoys would be disrupted and dispersed by storms in the northern seas.

In the month of November of 1765, we happened upon such a stray outbound ship, an impressive three-master called the *Barbersteyn*. When she was sighted, she stood out clearly above the horizon. Approaching her, we saw that she rode the waves majestically, sailing under ballast. This made her look even grander and more impressive. Faced with such a prey, Trench adapted his hunting technique. When attacking the *Sultana*, we had acted in a straightforward way, outrunning her and giving battle in military style. With the Barbersteyn, Trench changed us from lions into hyenas. We chased her for a full day, pouncing and retreating, exhausting her crew with constant diversions, repeatedly creating the illusion that we gave up the chase—only to reappear alongside at odd angles so as to avoid her forty-odd guns—for she was well armed, too.

This deadly game continued into the night when the crew of our victim must have lost any notion of safety or escape. We would trail her for several hours with our lanterns dimmed, then light all our flames suddenly at their brightest—and reappear to her startled mariners and passengers like the very devil. This long, protracted and cruel chase also played out in my mind. While during previous attacks I had stood apart, the privileged observer, now I began to feel part of the pack. I admired Trench's seamanship, for the mode of pursuit he'd chosen forced him to manoeuvre the *Vision Quest* with unprecedented swiftness and agility. His every command was meditated for efficiency and effect, and all his intuitions proved right. These moves were even more impressive when carried out in silence and darkness, after night fell on our chase; and our sudden reappearances as a blazing comet in the eyes of the Barbersteyn were also planned, timed and carried out to perfection.

My excitement grew with every heartbeat, anticipating the moment of the kill. When the moment was near, and command was given to check arms, I asked to be given one of the solid iron swords kept especially for the boarding.

Our attack, at dawn, must have come as a relief to the exhausted people on board the Barbersteyn. Avoiding her broadsides, our men ascended her from behind, killing the captain and the first officer in the first moments and thus throwing the entire ship into screaming confusion. When I made it to her quarterdeck, heavy sword in hand, it was like diving into hell.

The enormous sails of the ship, flapping aimlessly as she started to drift, drove clouds of gun smoke in my eyes. With odd precision, I heard the screams of women above the din of battle, and realized with added excitement that female passengers were being raped. The early hour and the sun just rising added extra cruelty to this orgy of sex and blood. Cutting and slashing my way forward, I felt immortal, part of a grand and eternal fraternity, my thinking self utterly abolished by a rush of instincts. My lack of experience must have protected me. Unable to see with any precision, I was reduced to the *smells and sounds* of battle, those senses closest to the animal soul taking over and adding to the blinding of judgement.

I attacked writhing bodies in the mass, hacking indistinctively—till, upon reaching the main deck, I came all of a sudden face to face with one of the Barbersteyn's soldiers—a mere boy-pointing a pistol at me, but so clearly shaken by the events that the gun went off without him taking proper aim. The shot went way over my head. As he struggled with the scabbard while trying to draw his sabre, and as I was carried forward on the momentum of my own physical and mental rush—I ran him through with the sword. About the same moment, the shrill boatswain's whistle called us back through the thick haze of the battle. I had killed a person.

The sudden realization came when I had to draw the heavy sword from the body. I could not manage without putting my foot on the dead boy's chest. But a sudden wave of scruple now stopped me from doing so. I abandoned the sword and ran back aft, covered in blood.

My fellow pirates had already emptied the captain's coffers. Large chests of gold and silver were rowed across to the *Vision Quest*. Upon inspection and while making the inventory, I found every single coin neatly marked with the VoC (*Vereenigde Oost-Indische Compagnie*) monogram. The coins were well made, regular in shape even down to the copper pennies, whereas the Spanish *Reals* were often of a sloppy workmanship.

As the other ship was of no value to us, and as this attack had taken place on a busy route, no trace of our passage could remain. This Trench determined with the utmost calm and composure. His ranting and raving was no longer necessary to himself: now it was his efficient and administrative side perpetrating massive evil with cold rationality.

While we regrouped on board the Vision Quest and counted our own dead and wounded, the Barbersteyn was set on fire, amid the cries of the wounded and the dying and, worse still, those who were fully intact and alive to witness the last stages of horror. The ship was soon transformed into a magnificent and loud pyre—cracking and exploding, flames licking the waves.

As we were sailing on and I looked over my shoulder, the burning wreck engulfed in fire amid choppy seas looked like the devil's own island. All souls on board burned and went down into the Deep.

CHAPTER 15

▼

I felt immensely relieved after confessing these horrors to Epifania. Having participated in the collective cruelty of battle was one thing. The conscious killing of one person created a very different responsibility.

Late one night, Epifania finally took me to the secret *Casa Babalao* hidden in the bowels of the Solar Sarabanda. I had not known what to expect. In the light of the single candle she carried, the interior was revealed to be fully painted in whirling and colorful images. She pointed out the likenesses of the various *Orishas* or spirits: Red-and-black *Eleggua*, the Lord of the Crossroads, Blue-and-White *Yemayá* the Mother of the Ocean; golden *Ochún* the River of Love; white-and-red *Shangó* the Master of Thunder ... And dominating the back wall, facing the entrance, one-armed *Sarabanda* whose motto read: *'why do you call me if you don't know me ...* It sounded like a warning to the non-initiated.

"Listen carefully now, Rey. And you have to swear secrecy to me— as my *Babalao* would never forgive me for having informed a stranger about these things. I am one of the queens of my *Cabildo* ... But first I will clean you of your burdens ..."

She undressed and told me to do the same. But while she folded her own clothes carefully and put them in a corner, she instructed me to stand on my old shirt and breeches and trample them thoroughly.

Meanwhile she tied a long strand of colorful beads and various amulets around her waist, and produced a handful of twigs. She also took a bucket full of water from a corner of the room and placed it near my feet.

"We enter a forest of spirits. You have to be naked to abandon your ego and to be defenceless. This here (indicating the belt around her waist) is my *collar bandera,* which I received at my initiation. I will clean you with these herbs. They are called *Escoba Amarga* and *Siempre Viva.* Keep on stepping on your clothes: they are your old self."

She passed the twigs over every part of my body, meanwhile whispering *"Con licencia de Obatalá, con licencia de Obatalá ..."* and various *"Maferefún", "Egún", Agguán", "Aikú ..."* In spite of the fact that we were both naked, there was nothing sexual in this procedure, even when the herbs touched my private parts. I was not aroused, Epifania was absorbed in her rôle and seemed totally to forget herself.

I was receptive to her rite, so much is obvious, but this by itself does not account for the effect it soon started to have on my thoughts and feelings. As she was progressing with the cleansing, and as I was trampling my clothes underfoot, an intense flow of energy went through my body. Soon this concentrated my inner eye on the worst visual images of my crimes: my cowardice in the presence of Mr. Trench; my single but conscious act of murder.

My old self fought back, invoking lies and pretexts for my behaviour: self-preservation, the suspension of conscience, the rush of battle ... But I was drawn irresistibly to discount these defences, to admit what I had done, to face it squarely. Then a wave of warmth brought the onset of a kind of acceptance and serenity.

I was about to collapse, and Epifania too seemed exhausted. But she collected her energies, and furiously tore to pieces the old clothes I had been trampling. She picked up the bucket of water, whirled it around me three times. Next she collected my shredded clothes and ran outdoors. She threw the clothes down at the intersection of two narrow alleys a few paces away from the door, and emptied the bucket. Running back inside, she collapsed against a wall.

After panting for a long time she put on her dress again and told me to sit down next to her. Now, clearly coming to the core of her secrets, she said:

"I've done a great many bad things myself, Rey, I admit. I've never killed anyone as far as I know, but short of that … I offer no excuse— I'm the animal I am, coming where I come from, and so are you. Can't change that; and God—that you must understand—*isn't watching;* He *is*, but He doesn't interfere. The distance *makes* God. *Los muertos y los Orishas*—the Dead and the Spirits, now that's another matter. They *do* care, they *do* interfere. They all drink rum; they smoke; they take their pleasure with me when they possess me; they help and they play tricks. And the Dead rule us all, since we are all descended from them. It's really as simple as that.

All the actions and qualities of the Ancestors have grown into solid characters, which we recognize by their colors and their attributes. They are the *Orishas.*

We all take after them, and each of us is ruled predominantly by one. It's not for me to say which *Orisha* rules your destiny. Take my own case: there isn't a girl in Havana but will tell you she's a *Hija de Ochún*, so you will bring her sunflowers and buy or steal gold for her. But when the *Babalaos* consulted for me, I was told I was ruled by *Ochósi*—the hunter, the protector of prisoners … See? As a traveller, a user of the crossroads, you may belong to *Elegguá*; yet, you're a warrior too—just as I will always be running from the law—and as such, you're just as likely a son of *Shangó* or even of *Ogún*, the Master of Iron. Aren't you disturbed and fascinated by knives …?"

"More important still, Rey: *this is no sorcery as the Whites see it.* All of this is *proper procedure.* There are rules. There are norms. The ancestors have practiced this for ages and ages, adapting and correcting their visions, back in the old country …"

"Third, *about good and evil:* they don't exist in themselves; they are sides of a coin, or rather—facets of a diamond; for every deed is a cycle and a series, a faraway consequence from faraway causes, becoming infinite cause itself the moment it is acted out ..."

I objected in my thoughts that this was a dangerous doctrine, since it could justify any deed—precisely the question I'd been struggling with. "No," she answered, reading my argument off my face without the slightest effort: "you will learn to *know by instinct what's right for you, when you follow the paths of your Orisha. That's what the oracles are for.*"

By instinct? I thought, and what if my instinct makes me into a killer? Indeed: for a long time I had feared that violence *is* our ultimate instinct and our final demon, and my own *progress* on the Vision Quest seemed to bear this out.

But absorbing the rules of Epifania's system, I now saw that maybe my energies had been misdirected, or had lacked direction altogether, since I had not been an initiate. The link with my former life became evident: Trench had been able to corrupt me because I *had* lacked my own sense of purpose.

Was this, then, the most profound exchange between the girl and myself: I had saved her from opium and the slave-hunters; would she save me from the temptation of violence?

CHAPTER 16

▼

In retrospect, the scariest part of my piracy experiences had been Trench's speeches at the moments of attack. They had to be, for a simple reason. I had to admit I had been scared to death before each battle, yet Trench's words had always had such a hypnotic effect on me *as to do away with the fear.*

This illustrates that his very words, and the way he shouted them, granted him in those moments a power greater than death itself, a power such as to render our natural defences against transgression inoperative.

If a man could wield such power, if he could provoke at will other men's' indifference towards their own death and towards the infliction of untold misery, was he not a god or a devil in his own right? This I debated for long hours with myself, especially when the smoking of Ras Fasil's herb carried me on waves of clairvoyance or the illusion thereof. One conclusion I came to, was that Captain Trench could only have acquired such powers *because we of the crew consented to give them to him.* This would have been easier to understand if Trench had been an obvious demigod or Lucifer. But he was quite the opposite: physically unremarkable, addicted to sugary foods, unclean in many of his personal habits, none too natural in his desires of women. Such traits could not be kept secret on shipboard.

Yet we gave him the power in our direst moments. I gradually formed a hypothesis: if we made Trench our war-god, maybe it was precisely *because his own insignificance could channel our deadly energies*. If he had been a true torchbearer, he might have led us towards more light; but it took this insignificance of evil to concentrate our own darkness.

There are people shouting at the world—through their deeds: '*Stop me, or make me god!*' And as they mostly don't find the resistance they'd need to come to their senses, the world undergoes their deeds and suffers the destructions, till the aspiring gods destroy themselves. All of this is unavoidable and has happened so many times in man's history that we should know better, but still we don't.

But this made it all the more difficult to define a private morality, and this was our real struggle. How difficult it is to be free! To attain freedom in the first place—the immediate absence of hardship and pressure—is hard enough. But a slave after freeing himself of those first shackles, still has to eat and drink, accepting new limits in the process—and still has to have a code of conduct, however different from the one imposed by the former master. In that situation I found myself, having to construct from scratch a complete structure of beliefs, with no useful materials from education or example. But it remained my conviction *that man needs to believe*. I was often envious of Duchesse's idealism, her unshakable conviction that the advent of the Black Republic in St. Domingue would be the ultimate guarantee of freedom for her people. It would have been a crime to rob her of that conviction, and yet I shared Epifania's cynical doubts about the whole idea.

Even in the middle of all these anxieties and doubts, I now found the strength to fight feelings of despondency. Just as I had recognized myself as a naturally religious soul, I *knew* I was made to be happy— to feel & greet the bliss of every morning, to delight in small details & intimate intuitions; and to accept without illusion the absence of eternity. And what drew me near to Epifania, even in the darkest hours of her self-destructive habits, was that I sensed that she carried the same conviction: that we were, ultimately, creatures of light and not of darkness; that for all the real evil we'd witnessed and committed, we could also be agents of our own redemption; and that our innate intensity as well could be turned from dark to bright. This I now resolved: I would never let my natural happiness be destroyed by loneliness and self-pity.

CHAPTER 17

▼

But to return to the *Vision Quest* and the last leg of our voyage before reaching Cuba: The time we spent in Jamaica was a pilgrimage of sorts to the origins of the ship: the Vision Quest—or, rather, the original *Dragon*—had been built of Jamaican redwood, as I knew from her books and as had been ascertained during her careening in Angola. This hardwood was famously fit for warships, as it did not splinter under impact of even close-range cannon fire. It was also resistant to woodworm and other tunnelling parasites.

As for Port Royal—this harbour's fame, in sailors' tales, still rested on the 1692 earthquake, as being an event rich in meaning and foreboding. At the time of the earthquake, Port Royal had notoriously been the *wickedest city in the Universe*, and a famous pirate haven. The city had never recovered from the devastation, as survivors had moved across the bay to the new town of Kingston. What remained of Port Royal, after a large portion of the city had sunk into the sea, was in fact an island. Sailors of our description avoided the place now, as there was a small garrison and it was a well-known place of execution.

But Trench was defiant. Port Royal had also been the base of Sir Henry Morgan, the only English pirate to have achieved respectability, having ended his life as Lieutenant-Governor of Jamaica. Mr. Wingate pleaded in vain that times had changed: since the 1720's those pirates who had chosen not to surrender under the Pardon

Edicts, had been persecuted mercilessly in these parts. Hangings had been frequent, and widely publicized: again, such news travelled the oceans and was sung and commented about in every port tavern.

But Trench was adamant to touch land in Jamaica. In the scheme of things he pretended to pursue, he was anticipating the day of his own respectability as a trans-Atlantic merchant; while at the same time, in his unspoken plans, he was courting disaster. We approached Jamaica from the southeast. It was a clear day, the heat alleviated by the Christmas breeze. The Blue Mountain peaks stood out majestically above the low buildings of Kingston Harbour. The cool off-land air carried sweet smells of wet earth and blossoms. In between the shore and the mountains, plumes of smoke rose from the densely wooded hills and gullies, where runaway slaves were hiding from bounty hunters and their bloodhounds. With its narrow coastal plain, filled with hard labour, and the impenetrable mountains beyond, the whole island appeared like a splendid prison.

One of the crew had sailed these waters frequently and acted the pilot, naming the sights. We steered clear of Lime Cay. The narrow line of the Palisadoes to the northeast marked the crossing between the mainland and Port Royal. We spied the flags of Fort Charles and Fort Clarence, and the ominous Gallows Point beyond the latter. Trench boasted that he had approached to within view of the birthplace of his ship, as the shipyards lay on the leeside of the Palisadoes tip, behind Fort Charles. Next, though, we hastily steered towards the cays and the dense mangroves west of Kingston, where we would be safe to haul water and find fresh food.

There were countless mango groves. Some old hand pointed at the *ackee* trees, indicating that the red-and-yellow fruit was an excellent and tasty vegetable, but poisonous till the shiny black seeds had popped out. The crew declared they'd rather starve than eat such devilish food. There were cashew nuts in abundance, and those we picked and roasted. We cut an amount of sugarcane from the fields of an abandoned and overgrown estate, the weeds lively with many rats and mongoose.

Further west, the beaches were grey as ash. Inland was a dry and thorny plain, reminding me of the savannahs we'd seen in East Africa during our apprenticeship as pirates. Those days seemed very remote now.

CHAPTER 18

▼

The Jamaica episode was the last part of my story to Epifania. With the piracy adventures behind me—or so I thought!—all our energies now went towards organizing our escape from Havana's ever-tightening grip. We were more than ever confined to Regla and the Solar Sarabanda. But the effectiveness of Duchesse Malenfant's networks increased as the repression and the controls in the city grew worse. Hence, we were even better informed than before about events elsewhere on the island and in the world beyond.

A number of large ships out of Cádiz had berthed on the Regla side of the harbour while the deportation of the Jesuits was in progress. As usual, Duchesse had her informers on board those vessels. Even ordinary mariners were more talkative than usual, many of them disgruntled about the fact that the city of Cádiz was losing its trading monopoly with the Spanish Americas. As these feelings were easily exploited, Duchesse—ready for action as always—cleverly recruited more informers.

I took advantage of these circumstances to hear out the sailors about ports on the mainland, trying to find out what life was like in Savannah, Charleston and the New Orleans (which had recently fallen to Spain). Charleston, I was told, was frequently hanging pirates. Savannah was more sedate, being a river port in the middle of rice paddies. New Orleans was rowdy, bawdy and—due to recent changes in politics—lawless in many respects. Guessing my purpose, one sailor—a redhead, Irish by birth but speaking Spanish like an Andalúz—said the cities of New England were now the most rebellious against Kings & Taxes, and hence the places *he* would run away to; but he didn't recommend them to someone *of my name & complexion.* The Irishman also said that one of his shipmates had spent time in New Orleans during the carnivals, and had told colorful stories about wild parties, wonderfully indecent girls, a general ease of morals, and a proud and thriving class of Free Africans.

This sounded too good to be true. We asked to meet that sailor and the next day got the reply that, being French on his mother's side and peculiar in his habits, he refused to come to the *Solar* and would only talk to us *if we bought him wine in a proper tavern.* So, taking a chance, we left our lair and invited him to a bar on the far side of Regla church.

The man turned out to be in his fifties—dry, wrinkled and tanned but still lively in the eye, and green enough to be constantly staring at Epifania's generously exposed breasts. He drank his wine, found it to be lacking in quality, answered some of our easy questions and avoided many of the more pressing and urgent ones. On the crucial point—how Epifania would be treated under local laws in New Orleans—he proved more evasive or less informed than the Spanish Irishman had given to understand. The Blacks had misbehaved freely in the streets, he said, right next to the Cabildo, and the girls more than the men, showing their tits for beads and coins; but then again—it was Carnival time …

While this conversation was in progress, I was sitting with my back to the door of the tavern. The table was a small one, and Epifania would only sit and remain in such places if she could face the exit. I observed the comings and goings through the mirror of her reactions.

All of a sudden, I saw her body stiffen and her eyes go wild. Avoiding to turn around and to expose my face in full view towards the door, I *knew* that someone of importance to her had just entered the tavern. All my earlier distrust of her returned at once, overwhelming me and sucking me down like a sudden wave and its undertow. "This is the moment she's betraying me and handing me over to the guards. This is what she's been working towards all these months to save her own skin, and I've been the sucker falling for her confidence tricks"—such were my instinctive reactions when I observed her face during the time of those few heartbeats before I did turn around myself and recognized—*Mr. Wingate!* For months I had built great fears about his presence in Havana. There was one more instant during which my instincts accused Epifania of being in league with him—hadn't I seen them together in the Café Cantante?

But now, with one close look at his face, those fears dwindled to nothing. He looked neither hateful nor dangerous, but rather immensely relieved. Nor was there any sign of collusion between Mr. Wingate and Epifania. Quite the opposite: she looked more scared than me. I had completely misread her reactions. Both my fears and my renewed suspicions were unfounded. For the first time, I felt deeply embarrassed at my own lack of trust.

"I've been looking for you all over. You *must* hear my story!" Mr. Wingate said in a passionate whisper. The French sailor, failing to understand what was going on, but sensing trouble at the sight of Wingate's respectable clothes, made a quick exit. Wingate was wiping imaginary dust from his coat shoulders and tugging at his wig. His well-known efforts to look like a merchant were badly out of place in Regla—if anything, the dark coat and yellow breeches made him stand out even more.

"Mr. Wingate ..." I began, but he immediately looked over his shoulder and whispered even more urgently: "Please, please: I'm called *Philips* now. Don't mention that other name ever again ..."

When he had calmed down and after we urged him to take off the coat and roll up his sleeves, he told us that he had jumped ship while the Vision Quest was marauding around Savannah, and that he had laboriously made his way back to Cuba, taking advantage of the increased shipping resulting from the sugar trade between the island and the American colonies.

Providence had been on his side, he said—for only a few weeks later the Vision Quest had been engaged by the coast guards and had been destroyed, her crew killed or captured, and Captain Trench hanged shortly afterwards at Charleston.

Epifania shuddered at the hanging part and impulsively grabbed my hand. She called for rum, and drank a good swig. Wingate—or rather Philips—followed suit; only then was he able to talk more.

CHAPTER 19

▼

This was Mr. Wingate's story as far as Captain Trench was concerned: Wingate had met Mr Trench in the year 1760, in the backroom of a certain tavern in Bristol where a fashionable *Hell-Fire Club* was holding weekly meetings.

Such clubs of anti-moralists were much *en vogue*, following the example given by notorious aristocrats congregating at Medmenham Abbey for secret rites whispered to be satanic and erotic in nature. In a port city like Bristol, collecting colonial adventurers and the usual quayside parasites, dollymops & catamites, such a club was likely to become nothing more than a slightly perverted brothel—which it had. A disgraced teacher and two drunken students provided it with some pornographic Latin inscriptions. The landlord of the tavern procured young girls willing to be stripped, smeared with chicken blood and fucked on an improvised altar.

Following the ruin of his family, Mr. Trench had been on a quest for real moral and political alternatives. He was disappointed and disgusted after two sessions of the club. He had convinced Mr. Wingate to follow him to more worthy experiments. Yet, Mr. Wingate was convinced that the Hell-Fire Clubs had inspired Trench's actions from then on. The example set by the highest classes of the country had convinced him that conventional morality was indeed a shambles and a fraud. Philosophically, he subscribed to the *wholeness of nature:*

whatever is, is right. This doctrine tended to justify his every impulse, all the way to the darkest and most murderous.

Mr. Wingate's tale set me thinking. Having been raised in the Netherlands, as a child I had heard whispers and had indeed known the remnants of crazy and violent heresies of ages past: the Adamites, the Münster Anabaptists ... All of them mixing sex and crazy justifications for murder and mayhem. Supposedly in Holland these had been wiped out under the orderly rule of the Republic and the Gentlemen XVII of the East India Company; but remnants of all those sects probably had survived underground; and where would such secret currents meet, but in port taverns and on shipboard? I now realised that Hans, our fake monk back in Antwerp peddling his pornography and his anarchy, was in all likelihood a survivor of those wild beliefs.

Thus my thoughts came full circle—for Trench, even if he had indeed been illiterate—had certainly absorbed the essence of Captain Johnson's pirate history. If he saw himself as a philosophical and political pirate, his great example must have been Captain Sam Bellamy, whose scornful speeches against kings and their power had been widely publicized in broadsheets and books following his death in the shipwreck of his vessel the *Whydah* off Cape Cod in 1717—and whose rhetoric had been the core of the book Inky and I had peddled back in Antwerp, and which had set me on my own adventurous course.

What strange, *personal* trajectories Fate had mapped out for me! Then and there, in the Regla tavern, I was reminded of the secret belief of my lonely childhood—that the circumstances of the world somehow would follow my own obsessions. This was a brief and penetrating moment of deep intuition. Mr. Wingate was finishing his tale:

"... But Trench was given to self-contemplation, even to the point of narcissism. This made his violence worse—for every deed is poisoned by self-consciousness—and acts of cruelty even more so, as they can only be justified by unreasoned urges or needs."

We drank our rum in silence. Epifania was still holding my hand, as if to ward off evil or to share my dangers. She was following only tiny fragments of the conversation in English, but her eyes told us that she was aware of the gravity of our words.

We took Mr. Wingate inside the Solar for the night, and put him up in the veterans' quarters near the first patio. I had more questions for him.

CHAPTER 20

▼

That night I couldn't sleep. The day had been too eventful, and too many demons of every size and description were whirling around in my head. I quietly left Epifania, sleeping with abandon next to me, and climbed up a flat section of the roof of the *Solar*. There I sat smoking and musing under the stars for a long time.

My thoughts kept on running their own course, going back to Mr. Wingate's revelations. Captain Bellamy's fine rhetoric—whether or not embellished by the writers and publishers—was of course unknown in Havana. But during the war, Spain had justified even piracy against the British and their ambitions to rule every sea and every island.

A man from the Low Countries—of all places!—had set up a printing press in Havana in 1723. Pamphlets with anti-British propaganda had been printed there. Some copies were still around in the Havana underworld, as they had been circulating under the cloak during the occupation.

These tracts, glorifying every deed of resistances against the invader, had become embarrassingly provocative after the British withdrawal—as their questioning of established authority could easily be construed to apply to any ruler, especially to remote and often inept monarchs in Madrid. The censors and the Inquisition had destroyed most of the pamphlets; but the odd copy still around was cherished by some revolutionary intellectuals as a precious illustration of the opportunism of the monarchies, and the shaky foundations of their power.

Following this train of thought, now I remembered the full extent of pirate politics as I had absorbed them as a youth. The mysterious Captain Johnson, speaking under the cloak of his characters, had gone further than the mere questioning or royal authority. In the chapters dealing with the French buccaneer Misson and his associate Carracioli, Christian religion fares no better than the monarchy when described by Captain Bellamy.

The night, the smoke of countless strong cigars, and the stars above, encouraged vast and abstract schemes in my mind. Even now, as I write down my youthful adventures so many years later, I still remember the intensity of my reasoning during those hours, as they contained the ultimate key to the meaning of my wanderings.

I was deeply convinced of the utter failure of the Christian religion, easily the greatest scam and lie of human history. When the Romans ruled, their gods didn't induce war in the name of peace and brotherhood. Nor did tribal leaders anywhere, who followed clear objectives in line with their ancestral religions however cruel towards outsiders—but never building on fundamental hypocrisies as Christianity has been doing for so many centuries, its effects *always and everywhere diametrically opposed to its tenets.* Yet—what to replace it with?

I am sure now that in Captain Trench's case, his excessively contemplative nature did away with the purity of the hunter's instincts. Hence, his road of excess became a secret quest for self-destruction as well. Having forsaken Christianity, Captain Trench was at a loss to maintain himself above an enormous emptiness, far deeper than the oceans he was roving. The first half of his life he may have lived in a world too rigid and lawful to accommodate himself of his own later chaos. His painful sticking to certain details of a good sailor's duties (while pursuing a life of murder, rape and plunder) had long confirmed me in that impression. In contrast, I had had the advantage and the burden of seeing all the official truths from the backside from childhood on.

Trench was one of those men who, on discovering belatedly that all is lie and deception, turn profoundly against the world—but also against their former, believing selves. I had heard every argument against the Christian religion from a renegade monk turned philosopher whom I'd met in a brothel in Nantes, one more representative of the secret travelling brotherhood of revolutionaries. The monk had argued that the Christian doctrine of the Holy Trinity had been devised specifically to deceive the people—establishing the church both as a necessary power from above and as an alleged defender of the meek. In short—it was a cunning lie aimed at serving the powerful while pretending at the same time to be on the side of the oppressed. God the old patriarch was always there, and at the same time the adventurous and subversive son; both were always right; this could not be.

On that drunken night I had agreed with the renegade monk, of course. He *was* right, moreover—but it was old news, a neatly formulated confirmation of a truth I'd long reached through my own instincts.

Yet, now that I lived immersed in the African religions, I was again strongly reminded that I was a naturally religious soul. I also discovered that religion—though not Christianity—is so deeply embedded in our brains as to make us feel reduced and amputated when we reject it.

Compared with captain Trench's purely negative attitudes, and the void they caused in his life, the rhythms, the chants, the joys and the ecstasies of religion in Regla were overwhelmingly beautiful— even though no one knew better than I the matters of money, power and jealousy accompanying them: these matters just made Epifania's religion more unavoidably human.

I had confronted Epifania's demons in order to calm my own. Now I wanted finally to get to the bottom of all the intrigues on board the Vision Quest. I climbed down from the roof and made my way to the room shared by the former Mr. Wingate.

CHAPTER 21

▼

Mr. Philips was obviously a light sleeper; or maybe his mind was as disturbed as my own by the quest for revelations. When I knocked at his door, he was up in a moment, almost as if he had been expecting my visit.

To enjoy the cool air again, I took him up on the roof with me. He still climbed nimbly enough for a man his age, yet he said with a sigh that he hoped never again to go up a mast. I handed him a cigar, and we smoked together now. The silence between us was full of distrust and denial at first. Slowly though, as night took possession of our souls, the unspoken wariness began to dissolve.

All around and below us, the organic structures of the *Solar*'s wild architecture were outlined against the luminous night sky. The waters of the harbour scintillated beyond Regla church.

There emanated from this scene a strong sense of completeness, a sense of definite time and place which I had rarely, all too rarely, experienced since my flight from Antwerp. This was a moment of special grace, not to be left unexplored. I further pressed and interrogated Mr. Wingate. This was what I found out next.

CHAPTER 22

▼

In December 1765, during the Atlantic passage, Trench had made elaborate plans for the sale of the opium taken from the *Sultana*. Wingate had been in his confidence—Trench had carefully avoided sharing his intentions with me, for very specific reasons; but he needed an associate.

The plan was astute. I would be set ashore supposedly to contact importers and dealers in Havana, carrying a sufficient amount of the merchandise as a sample of quality and origin. After they sent me off, the *Vision Quest*—avoiding the port of Havana—would make a brief stop at Matanzas, where Wingate would go ashore under his respectable guise, and would alert the Port Captaincy that a major shipment of the drug was about to be brought into the capital. Then the Vision Quest would sail on to New Orleans, where the bulk of the opium would be sold.

The purpose of this diversion was clear. Trench was confident that word about the opium reaching Havana through me would spread rapidly and effectively enough to clear his ship of the suspicion that he still carried the drug; and so he would sell the goods without any hindrance or pressure in a future port.

The timing of these moves was important. A fast courier from Matanzas would reach Havana within hours. When he decided to put me ashore in Bahia Honda—invoking the safe distance from

Havana—probably Trench had planned for me to be caught as I entered the city with my wares—for by then, the courier from Matanzas should have reached the capital. But that part had gone wrong for him, simply because the women on the banks of the Almendares River had helped me disguising the opium as goava jelly. After that, once I was inside, the Authorities knew about the theft of the opium—since the thief was also a police informer—and hence they had lost interest in me.

The reader may well imagine the confusion these discoveries brought to my mind. All the time, I had felt guilty of betrayal, and I had been the victim of a far worse plot than I had devised myself! I had always felt a kind of loyalty towards Trench—first, because of my oath to the Articles of the Vision Quest; next, because he had been instrumental in revealing my violent instincts; this revelation, however troubling, had nevertheless created a bond the depth of which I considered with awe. But I was now revealed as utterly naive.

CHAPTER 23

▼

While I was digesting this, with a mixture of anger and embarrassment, a slight noise from the backside of the roof drew my attention. I crept to the edge and as I was about to look down into the patio below, Epifania climbed upon the roof.

"I couldn't sleep either," she said.

A child started to cry somewhere in the *Solar*. It must have been Mildrey's baby, for now I heard Cecilia's voice trying to soothe the child with a melancholy lullaby which ran thus:

> *"A mi me duele la vida*
> *Como una enfermedad*
> *De día como de noche*
> *Sola con mi soledad ..."*

Epifania, who knew every song ever sung in Havana, softly chimed in:

> *"... Casi no tengo sombra*
> *Casi no tengo edad*
> *A mi me duele la vida*
> *Como una enfermedad."*

'Sola con mi soledad ...'

Across immense distances—yes, maybe across the cosmic boundaries of Death, suddenly it seemed to me that it was *my mother's voice singing the lullaby*. And circumstances *in the objective world* once again conspiring to confirm the private clockworks of my fate, at that very moment Mr. Wingate cleared his throat and said he had something further to tell me.

Next he hesitated and the three of us smoked again in silence for a long moment. The night felt different at each revelation. Mr. Wingate also seemed to sense this. Epifania's presence embarrassed him at first. But I felt something more in his attitude now—some further secret the disclosure of which was actually *encouraged* by the presence of a woman.

He cleared his throat again, reached into his coat pocket and handed me a much crumbled letter folded in four, ragged along the edges and the folds; but still clearly legible on the outside was my name, somewhat faded *but clearly written in my mother's rounded hand*. I started to cry.

Epifania, reading the situation correctly with her fast intuition, said: "*Dios mio! Carta de tu mama?*"

I nodded. How it was possible that this letter should have followed me from ship to ship, from port to port—I still cannot comprehend. The message was not dated, and ran thus.

CHAPTER 24

▼

'My dearest son,

I have known the most cruel fate any woman can face. Failing to retain a husband at one's side is a common enough lot. A husband is, after all, but a stranger chosen by fate and instinct to enter one's intimacy. But the bond between a woman and the son she has carried in her womb is far more necessary. I admit that through you, I hoped to control your father. I nourished the illusion that I would at least be completely loved and trusted by one male creature during my lifetime, and that the son would give me the joys denied by the father.

Your sudden departure has left me alone and desolate. The offence to my person was deep, but I try to understand. Your father too, was driven by forces of the blood, stronger than his conscious will could pretend to control.

Now certain indications have led me to believe that he was wanted for murder in Spain, but being a Hijo de Algo, was allowed to exile himself to the Army or the Colonies instead of being judged. The blood I have passed on to you may be bad; your disappearance made me fear the worst. I felt therefore I had to send this message, however slim the chance that it should ever reach you. If you are alive and read this, you must search the truth in your own soul. Maybe you have already committed acts to be blamed on your blood. I would not condone them, holding that the blood inclines, but does not compel; and thus encouraging you, whatever the excuses available, to always take responsibility for even your worst deeds.

I bore you under signs of solitude, and under such signs I will die. My last thoughts will be for you, with the tenuous hope that my fears were mistaken, and that a mere accident or circumstance outside your will drove you from Antwerp, and that—wherever good or bad winds have blown you—you have had an occasional thought for your ever loving,

Mother.'

CHAPTER 25

▼

Tears in my eyes, I pressed Wingate—*"Philips, sir, please!"* he insisted—to enlighten me about the letter. As it was without a date, when had it reached the ship? For from this date I thought it possible to determine whether my poor mother could still be alive. Philips said the letter had been in Trench's hands when the Vision Quest was still called The Dragon. This explained the letter's trajectory: it had followed me from legitimate ship to legitimate ship ever since I had left Ostend on board the coastal trader.

But a mystery remained: had Trench known the contents? He was supposedly illiterate himself, and could not possibly consult me in this circumstance, if he had decided to keep the letter secret. But he may have had an opportunity to seek help from another scribe in a port of call—although such possibilities must have shrunk considerably after he turned pirate and changed the name of the vessel.

If Trench had known the contents, had he decided to keep the letter from me so as to avoid the discussion about the moral responsibility for our coming cruelties? Had he felt—even without knowing the contents—that any message received by me from my former life would undermine the total control he wanted over my soul, so as to render me a more helpless accomplice of his crimes? He had considered me an innocent: so much was clear from the part he had assigned me in the opium deal. Hence, corrupting me would have been a kind of perverse game for him, deepened by his plan to send me to my doom once I'd served his darkest purpose: to see his own lust for blood revealed in a younger man.

Mr. Wingate whispered even more confidentially now: "It sounds farfetched even as I'm saying it, Rey—but in a strange and inexplicable way it now seems to me that Trench lost his sense of purpose the moment you left the ship … You know, that aimless sailing up and down the Savannah river, stealing some bags of rice from the coolies was just not like him anymore … And on a ship which had sailed and seen so much … Which leads me to suppose …" "Speak, Philips, speak," I insisted.

He swallowed hard and shook his head, still in disbelief of his own thoughts, then he answered: *"You, Rey, were Trench's greatest undertaking.* More than any ship, he wanted to take *you.* You had every advantage over him, but your soul was available. If he could corrupt *you,* he could take anything."

I was stunned by this confession. At the same time my vanity wanted to glow in the dark at the thought of having been so important in the pirate's progress; but it also increased my shame in exactly the same proportion. If taking my soul had been Trench's greatest prize, my letting him have it (at least to the extent that he'd turned me into a killer) was my own worst defeat.

Thus I came to judge Mr. Trench in the end. His many excellent qualities, such as displayed by his sanitary measures against the scurvy, his management of the ship in general, his remarkable political talents, his careful navigation, his commercial plans—all of it had been subordinate to his deeper, destructive and self-destructive urges. And into that abyss he had wanted to drag me down as well.

Wingate must have sensed this conflict on my face, for now he said: "We're all very guilty, Rey; and since we've been spared the rope so far, we have to redeem ourselves …" Looking sideways at Epifania, he added: "That girl, Rey, may be your way to go; she obviously trusts you. I say—*I* probably won't get such a second chance at my age …" With that he got up and climbed down the roof.

CHAPTER 26

▼

Deep as these revelations had been, they still left one question unresolved. Since I'd come to trust Epifania almost completely, the part she may or may not have played in the disappearance of my most precious contraband—infinitely more valuable than the opium—still had to be clarified.

In order to do this, I tried to reconstruct, with painful accuracy, my last moments on board the *Vision Quest* before my landing.

The opium samples had been packed and sealed the day before. The two leather pouches were on the table in the captain's cabin. On the same table were the slates with my last observations, and the open logbook. It had been agreed that I would fill out the observations up to date, as the ship would pick me up on the same spot ten days later. Trench would supposedly sail the *Vision Quest* around the western edge of the island, and spend the time on one of the southern cays, where there were discreet sources of water. It was even rumoured that there was a fresh-water source spouting in the very sea, allowing a ship to water without touching land. This trip was mostly within sight of the shore, and could be undertaken without a skilled navigator.

I had delayed the transcription of the last observations from the slate to the book to the very last moment for my own purposes. In all the various acts of treason, I had pretended to count on the Vision Quest's return because my presence on board was supposedly necessary to sail the ship away safely over great distances, after the opium deal would be concluded.

But now, doubts started creeping in about the very fundamentals of this understanding. What if Trench had not been illiterate as he pretended? What if Wingate, or some other crew member, had observed the dead reckoning procedures with sufficient zeal to learn them from me? All these suspicions were possibly true; and of course, every such suspicion led to others, more insidious and more poisonous … I willed myself again to concentrate on my last moments on the ship.

The transcription of the data in the logbook had allowed me a few minutes alone in the cabin just prior to being rowed ashore. Trench tolerating my being alone in the cabin was part of his blackmail on my honour—or so I had thought. The time had been sufficient for me to take the diamonds out of their hiding place, undo the wrappings of one of the packages of opium, press the diamonds deep into the mass, and seal the package again. There had been no interruption while I carried out that part of the plan.

But there had been a brief delay—not more than a few seconds, really—just afterwards, before I climbed into the boat. Mr. Wingate had called me upstairs. I had left the packages on the table. The mate said only a few words—a routine question, to which I nodded my assent, and immediately re-entered the cabin. The leather pouches were on the table just as I had left them. I strapped them to my body under the long coat, and left the cabin and the ship. But now my suspicions had revealed that the pouch with the diamonds in it had been on the table in the cabin for a time—however short—which may have been sufficient for someone to remove the diamonds again.

In other words: it now and only now dawned on me that I had never brought the diamonds ashore, and that I'd been duped from the very outset.

CHAPTER 27

▼

Confirmation of Captain Trench's trial and of his hanging in Charleston first reached Havana and Regla through the ever-mysterious channels of port-to-port communication. It was Epifania who brought in the news from the warehouses, where she had heard it from an American sailor coming off the *lancha*.

My first reaction was one of immense relief. I felt myself free from whatever commitment I might still have had towards the pirate company and its Articles. The merchandise I had stolen from the Vision Quest—although nothing was left of it—I now considered my rightful property.

Also, Trench would have gone to the gallows carrying the secret of my own misdeeds and my own secret adherence to extreme violence. But next, I got new worries. Had all of the crew been hanged? What if survivors traced me? Had my name been mentioned at the trials?

It was several weeks later that a transcript of the trials, hastily and badly translated, was offered for sale by the printers' shop in Havana in *Calle Aguacate*. Again it was Epifania who got me a copy, free of charge I have to say, as she stole it from the pocket of yet another *lancha* passenger who was peddling contraband to the very Customs agents at the warehouse.

The broadsheet was crudely illustrated with a supposed portrait of Captain Trench—which was, I saw all too well—a slightly redrawn picture of the late Blackbeard. I quickly ran over the account and then, urged on by Epifania's impatience, read it out to her. The indictment brought by the jury ran thus:

'The Jurors for our Sovereign the King, upon their oath, present that Edward Trench, mariner, late of Bristol, and members of his crew named hereafter, in the years of Our Lord 1765 and 1766, by force of arms upon the High Seas, did piratically & feloniously set upon, break, board and enter various ships and vessels, with great loss of life & property; among such vessels, according to testimony by the said Trench himself, being the merchantman *The Dragon,* out of Nantes, Mr. Zénobe Dandélion, owner and master; and the East-Indiamen *Sultana* and *Barbersteyn;* the exact location of these crimes being unknown given the loss of all related log books; and within the jurisdiction of the Court of Vice Admirality of South Carolina, did engage in similar acts of piracy against a merchant sloop called *The Nymph,* killing in the process the mariners Zachariah Long, late of Charleston; William Hewet, late of Savannah; and John-William Smith, late of Boston; moreover, within the jurisdiction of the Civilian Courts of the foresaid Commonwealth, while sailing up the Savannah River, did sack & plunder various establishments, stealing ten casks of rice and other supplies, and beating up slaves and coolies belonging to the establishment of Mr. Nicholas Trot, Esq.; all acts foresaid committed against the peace and security of Commerce and offending the Crown and dignity of our Sovereign.'

The judgment, quoting applicable laws but also entire chapters of Scripture, began as follows:

'Observing that the Sea was given by God for the use of men and is subject to dominion and property, as well as the land; That as commerce and navigation cannot be carried out without laws; so there have always been particular laws for the better ordering and regulating of maritime affairs; That hence there have been particular Courts and Judges appointed; to whose jurisdiction maritime causes belong; Given the Constitution and Jurisdiction of this Admiralty Court, duly

appointed and sworn; Given that the crimes committed are
cognizable therein ...'

The judgment concluded thus:

> *'That you, the said Edward Trench, shall go from hence to the
> place from whence you came, and from thence to the place of
> execution at White Point, where you shall be hanged by the
> neck till you are dead, dead, dead. And the God of Infinite
> Mercy be merciful to your soul.'*

CHAPTER 28

▼

Attached to the account of the trial was a list of the men hanged as its outcome. I feverishly counted the names before even reading them. Much to my relief—I must admit—it seemed that none of my former shipmates, other than Mr. Wingate, had escaped. The account of Trench's capture had been somewhat vague. Obviously the authorities would have embellished the facts if they had been less than successful in apprehending the whole crew. But on the whole, it seemed fairly certain that no witnesses of my crimes were left alive.

I mostly discounted Mr. Wingate, whose sincerity had seemed genuine. He had disappeared from the Solar the very night of all his revelations. I supposed him to be in quest of his own redemption. But I remained mistrustful after all. How solid is sincerity? Certainly it is not permanent. I didn't know the first word about his circumstances or his plans. What if he was still in Havana, and was apprehended sooner or later? What if, driven by poverty or remorse, he gave himself up?

It was wise for me to leave Havana as soon as possible, even with all the unsettled questions about our future destination. The sugar trade offered some new possibilities, as it was mostly carried out by small vessels, and as the Authorities in Havana didn't care too much about sending subversives over into British lands.

Duchesse set up our escape, in exchange for Epifania becoming her permanent agent in whatever port we would end up in. Duchesse was now very keen to develop her network in and near the British mainland Colonies, as she had become convinced that revolution was imminent there.

We would sail as stowaways on a Cuban snow carrying sugar and molasses to the Colonies and returning from the Carolinas with rice for the Cuban slaves. It seemed foolhardy and dangerous to run away to the very territories where Trench and so many of my former shipmates had been hanged; but this was the only escape available.

Also, it was unlikely that the same trial would be re-opened. We wanted to try our luck in New Orleans, hoping to start a new life there—with me speaking several languages and Epifania planning on establishing contact with her free Yoruba brothers and sisters, and hoping to help them to maintain the traditions of their ancestors.

This was very much encouraged by Duchesse, for she said that the soon-to-be freeing of the slaves had to be followed by a return to their own beliefs. The night before we shipped out, Duchesse took Epifania apart and gave her long and detailed instructions about how to maintain contact with her. This happened in whispers and with sidelong glances, as Duchesse would never really trust one not fully of her own blood.

I thought with irony about the fact that I resumed my maritime adventures as they had started: as a clandestine on a trading ship carrying victuals back and forth over short distances.

The new year had just been celebrated. The Christian calendar called it 1767. To Duchesse it was the *Year of Great Hope*. She even included our modest migration in the future mythology of her Revolution. The confusion of the upcoming *Noche de Reyes*, Duchesse said, was the ideal moment to leave the city.

CHAPTER 29

▼

It was hard to believe that a full year had passed since I had waded ashore in Bahia Honda. Now, as the *Noche de Reyes* was in full swing again, we took advantage of the general confusion and rowdiness to cross the inner bay and board the ship as it was ready to set sail. The guards were drunk. The customs officers were fucking *mulatas* in the warehouses along the *Muelle De La Luz*. We paid off the ship's mate as agreed and took up our quarters between the hogsheads of sugar in the hold.

As the ship was slowly making its way toward the open sea, and as the faraway sounds of the city in uproar accompanied us, we made love on the hard wooden floor, hitting limbs, knees and feet against the bulkheads. I was reminded of Sra. Marisél's song about the British occupation: '*Havana's girls have no shame and lie with their lovers between casks of rice.*' But is was casks of sugar now, I thought. Maybe the future would be sweeter.

CHAPTER 30

▼

The Pedroso brothers, Arrango and the Captain-general were standing on the high balcony of the Pedroso Palace, surveying the dancing and drumming in the streets below. It had become a ritual now, their own way of celebrating the night they saw devoted to strange demons. After Captain-general Bucarely had received the salutes of the *Cabildos* and thrown his handfuls of coins from the ramparts of the *Fuerza,* the conspirators met here to congratulate themselves.

The *iremes* or *diablitos* were dancing on the Plaza, scaring women and children, provoking high shrieks from the crowd. The wildest phase of the dancing again showed women and girls in sensual and spiritual abandon, the men exhausted into their own muscular trances as they ceaselessly maintained the rhythms of the drums. But high on the Pedrosos' balcony, the smells were lost, the sounds were muffled.

There were notable changes in the appearance of all these *caballeros*. Arrango was dressed richer now, with a greater display of gold and even diamonds on his person. He had become a more substantial man too, thicker in the waist and the neck, moving with the slow arrogance of overfed success. Bucarely on the contrary seemed shrunken and his official uniform, worn without self-assurance, looked uncannily like a servant's livery. The Pedrosos were dressed richly but discreetly, as befits men who are aware of the subtleties of real power.

"Why all those demons? What do they dance for? It's always a mystery to me," Bucarely said naively. Arrango lifted one eyebrow: did it matter in the least what happened down there in the streets?

As the Pedrosos kept their knowing silence, Arrango finally slapped the Captain-general on the back and answered: "Don't you worry, Don Franciso. *The real devil works for us now.* Yes he does."

FROM THE 'SAVANNAH ENQUIRER', FEBRUARY 2, 1767

Among foreign undesirables & Hereticks brought to our shores and appre-hended by the Provost there was a Dutchman by the name of Hans who, while under the devilish influence of strong liquors at a notorious portside tavern, was heard boasting about illicit Literature he was offering for sale to depraved members of the Publick.

Upon a timely denunciation by a true Christian Soul, displaying a deep commitment to the innocence of our Children & the chastity of the Community, the Miscreant was arrested and put in chains.

After sobering from his Hellish Ingestions, and after thorough ques-tioning, he led the Provost's Posse to a room in Mme Trousseaux' board-ing house where, upon inspection, various Utterly Pornographick volumes in print were found located under the floor boards.

Apart from these writings—so corrosive to the Soul as to lead to the very rotting of the Body through the Impure Practices they seek to induce—in the same hiding place there were also found a number of pri-vately printed broadsheets glorifying some Pyrates lately executed at Charleston, and utterly misrepresenting the Truly Christian declarations these criminal but repented souls had made before meeting their Lord.

As the Publick has been fully informed in these pages of the true con-tent of these declarations, there can be no doubt that such Odious Fabri-cations will be regarded with all the contempt they deserve.

The Pornographer was heard by HM's Magistrate and, offering no defence the terms of which can be repeated here, was sentenced to the Pil-lory and to Deportation to Jamaica, there to be sold into slavery.

FROM THE '*SAVANNAH ENQUIRER*', FEBRUARY 15, 1767

As this Newspaper has reported in due course, a foreign pornographer was apprehended in our City and his merchandise found at a boarding house of ill repute.

From investigations undertaken by this Newspaper, it appears that the perverted character was not without the usual accomplices. Indeed, several Witnesses in good standing attest to the fact that the named Hans was sharing the room at Mme Trousseaux' with a young Negro prostitute and her companion, a Spanish sailor recently shipped here from the Habanas.

Both went missing after the said Hans was arrested and have not revisited the premises.

From further investigations, it would seem that these young rascals fled south, having taken the mail coach bound for the New Orleans. They were last seen running hand in hand to catch the departing conveyance yesterday at sunrise, utterly devoid of any luggage, the girl barefoot and barely dressed, and both laughing like two children possessed.

While deploring their impunity, we can only applaud their departure.

It is believed that the general lawlessness prevailing in said city of the South will give them ample opportunity to exercise their highly questionable talents.

BROADSHEET FOUND IN HANS' ROOM IN MME TROUSSEAUX' BOARDING HOUSE

CAPTAIN TRENCH'S LAST STAND

The pyrate commander, being led from the Provost Dungeon at the Old Exchange, walked up to the place of execution swiftly and with a proud bearing. He was dressed in his finest, and his hair and beard adorned with red ribbons. Standing under the gallows, he asked for rum, which he was given; next he offered his shoes as a present to the hangman's son, but the boy refused; and given the opportunity to say his last words, he addressed the numerous crowd in the following terms:

"My corpse will keep you company for a while, as your lords of the Admiralty have promised to hang it in chains above the harbour. This I appreciate as a grand gesture: my remains are not nearly as important to myself as they seem to be to their lordships. As I do not believe in your god, I accept henceforth to be reduced to inanimate particles of matter. But since subtleties need to be expressed now, let me argue that even if I believed in your god, this would still not convince me of the immortality of the soul. Yes, your god may exist after all, but he may be infinitely remote from our concerns. This world ends with me: so it is unto every one of us. Yet, the world exists inexorably. This is our fiercest burden.

This world, my friends, is full of innocent pleasures. Innocent it is to love many beautiful girls; innocent to partake of the substances that bring rapture to the senses and the mind. Just so you know: I have fucked every kind of girl on every island & continent, and I have smoked and ingested every intoxicating substance. But if this world is so full of innocent pleasures, why then do we crave the evil ones? Yes, I have murdered. Yes, I have enjoyed to the full the terrors of power. But compared to those who rule over you, my power was innocent enough. Blame them for their example: next to their armies and weapons, next to their eternal wars over lies and vanities—I was but a butterfly next to their dragon.

I am now far, too far beyond the beauty of the world, seeing only the meanest clockworks behind every wonder. In conclusion therefore it befits that I should quote the scriptures:

'As it happens to the fool, so it happens unto me: but why then have I been more wise?'. Your skulls and skeletons, good people, will look just like mine. Mind I have done society a great favour: I have given you one to hate, which you need far more than one to love. Amen.'"

THE END

978-0-595-70340-1
0-595-70340-2

Lightning Source UK Ltd.
Milton Keynes UK
UKOW05n0434250214

227073UK00002B/13/P